JUDY

A NOVEL

THAT EVER DIED
Y(SO)UNG

Maple Creek Media
Hampstead ◊ Maryland ◊ United States

ISBN-13: 9780991244201
ISBN-10: 0991244206

This book is a work of fiction. Any references to real people, events, establishments, organizations, or locales are intended solely to provide a sense of authenticity and are used fictitiously. All other characters, incidents, and dialogue are drawn from the author's imagination and are not to be construed as real.

MAPLE CREEK MEDIA

A part of the Author Resource Network
P.O. Box 624
Hampstead, MD 21074
Toll-Free Phone: 1-877-866-8820
Toll-Free Fax: 1-877-778-3756
Email: info@maplecreekmedia.com
Website: www.maplecreekmedia.com

Dedication

To Steph, whose positive attitude encouraged me.

Acknowledgements

Thanks to everyone who helped in some way with the story —
Rupa Basra, Joe Radko, the Antioch Writers, Reston Writers and
Rockville Writers.

Chapter 1

Scott

Tires screeching, car swaying, Scott could hardly keep up as he sped directly behind his father weaving through the intersections and veering around cars. Cameron Kersey took the next corner on two wheels, made a wide right turn into the Wayside Park parking lot, and raced toward the entrance to the bike and walk path at what seemed like 100 mph. The police and few walkers and joggers using the trail at this hour of the cold January morning heard the screeching noise, saw the car, and one by one ran to get out of Cameron's way. He suddenly braked and his car came to a full stop near the yellow tape the police used to seal off the crime area.

When Cameron jumped out of his car leaving the door open and engine running, Scott saw that his father was still in his pajama shirt — but half-tucked into his Dockers — and dress shoes left untied. Scott slammed on his brakes, car bobbing as he pulled up beside his father's car. Cameron, half-walking, half-running, headed first toward the group of walkers and runners all standing in the entrance of the trail, but then turned around and rushed over to the group of policemen talking and pointing.

"Someone said my wife was hurt?" He stood away from them. "Where's my wife?" asked Cameron loudly, turning from officer to officer.

Scott looked at the crowd, and tried to remember what his mother told him about the running event that morning. She didn't race, he knew, nor did she speed jog. He rubbed his eyes. Things going on around him seemed fuzzy unfocused, and if he could just turn the knob and adjust the lens he would understand. He looked harder and saw two men, both wearing black jackets — with some kind of lettering on the back that he couldn't make out — taking pictures of a car parked next to the entrance of the trail, the space where his mother usually parked. Another man had what looked to Scott like some kind of measuring instrument that he pushed in front of him from the car to some point. The car; it was his mother's car. Scott took a step closer to see what they were doing to her car and saw two other men wiping or scraping on its left rear side. He didn't see his mother standing or sitting in the car. On the way out of the house, his father said that his mother was hurt. Where was she? He searched the small crowd again. The man in the black jacket taking pictures stood up, and the other people shifted and Scott could see something on the ground just in front of his mother's car. Then he heard his father.

"Where's my wife?" Without waiting for a response, he moved toward the ambulance just outside the yellow tape.

An ambulance. They put her in the ambulance already. Scott wanted to see inside the ambulance and say something to his mother. He wanted to see how she was hurt. Perhaps she only fell; after all, runners fall and hurt themselves all the time. His mother, no doubt, tripped over something on the trail during her run, and fell and twisted her ankle. She'd done that before. A trip or fall never stopped her from her run in the past. She always made herself stand, walked around a bit, and continued her run.

Two men inside the yellow tape lifted a body bag off the ground - several brunette tresses exposed - and placed it onto a gurney just as Cameron moved nearer to the gurney.

"Where's my wife? They told me that my wife was hurt." He seemed to ignore the body on the gurney and in his "Please don't tell me this is true" voice, Cameron asked again, "Where's my wife?" shaking his head and taking a step back. He looked at the two men who Scott now saw were paramedics and then he heard his father again, "I want to see Laurie . . . I want to see Laurie. Laurie? Laurie?" voice cracking. Taking a step forward and touching the yellow tape, he paced aimlessly in front of the gurney, refusing to look down in front of him.

Standing in shock and moving from side to side, a runner ready to take off at the sound of the gun, Scott gaped at the brunette tresses. He recognized his mother's curls, but he had to see who was inside to confirm that the body inside was his mother. Many people and people who ran on that trail had brunette curls. His mother wasn't the only person. The two paramedics looked at each other but neither one of them spoke. Then, a police officer approached them.

"Are you Mr. Kersey?" the officer asked. He motioned to two men in street clothes, who were standing near the yellow tape, to join them.

"Yes, Cameron Kersey. Is my wife hurt? I want to see her. Please, where is my wife, Laurie?" his voice sounding thick.

9

"I'm Officer Morris. This is Detective Haines and Detective Charles. They're from homicide."

"But, I want to see Laurie."

Cameron stared at the two detectives. Perhaps he wished that they had the wrong person, expected them to somehow, change their minds. No matter how much experience police officers have in delivering bad news, there must be a time when the officers can't think of anything to say. Possibly, they think it best to say nothing and let the person figure it out for him/herself. That's what happened. Laurie on the gurney in front of them — her husband and son — and the two detectives just stood there looking from Cameron to Scott until both men figured it out. Scott tried hard not to focus. He knew that after a night out drinking and hard partying, even with an hour or two of sleep, he had misunderstood. His head pounded and he was unsteady on his feet, reeling slightly. He stood there as the detectives looked at him, and knew something was wrong. His heart began to beat so hard that he felt it in his throat, his ears, his head and he thought that he was having a heart attack. Scott realized that the body hidden under that bag with the brunette tresses was his mother; something serious had happened to his mother. He didn't want to believe that anything had happened to her and at the point when he wanted the police officers to say it was all a mistake, he heard his father let out a gut-wrenching scream, something he had never ever heard from his father. And Scott knew. He didn't want to know, but he knew his mother was not hurt. Her being hurt would have been good news.

Before the paramedics rolled her away, Scott, tears rushing down his face, watched as his father turned to the gurney, his eyes begging to take one last look at his Laurie, the woman whom he adored so much. Detective Haines saw him and nodded to the paramedics. One paramedic unzipped the bag, slowly pulled it down, exposing Laurie's face. Scott took a step closer, reached out his hand to touch his mother's face. The face that smiled at him just because, the face that showed anger when he took advantage, the face that had shown him love for his entire life, the face that was full of laughter and happiness.

Cameron Kersey a powerful, fifty-nine-year- old man with piercing blue eyes who had built an empire of shopping malls, corporate housing, hotels, and rental developments; who had handled the most sensitive deals; who had met every problem head on; who had worked around squashed deals, and deals that almost fell through, stood in that parking lot looking down on his lifeless wife, numbed by the sight of her. At this moment, he was something that Scott had never ever seen from his father. Cameron was paralyzed, powerless to help the woman for whom he would give his life.

"No! That can't be!" Cameron yelled after a moment. "She just went out for a run. She promised she'd be back. No, no, no, just a run."

On this frigid morning in mid-January where the clouds receded and the sun sprinkled itself between the bare trees and evergreens that surrounded the parking lot, Scott and his father, Cameron, stood side by side in that parking lot where Laurie Kersey mother and wife ran almost every morning; her once vibrant body now lifeless; her eyes closed. Cameron reached out his hand, an attempt to touch his wife, but he drew his hand back as if he thought that touching her would mean that he believed she was gone; as if he thought that touching her would confirm what he couldn't allow himself to believe. Scott saw that his father pulled his hand back and drew a sigh of relief. One of the paramedics pulled the bag over Laurie's head, zipped it up and the two of them rolled her to the waiting ambulance, and put her inside. Without purpose of mind, Cameron and Scott followed their Laurie to the ambulance, the two of them still in shock as they watched the ambulance drive off carrying what used to be their wife and mother. Scott could feel the air seep out of his body, like the vacuum of a plastic bag, leaving him feeling lifeless. He almost yelled out after the ambulance, "I'll see you at home, Mom," but then he knew that the two men must have been from the Medical Examiner's Office and the Medical Examiner gave them permission to move the body after he pronounced her . . . no he couldn't say it.

Detective Haines, in his dark gray overcoat that seemed too short for his height, approached. "I'm sorry, Mr. Kersey." He took Cameron's elbow and directed him away from the area, leaving Scott standing there. Scott watched the ambulance until it was out of sight, a sick, empty feeling still inside him. Confused, puzzled, he ran his hand through his thick brown hair. Then he walked toward his father and the detective.

"What happened?" Cameron asked. He stopped walking and turned to face Detective Haines, who looked too young for a man with a receding hairline.

"We think that she was hit by a car. It looks like she finished her run and was on her way home when this happened. We found her there . . . uh, near her car. Looks like the same tread marks across her in two directions. Is that your car Mr. Kersey?" pointing to a late model dark blue Jaguar.

Cameron turned to his car as if he had forgotten it was there. "Yes."

"And that one?" pointing to an older dark green Jaguar.

"My son."

"Get pictures of those two cars," said Haines to Officer Morris. "And cut the motor off for him."

Cameron gave Officer Haines a questioning look.

"You don't mind, do you? We want to be thorough."

"Oh, I guess not," said Cameron still sounding lost as if he didn't understand. He looked around the parking lot, at Scott and then turned to Detective Haines again. "Did anyone see what happened?" asked Cameron.

"We have someone who thinks she knows the woman who might have seen the car. That's all we have right now," said Detective Haines.

"Find the person Detective. Find the person who did this."

"Not so fast. Let's take it one step at a time. We have to question everyone here and anyone we think may have information."

"But, you said someone saw the car. Where is that person? She? You said she," said Scott, loudly.

Cameron turned toward Scott as Scott walked toward the bystanders.

"Stop him." Detective Haines said to one of the officers standing nearby. The police officer stuck out his hand in an attempt to keep Scott from walking further. Scott turned toward Detective Haines and his father.

"I can't let you do that. The police will conduct the investigation," said Detective Haines.

"I've got to go with her. She needs me. I wanna be with her now." Cameron started toward his car.

Detective Haines blocked his path. "We have to ask you some questions before you go."

"I understand that, but I can't, I have to, you see, I, I . . ." Cameron shifted his weight from one leg to the other, turned around several times, and pinched his eyes shut as he tried to stop himself from breaking down.

Detective Haines looked down at the ground. He cast a sideways glance at Cameron.

"Mr. Kersey, we'll come to your house when we finish here," said Detective Charles, walking over to Cameron. "You can go for now." He shrugged his shoulders as he looked at Detective Haines. Detective Haines nodded back.

Cameron wiped his eyes with the back of his hand as he ran to his car and took off to try to catch up with the ambulance.

Scott watched as the tow truck backed up to the yellow tape. When a police officer took the tape down, the truck continued backing to Laurie's car. The driver got out and pushed a button to lower the bed. The other man opened the door to Laurie's car and got inside. Scott's body shook and a wave of heat flowed through him. He wanted to stop the man from getting in his mother's car. The man had no right. That was his mother's car, only she could drive it. He took a deep breath and made himself calm down.

After the truck pulled away he couldn't help himself, he had an uncontrollable urge to be where his mother was, where they found her on the ground. He lifted the yellow tape the officer had just put back and stood in almost the spot where his mother was hit. Another feeling from long ago tugged at him. He refused to recognize it and tried hard to focus his thoughts on his mother. Scott couldn't bear the thought of his mother being hurt, part of her body smashed by a two ton automobile. He didn't want her to suffer. He didn't want her to have to cry out for help, to cry out for him to save her. He wanted her to have been spared of all that.

When he looked down on the ground, Scott saw the chalk outline of the last position of her body and a tremor went through him. He saw the blood that must have spilled out from her and saw parts of clothing torn from her. He felt like bending down and scooping up the remnants of the blood that had oozed from her body to return to her to make her whole again to make her alive again. He stood in the place where he could almost hear his mother scream out for help, where she must have struggled, maybe even tried to run away from what she saw coming. Anger clouded his thoughts. He felt like he wanted to kill the person who took his mother's life – an eye for an eye, a life for a life. His mother was just killed, run over by some law breaking low life. Scott knew that no matter what, he would have to find the person who took away his mother's life. If his mother had to give up her life, so should the person who ran her down. Maybe he would lure that person right back to the site of the incident and mow them down just the way they did his mother. But, knowing his mother, she would be ashamed of him for thinking of such a revengeful act.

He thought of himself as unreliable; never there when his family needed him, the deadbeat son. His family must hate that in him, but somehow, he couldn't help being that way. Now, he had proven it again. The fact that he had allowed this to happen to his mother made him feel like he was the low life who ran her down. Did he have to go out drinking last night? Even if he did, did he have to stay out so late? How many times had she told him that? He heard the sound of his mother's voice so loud that he looked around. "Don't forget you have to get up early in the morning." He looked down on the ground at the outline of her body, tears streamed down his face, again. "Scott, a good daily workout and you wouldn't want to drink. You should run with me more often."

Scott ran with his mother as often as he could, but not because running was necessarily good for him. He hated running and thought that it was one of the most brutal things a person who took good care of their body could do to their body. He went along as often as he could to keep his mother happy because she loved running and to keep her company because she ran so early in the morning and he thought it was unsafe.

But, he didn't on this morning. On this morning, he arrived home late, or early and had just made it to bed when his mother knocked on his door to see if he was ready. He heard her knock, but pretended that he didn't and when he didn't respond, she left without him. Right after she left, he fell asleep and didn't wake up again until his father woke him after the phone call, almost an hour later. He looked down at himself and saw that he was still dressed in his clothes from the night before and now, a little hung over. He wanted to feel hung over. He wanted this entire morning to be a dream or better, something that his mother arranged as a way to help him stop drinking. That's what it was. Why didn't he see that at first? None of this was real. He found that he desperately needed to believe that.

But, as he stood there thinking about that morning, trying to believe that he was in a dream, another feeling came over him, one that he tried to ignore, but wouldn't go away. It was a feeling that always haunted him during trying times like this one. He was in the same spot where his mother's life was just taken away from her and all he wanted to do was to take a drink. He needed a drink; maybe several, yes several.

"Are you okay, Mr. Kersey? Mr. Kersey? Mr. Kersey?"

When he realized that someone was calling him, Scott wiped his faced with the back of his hand and turned around.

"Are you okay, sir?" asked Detective Haines.

Scott stared intently at the detective for a long moment. "Yes." He finally said.

"You need to come out of there. You don't wanna destroy the crime scene."

Scott looked at the detective and gave him the same pleading look that his father had given the detective earlier. The detective held up the yellow tape for Scott. Scott pulled his jacket collar closed and bent down to walk under the yellow tape. When he stood up, a momentary look of helplessness washed across his face.

"What . . . can I . . . ?"

"We will contact you at your home."

"Do I —?"

"Are you okay, sir? Would you like someone to drive you, sir?"

Scott cleared his throat. "Thank you, no. I can drive myself." He turned slowly and walked toward his car. His mother's death was too sudden. He needed time, time to tell her how much he loved her, time to run with her, time to tell her that he lied to her when he pretended he was asleep, time to stop this accident from happening. He got into his car and started it up, but he felt misplaced like lost keys. Then he realized that he had to go see where they took his mother, find his father. He drove out of the parking lot.

Just as he turned onto the street, a female runner ran out of the bushes and down the slight incline onto the street. He slammed on the brakes and she fell to the ground just in front of the car. His stomach seemed to turn inside out. He couldn't have hit her. Help her; he needed to help the woman.

"Miss, are you hurt? I'm so sorry. I didn't see you . . ." Scott was frantic. He'd just left the place where his own mother lost her life, now this woman.

"I couldn't stop. I couldn't stop myself coming down that hill." She pulled her earmuff back behind her ears and pointed back toward the bushes, slightly out of breath.

"Are you all right? Are you hurt?" He was in a panic. He tried to look at her, to see if she was hurt. "Are you okay?"

"Yes, I just fell." She scowled her face as if to ask what was wrong with him.

"Can you stand? Why don't you try to stand up?" Scott bent down to take her by the arm.

"I think I can." She reached out her hand to him and he took it instead. She tried to stand but her ankle didn't want to support her.

"My ankle. I hurt my ankle." She took off her wool gloves, pulled up her running pants to expose her ankle, and rubbed it.

"Let me get you to the car. I'll drive you to the hospital. I can have you there —" He got her up and tried to steer her to the car.

"No, I'll be okay." She tried to walk off.

He took hold of her elbow and supported her. "I'll drive you to the hospital."

"No, I'll be okay." She broke free of his hand and tried to walk off, but her ankle gave out again and she almost fell.

Scott took hold of her arm again to help her stand up. "I'll drive you to the hospital."

"Listen, I said I'm okay. Didn't you hear what I said? What's wrong with you?"

Scott stared at her. "What are you doing running through here anyway?" He felt the warmth of his blood rushing through him and beads of perspiration broke out on his forehead. His palms were sweaty and without thought, he wiped them on his pants. When he realized he was staring, he tried to think of something to say to her, but she spoke first.

"The entrance to the parking lot is all blocked off. I couldn't get through so I decided to cut through here." She pointed to the wooded area that hid the bike and walk path. "I didn't realize it was an incline."

"I'm Scott Kersey." He stretched out his hand. "Please, let me drive you to the hospital," Scott continued, his frustration diminishing.

"Kathryn Milner." She accepted his hand. "I'm okay." She walked around a little, as if forcing her ankle to work. "See? It's okay. Thanks, anyway." She pulled her earmuff down as she half ran and half limped off down the street.

Scott started back to his car when he noticed something black in the bushes where she had her tumble. It was a small identification folder like walkers, bikers, and runners carried with them when they exercised. He recognized it because his mother also carried one. It must have fallen out of her fanny pack that he saw around her waist. He picked it up, turned to hand it to her, but she was already gone.

Chapter 2
Kathryn

Kathryn Milner hobbled the two blocks to her home as fast as she was able, occasionally checking to see that she wasn't followed. When she reached her driveway, she was tempted to turn around, again. She could peep over the hibiscus bushes that lined the driveway, but she forced herself to keep her head straight and walk up the five steps to the antebellum-style porch and to the front door. Then she turned around. No one. She held onto the porch railing as she lifted her foot; turned and stretched it in several directions feeling for the pain. Maybe she should have it looked at. But it felt better; almost no pain. She had walked it out just what she thought she once read in her exercise books.

Kathryn turned toward the street one more time to look for the man with whom she had just had a colliding encounter. She remembered that he looked at her with somber blue-green eyes that seemed full of pain and anger. When he moved closer to help her up, she noticed that he reeked of a mixture of cigarette smoke, sweat, and alcohol, the day after boozing it up, an odor even worse than what she probably smelled like after her run.

Kathryn had to admit that amid all the sadness and even his odor there was something about that man, something that felt more like some kind of magnet, or magic even, that seemed to catch her attention. She looked around again, almost as if she had hoped he had followed her. He should have frightened her, but he didn't. A strange man practically ran her down in the park, or maybe she almost ran into him, tried to get her into his car, and she was not afraid of him. She supposed that it had something to do with his magnetism and his eyes.

She searched the zipper on her fanny pack to get out her door key and, out of habit, turned the doorknob at the same time. Surprisingly, the door was unlocked, so she was unaware that her identification folder was missing.

"Kat, you're back," said Betty, her stepsister, coming to the door to meet her. Kathryn stepped into the foyer, closed the front door. She moved toward Betty.

"Yes," said Kathryn. "I went for my run." She unleashed her golden brown hair and shook it several times, as it cascaded down to her shoulders.

Betty walked toward her dressed in jeans and a sweatshirt, dark eyes wide and her twenty-one-year-old body held stiff as if she were in the doctor's office waiting for a doctor to stick a needle in her arm.

"What's wrong?" asked Kathryn.

"Nothing. Why do you think something is wrong?" Perspiration formed on her brow; she stood tightly wringing her hands as if she was trying to get all the excess water out of a towel.

"Look at you. You look . . . Oh, no! Dad? Is my Dad okay?" Kathryn raced down the hallway to the kitchen leaving Betty standing near the front door, a forgotten toy.

21

Kathryn's father, Martin Milner sat at the kitchen table in his blue and white striped pajamas, pouring low fat milk over a bowl of oat flakes. The newspaper, unfolded and ready to read, lay on the table next to the bowl. Behind him on the stove, steam emanating from a teakettle, emerged upward and dissolved in the air.

"Dad? How long have you been out of bed? Did the doctor tell you it was okay to get out of bed?" She realized she sounded more like his mother than daughter; but she had to take care of her father.

Martin turned around and looked up at his daughter as if startled by her rush. "Good morning Sweetheart. No, the doctor didn't have to tell me. I'm feeling better so I thought I'd get up and get myself a breakfast. How was your run?"

The sun stretched itself through the sliding glass doors and filled the room with light.

"Dad, let me get you back to bed. I'll bring your cereal." Kathryn, one third of her father's strapping size, took her father by the arm and tried to get him up out of the chair. Betty appeared and stood watching in the doorway.

Martin snatched his arm back. "Sweetheart, I'm feeling so much better."

"Dad, yesterday you were almost delirious, with the worse case of the flu you've ever had. You need to stay in bed. Betty, help me get him back in bed."

During times like this, Kathryn realized that even with her new family, her father was all she had.

"Oh, stop babying him. He's a grown man. He knows what he's doing," said Sylvia, Martin's second wife and Kathryn's stepmother, as she entered the kitchen, both hands puffing up her greatly teased dyed blond hair. Her chiffon robe trailed behind over her ponderous body, as she seemed to glide over to the kitchen table.

"I just don't want him to have a relapse," said Kathryn, standing beside her father, one hand on his shoulder.

Martin put a spoonful of cereal in his mouth.

"I'll take care of my husband, if you don't mind," said Sylvia with a pompous air. She moved to the cabinets on the other side of the kitchen, took out a teacup and saucer, and sat them on the granite counter.

"He shouldn't be out of bed. Yesterday he was so sick he couldn't sit up," said Kathryn, an apologetic tone.

"Well, today he's not, as you can see." Sylvia slammed that teacup and saucer on that glass top table so hard that it was a wonder that neither one of them — the cup or table — shattered into smithereens.

Martin jumped and looked up at Sylvia. This time, he had just put an oversize spoonful of cereal into his mouth. He chewed hurriedly as if he wanted to say something.

"You know how my father is Sylvia. Never taking the time to recuperate and then he's sick again. I just don't want that to happen. That's all," said Kathryn, softening up a bit more. She never wanted to put her father in a position where he had to choose one over the other or ever wanted to come between her father and his wife, so she was always the one to back down whenever Sylvia challenged her. This really bothered her and she hated herself for doing that especially when she knew she was right and because she thought that Sylvia was a selfish, hard-hearted woman who didn't care for her father at all. According to Kathryn, Sylvia only looked after her two daughters, Betty and Mary, and herself. Without Martin and whatever money he had, Sylvia and her two daughters would be living in a one-room trailer. Whether or not Sylvia loved Martin, Kathryn knew that Martin cared for Sylvia.

"Well, you don't need to worry," said Sylvia.

"Okay, you two. Please don't start. Kat, since it'll make you happy, I'll go back to bed," said Martin. He stood up and started out of the kitchen with the newspaper under his arm.

"Yes, it'll make me very happy," said Kathryn smiling at her father.

"Don't forget to bring my cereal."

"I'm on that right now." Kathryn went to the cabinet and pulled out a tray. She poured water from the teakettle on to a tea bag in the cup. She cast a sideways glance at Sylvia who by now was buttering her toast.

"My father has a bad case of the flu, Sylvia, in case you haven't noticed." She placed Martin's cereal on the tray.

"Yes, I have noticed," said Sylvia turning to face Kathryn. "I've noticed that every time anything happens to him you're all over him. 'Here, Dad, have some soup. Here, Dad, take your medicine.'" Sylvia tried to imitate the way she thought Kathryn said it to her father.

"I'm just trying to keep him well." She put more cereal in the bowl, a little angry over Sylvia's comments.

"Are you sure that's all?" She replenished her teacup with water and reached for her tea bag.

"Yes Sylvia. That is all. I know you don't love my father and maybe you never will, but I love him and care about him —"

"You won't let yourself believe that I love him. You're not the only one. I love your father, too. I'm his wife now, whether you want that or not, doesn't matter. I'm his wife and it's my job to take care of him when he's sick, not your job."

"I'm just trying —"

"I don't care what you're just trying. I know that every time anything happens to him you're right there, stepping on my toes. Every time anything happens to you, he's right there. Neither one of you have given me a chance."

Kathryn poured low fat milk into a cruet for Martin's cereal. She had to get out of the kitchen. What did this woman know?

"You can't bring back your mother and you can't save your father from an illness that might take his life. Martin told me that your mother died when you were five years old. But she was sick, Kathryn; she had a very serious illness. Can't you see that?" She looked over at Kathryn, lowered her voice to a decibel Kathryn had never heard from her.

"I'm sorry you both miss your mother and if I've found out anything during this marriage with your father it's that neither you, nor your father has gotten over the loss of your mother. But, Kathryn, I'm still here." Sylvia took a step toward Kathryn to touch her arm.

Kathryn pulled back, not sure how to take what she just heard. Sylvia had gone too far.

"Whether you like it or not, I do love your father. I know you think I just want his money, I've heard you say that enough times."

"You've given me that impression."

"Under the circumstances, aren't I owed something for my situation? The one you've put me in?"

Kathryn picked up the tray and turned to go to her father.

"You don't have to worry about telling your father about our conversation. He and I have talked about this before."

"So have we," said Kathryn.

"Ah, what the hell," said Sylvia waving her hand at Kathryn in a dismissive way. She walked out of the kitchen.

Kathryn took the tray up the stairs and stopped just outside the bedroom. She put a smile on her face and took a deep breath to relax herself before she knocked on the door.

"Come in, sweetheart."

When she entered, Martin was seated at the table in the sitting area reading the newspaper. Kathryn sat the tray on the table beside Martin.

"Dad, I want you to get well. You should be in bed."

"I know you do, Sweetheart. I know you do. I'll go back to bed just as soon as I finish this cereal. How's that?"

Kathryn leaned down to hug her father around his neck. He rested his head on her arm and patted her hand.

"Now will you go to work?" asked Martin.

"Now, I can."

~~~~~~~~~~

Kathryn stepped out of the shower and toweled off. She wrapped the oversize towel twice around her long thin body and tucked it in under her arm. Sylvia's words lay on her the way contaminated food sat in a stomach. She was right about Sylvia, at least, partially anyway. Sylvia was right about her. Kathryn never knew her mother so how could she miss her. Her father had always spoken so lovingly about her that it made her miss her mother more. She had always wondered what secrets they would have had together, how her mother would have appreciated her wanting to be a fashion designer and about her choice in boyfriends. Kathryn didn't really know what her mother's personal likes and dislikes were or how much she and her mother were alike. She wasn't able to get much from the few pictures that her father had shown her. She often wondered whether they wore their hair alike or whether they smiled alike, laughed alike, or had the same voice quality. Kathryn didn't know firsthand and for that, she had always felt deprived of a relationship with her mother. She envied her stepsisters, Betty and Mary. They took their relationship for granted. Kathryn found it difficult to sit back and watch Betty and Mary go at it with Sylvia while she wished she had a mother. Kathryn also knew that her father still missed her mother very much and knew that Sylvia was right. Her father had never gotten over the loss of his first wife.

Kathryn remembered the times her father left her home alone because he couldn't stand coming home after her mother died. She remembered that he smelled strange like liquor, she heard her aunt say to him, and that his clothes were always wrinkled as if he had slept in them. She remembered the many times her aunt had to pick her up from school or take her to her house for the weekend and holidays because no one could find Martin. When she was five, she thought her father didn't love her without her mother. Later, she found out that he loved his wife so much and couldn't deal with the loss of her. When Kathryn was eight, she ran away from home. She took the money she had saved from her grandmother's birthday gifts, and on a warm fall Sunday, didn't come home after church. She was able to use the phone and called her aunt to tell her that her dad had decided to pick her up. It was the only way she knew how to let her father know how much she missed her mother and how much she needed him. She was gone one day before her father found her. When she didn't show up for school on Monday, the teacher called Martin. Martin called the church and found out that she was there, but no one had seen her leave. Martin rushed to the church where after searching the place, found her hidden in an inner room in the basement. Martin picked up his little girl, hungry, scared, and frightened and held her as tightly as he could. He wouldn't stop kissing her and told her how much he loved her and how sorry he was. He promised to straighten up and that he would always keep her safe. She remembered how tightly she held on to him, needing her father to show his love for her. Martin kept his promise and the two of them had been inseparable since then.

Kathryn wiped the fog from the mirror. She loved the relationship that she had with her father now, but she thought he deserved a woman who loved him with the same depth and completeness her mother loved him and a woman whom he could love with the same intensity and puissance he loved her mother. Kathryn never felt that that person was Sylvia.

Chapter 3
Kathryn

Kathryn drove into The Grove, an exclusive shopping mall in Georgetown. She parked on the back lot and entered through the employee entrance. Getting off the escalator on the second floor, she found Frankie Sanchez, designer and boutique manager, unbuttoning the first three buttons of the beige linen shirt on one of the mannequins in the window of his women's shop. When he saw Kathryn, he bent the arm of the model so that its hand was on its hip. He laughed and waved Kathryn to the door. Kathryn chuckled back and pushed in the heavy glass door to enter the store. She looked at her watch and noticed that the store and the mall wouldn't open for another half hour.

"Good morning, Frankie. Flirting with the dummies again, huh?" said Kathryn, smiling back at Frankie

"Don't you look gorgeous today? You're working that long sleeve dark gray dress honey. Look at that. Showing off that body." Frankie snapped his fingers and gave an expression of approval as he met her in the entranceway.

She walked up the steps to the top floor and the rapidly dwindling design studio above the boutique. She opened the door to the workroom stepping around bolts of material and walking around undressed and half-dressed mannequins as she found what some time ago, she declared to be "her desk." With definite ownership, as she routinely did, she cleared a space on the desk and slapped down her handbag, draped her coat over the back of the chair.

"Kat," said Michelle, an assistant in the shop who seemed dressed to reveal every aspect of her large breasts and with large dangling earrings that seemed to accentuate them further. "Your fabric came in this morning. It's just beautiful. I opened it, just in case it wasn't what you ordered. Here it is." Michelle produced a bolt of imported lime green Chinese silk rolled on lightweight cardboard and with tissue paper between every other turn. She handed the bolt of silk to Kathryn.

Kathryn stared at the material, engulfed by its exquisiteness. "This is so beautiful, just stunning. And this is gold." She unrolled the silk two turns, removed the tissue paper, and picked it up to give it a closer look.

"Yes, it is," responded Michelle.

"I love these gold lines. They look like they're barely present, but they give the lime green a hint of sparkle that wakes it up." Kathryn unrolled more of it and held it up in front of her. Stepping toward the table, Michelle grabbed the other end of the bolt that held the remaining silk. Kathryn moved to the window to look at the unrolled portion as the light cast through it and gave off a delicate flickering. Without saying a word, Frankie took the edge of the bolt with Michelle and the three of them stood at the window amazed, ineffable.

"That's going to be gorgeous with the cut and design. I think it's strong enough to work, too." Frankie looked at Michelle and gave her a nod as if letting her know that he would let go of the bolt. Michelle, hands lightly on each side of the bolt, Kathryn at the start and Frankie in the middle, together unrolled the silk two more turns. Frankie took some of the fabric and held it in his hands.

"Can you imagine the feel of this soft, delicate fabric up against your skin? It'll bring the feminine out of every woman, make her scream out, and drive the men crazy. Um hum, that's it. This is it," said Frankie.

With Michelle, he rolled the silk back onto the bolt with the paper and took a step back. Shifting his weight to his right leg, he tucked his right hand on his hip.

Kathryn stood quiet for a moment. She had been a fashion designer for The Boutique that Frankie managed since she graduated from college three years ago. She knew it was just her dumb luck that she got the position with Frankie in the first place. He and his partner, Robbie, whose full name was Robert Thomas Boyd, had just severed their partnership – both personal and business – when Kathryn, carrying her portfolio, a college recommendation, and a prospectus about her future creations, appeared answering an ad that Frankie put in the newspaper. Even though the ad specifically asked for someone well experienced, Kathryn decided to take a chance anyway. Why not? She'd been rejected by every agency so far.

During the interview, Frankie could no longer maintain his composure. He broke down and cried right in front of her. Kathryn didn't know what to do or say, especially since Frankie told her that he wanted to take his life. It was hard being gay and even harder being a monogamous gay person, he told her. Robbie wasn't ready to settle down with one person quite yet and according to Frankie, Robbie was his soul mate. Kathryn could see how hurt Frankie was and she just reached over and held his hand until his crying subsided. She didn't know what to say – whether he should call Robbie back or continue without him – but she just let him cry. Kathryn couldn't help feeling that she said or did something in the interview that brought on the whole thing and she felt partly responsible for his poignant fluxion. Frankie told her that he couldn't believe how overly kind and sweet she was during that time. He apologized to her over, and over again and let her know that he was so mortified and humiliated about how he just broke down. He was impressed with her recommendations and portfolio and especially with the way she handled him, and his embarrassment, he said, that he hired her right then and there.

Over the three years, Kathryn had proved herself to be just as good as Oleg Cassini or Vera Wang or Emilio Pucci, at least that's what Frankie said about her. Kathryn had been a fast learner, but she felt that she still had so much to learn about what fabrics were best for a particular cut, what fabrics made good dresses, what fabrics should not be used for skirts, or pants.

She wanted to learn all that she could and as fast as she could learn it, which meant that she had to work overtime often. Frankie told her that in time, he would sponsor her fashion show. This was any fashion designer's dream, it was certainly her dream as it had always been – to have her own fashion show where items of her creation were paraded down a runway and for everyone to see and marvel about how good she was. She wanted so badly to have Frankie Sanchez, an acclaimed fashion designer himself who had been in the business almost since fashion designing existed, as Frankie would tell it, to sanction her creations.

Kathryn stood there holding on to the fabric. She wanted to raise her hands and shout aloud, "I'm a fashion designer and I'm good at it." She smiled inside.

The phone rang and Frankie went to answer it while Kathryn laid the bolt down on the worktable next to her desk. She took out her design, the sketch of her dress and laid it beside the silk so that she could imagine the dress in that fabric. She couldn't get over the fact that she had been the one to pick this beautiful fabric. She had better instincts than she thought she had. With a smile on her face, she went to another table and cut off enough muslin to make the test garment. Frankie told her that an expert designer always cut the outfit using muslin first. See your mistakes on something else before destroying the material.

When Frankie completed his call, he came and stood next to Kathryn. Kathryn realized that he was silent, which was not the usual Frankie, and turned to him.

"What's the matter?"

"Nothin. It's not important." She noticed him trying to hide a smirk, and she knew she would have to guess.

"What's not?"

"Well, if you have to know, the mother-company needs someone to manage its boutique in France. The store is not doing well and they need someone to get the store in order while they find a buyer. It could be you, girl," said Frankie. With a bent wrist, he waved at Kathryn.

Kathryn looked at him. She almost laughed. It never took much to get any secret out of Frankie. Usually, he couldn't wait to spill the beans. So Kathryn couldn't understand why she was so surprised when he just came out with it this time.

"You're kidding?"

"No. That's what that call was about."

"They said me? I mean, they said I could manage the store for them?" asked Kathryn.

"They want a recommendation. I could recommend myself if you want me to. But I thought this could be your chance, girl, you know, to introduce your line." He looked at her out of the sides of his eyes.

"I can't believe this. When? When does this all start?" asked Kathryn.

"They didn't say. But you know the company. There won't be much turn-around time. I'd say max two, four weeks at most."

"My father isn't feeling well right now."

"Well, hey. Think about it. They said they'd call back."

The phone rang again and Michelle answered it.

"It's for you, Kathryn," said Michelle.

Kathryn went to her desk to answer the phone.

"Hello, this is Kathryn."

"Hello, Beautiful," said a voice on the other end.

"Harris, where have you been?" asked Kathryn. She twirled the telephone cord around her fingers.

"Miss me babe?"

"Harris Sweeney, of course I do. Are you calling to say that you're on your way back and that I should make dinner plans right away?" She made a joke out of it, but she wanted him to say yes.

Kathryn had met Harris Sweeney about a year ago at one of Frankie's "fashion parties" that he regularly held at the Hilton in downtown Washington, D.C. He was the advertising consultant for a company owned by one of Frankie's friends. Frankie introduced them and told her throughout the evening in between sips of wine, that he could see them together, that Harris was right for her. She wondered if Frankie wasn't telling Harris the same thing. Even though there were many single people at the party or people who appeared to be single, Harris stuck with her almost all night. He arrived alone and even though they left together, he went home alone. Soon after they met, they began dating in between his trips out of town, or her working over time.

"I wish I could. I have to stay another few days. This project is not turning out the way we thought it would and somebody has to straighten things out."

"And, so that's you, huh?" She was disappointed, but she tried not to let him hear it. She never wanted to be the kind of girlfriend who didn't understand why her boyfriend had to work late or overtime, and she didn't often question him when he said he would need to work late or stay out of town longer. She sometimes felt like that was one of her negative qualities and she got the feeling that he wanted her to express her disappointment. But, there were many times when she had to call him to tell him that she had to break their date because she had to work late. She knew that he must be let down with her sometimes, too. Or, at least, she had hoped that he was. She had to admit though, with Harris, it was sometimes hard to tell whether he was happy or disappointed with her.

"Yes. Don't be upset. When I do get back, I'll make it up to you, okay?"

"Okay. Harris, I . . . ."

"No, no that's not right, damnit."

Harris seemed to be talking to someone else.

"Babe, I gotta go. I'll call you later." Harris hung up.

Kathryn heard a click and the line went dead. He hung up without giving her a chance to respond. She held out the phone and looked at it as if she thought the line would reactivate itself and when it didn't she pushed the off button and put the phone back in its cradle. Kathryn sat down in the chair and stared out the large window that overlooked the employee parking lot.

"Kat, the shop just called. They said that some man is downstairs asking for you," said Michelle as she hung up the phone.

"Did they say who it was?" asked Kathryn.

When Kathryn approached the front of the store, she saw the man from earlier whose car she took a tumble with, standing on the other side of the cosmetics counter. She walked around to the now cleaned-up, tall, dark haired, intense looking man watching a lady having her face made over.

"Hi," said Kathryn. She recognized him right away, but she wondered how he knew where she worked.

"Hi," Scott's smile widened when he saw her. "Scott Kersey, remember? From this morning? I just wanted to return this." He held out her identification wallet with her home, and work addresses and phone numbers.

Kathryn let out a smile. "Yes. I remember. The front door was unlocked so I didn't miss it. Thank you. You didn't have to bring it. You could have mailed it or something."

"It was no problem. I just wanted to see that you're okay."

Kathryn stared at him for a long second. "That was . . . that was nice of you. I'm fine."

"Well, okay." He turned to leave.

"Wait a minute."

Scott turned around.

"Should I, I don't know what to do."

"What do you mean?' asked Scott.

"Well, should I offer you a reward or something?"

Scott stood staring into her eyes, making her feel uncomfortable and she wished she had more tact in forming her thoughts. She tried to look away but felt that magnetism again and couldn't move. She almost thought that he had given her something, some kind of magic that she didn't notice and that prevented her from moving.

"You've given me a reward," said Scott.

"I didn't mean it to sound . . ."

"It didn't.'

Kathryn felt like he'd just given her a long tight hug. She smiled at him, again.

"Thank you for bringing this by."

As she watched him walk away, she felt the same tingle in her heart and that same nervousness that she had felt earlier and she knew she had to see him again.

Chapter 4
Scott

If anyone had asked Scott why he had to take Kathryn her fanny pack on this day, the day he went to a crime scene to identify his mother, he would not have been able to say. But that was all he thought about on his drive home. When he first saw her in front of his car, just after he watched the paramedics take his mother away, a sense of calmness, an inner peace overtook him. That desideration pulled him to her, driving him to her work to return something in person that he could have mailed. Hence, it was because earlier he had seen his mother carried off in a body bag that urged him to seek out Kathryn. Perhaps it was the understanding or compassion or the care and concern that he saw in her eyes and face, and heard in her voice, that provided him with that calmness and serenity that he felt and needed. When he pulled up to the stoplight, he smiled slightly when he remembered that she asked him what was wrong with him which meant, to him, that she at least knew something was wrong. She seemed so different from Lisa, the woman he was currently seeing. Lisa never saw what he needed, never heard his cry for help.

The only person he thought clearly saw something was wrong was his mother. His father must have had some vague idea that Scott was troubled because he tried talking to him. He and his father were close; sometimes Scott thought they were "father and son" close. They went to ball games together, every now and then, took in horseracing, and even bet on a horse from time to time. During these times, they talked, but Scott found himself talking more with his mother. He was always nervous around his father, afraid that he wouldn't reach his father's expectations or more importantly, wouldn't be the man his father expected him to be.

After college, his father gave him a job in his real estate investment firm where he had been sitting for the past four years. Even though he worked for his father and earned a paycheck, his father never assigned him to a department or gave him specific duties. Scott thought that the only reason his father gave him the job was to keep him close and out of trouble.

He pulled his car behind another black car in the circular driveway in front of his house. As he walked by the car, he peeped in the Crown Victoria, and saw a computer mounted in front of the dashboard. He remembered that the police said they would have to ask more questions when he and his father returned from the coroner.

Inside the house, the housekeeper told him that the police officers were meeting with his father in the study. At the door, Scott took a deep breath first, and walked in. His father was talking as he entered and Scott took an armless chair in a corner near the door and behind the two police officers who sat facing Cameron. Scott noticed that his father used the neatly arranged desk to steady himself and as he talked he looked down at the desk as if reading notes.

"Tell us about this morning," said Detective Haines. He took out a notebook and pen and began writing.

"I, I, I don't . . . she left, she went, she . . ." began Cameron. He took a moment and pinched his eyelids shut.

"Take your time," said Detective Charles as he sat poised and confident. His dark brown suit and beige and brown tie blended with his cocoa-color skin. He adjusted his African horn necklace that lay neatly over his tie. "We just need to know when she left here, where she was going and what time . . ." He looked at Detective Haines who ran his hand over his receding mixed-gray hairline. "And anything else you want to tell us."

"Well, uh, she, every morning, well, almost every morning she goes for a run, sometimes with my son, Scott." He paused for another moment, tried to pull himself together.

"She likes to run. I used to, I didn't, I . . . She left at 5:30. She always leaves at 5:30 so she could get back before I leave." Cameron looked toward the door, cleared his throat, and started again, voice shaky. "When the alarm rings off at 5:15 she gets up. I cut the alarm off and she gets dressed to go run at 5:30. She runs for about an hour while I get dressed for work. When she returns I have the coffee brewing, a small breakfast ready, and then we talk about our plans for the day before I leave for work."

"What happened this morning?" asked Detective Haines as he continued to scribble in his notebook. He stopped, looked at his watch.

"She wanted us to buy this hotel for a project, housing for run-away teens, she was working on. We didn't have to meet the client until later, so I went back to sleep. I didn't get up, I usually get up."

"So you were here when it happened?" asked Detective Haines.

Detective Haines's questions made Scott feel like he didn't believe his father.

"Yes, I, I was here." Cameron pinched his eyes again, trying to stop his tears.

"Where were you this morning, Mr. Kersey?" asked Detective Haines turning around to Scott.

His question took Scott by surprise. He had eased into the room, unnoticed, he thought. "I, I was asleep."

"So, you both were asleep when the incident happened?" asked Detective Charles.

"That's right. Why are you asking us where we were?" asked Cameron in a steadier voice, somewhat angry.

"We just need to get an understanding of how your wife's morning went so we can get a picture of what happened, how and who may have been present during her run," said Haines. He wrote another note.

"I love Laurie, detectives. Loved, loved her. I loved my wife and family more than anything else in the world. Everything I did, I did for her and my children. I don't like your insinuations." His eyes rested on a picture of his wife that sat on his desk.

"Calm down, Mr. Kersey. We have to do our job. We have to eliminate possibilities and you're both considered until you answer our questions to our satisfaction and are eliminated," said Haines. He turned toward Scott, "Any problems you and your mother had?"

Cameron looked toward the door, stood up behind his desk, and opened his mouth as if to respond for Scott when Scott put his hand up to stop him. Scott moved forward in his chair.

"How can you sit here and ask us questions like that? My mother and I were very close. I ran with her in the morning sometimes." As soon as he said it, Scott wanted to take that statement back.

"But you didn't run with her this morning?" asked Charles.

At that question, Scott looked away, looked at his father, who was still looking toward the door, and then back at the two detectives waiting on him to respond. He tried to make a sound, say something that would make them stop looking at him, but when he opened his mouth, nothing came out. He wanted to run to his father, throw his arms around him, comfort him and tell his father that he was sorry, but he forced himself not to do that. He looked back at the detectives and tried to think of an answer to the question: "But you didn't run with her this morning?" He asked himself "Why?" Of all the mornings he could have begged out of going with her, why would he pick this morning, the morning she really needed him to be there? He looked down at the floor.

"No." was all he managed to squeak out.

The two detectives looked at each other. They didn't seem to know how to proceed from there. Scott swiped his face with the back of his hand.

"No, I didn't today."

"Did she run alone today, do you know?" asked Detective Charles.

Scott cleared his throat. "When I don't go with her, she tries to run with April, if April is running. They just meet up in the parking lot. Otherwise, she runs, ran with me, or by herself. I don't know about this morning." His voice was barely audible.

"So, you have no way of knowing whether or not she ran by herself or with this April?" asked Charles, almost friendly, almost as if he understood Scott.

Scott looked at him. He was not prepared for these questions. He could see now that his mother needed him and he wasn't there. He could see that he had let her down. "No."

Suddenly, he realized why his father kept looking toward the doorway. His father expected Laurie to walk in any minute. She always came in the study when he brought work home. Scott would sometimes hear them talking and giggling — she asking questions about his work, their plans, he asking questions about her plans, her day and Scott, Becky or Jack. After a while, he would hear his father playfully say to his mother that he had work to finish. It was a nice habit for them. They looked forward to their daily meeting in the study, a time to see each other, get out the business part of the family, a time to be in a family. He looked for her now.

"Do you know how to get in touch with this April woman?" asked Charles.

"No. They would just meet up at the trail."

"You mean that they ran together if they got there at the same time every day?" asked Charles.

"That's correct," said Scott.

"No last name?" asked Haines.

"I don't know it," said Scott.

"Okay," said Charles. He continued to watch Scott as Scott sat on the edge of his chair staring at the floor between his feet.

Haines stood up followed by Charles. Haines reached out his hand to Cameron and the two men shook. "If either of you think of anything else let us know." He took out his card and handed it to Cameron.

"What's next?" asked Cameron before they exited the room.

"We need to track down the woman who saw the car," said Haines. He put his notebook in the breast pocket of his jacket.

"The witness?" asked Cameron.

"Yes. It would help if we knew who else ran at that time of the morning," said Haines. He looked at Scott.

"When we did our run, we didn't run with anyone else. My mother went more often than I did and I didn't know the walkers and runners like she did. "

"Well, thank you both very much," said Haines.

"You'll let us know when you find that witness?" asked Cameron.

"Yes, we will. Meanwhile, you two need to come in soon and get fingerprinted. We need to eliminate you," said Haines.

"Eliminate us?" asked Cameron.

"Yes, you have to understand that everyone's a suspect," said Haines.

"And especially the family members, huh officers?" asked Scott.

The two officers looked at each other.

"Yes, that's correct. Statistics show that crimes like these are committed by family members," said Charles.

"You mean husbands. Just say it," said Cameron.

"Yes, husbands. Come in by tomorrow," said Haines.

The two officers left. Scott stood at the door wanting to say something to his father. He knew his father blamed him for his mother's death. His father told him often enough about being responsible and if ever there was a time he felt irresponsible, it was now.

44

Cameron went back to his desk and slammed himself down in the chair. He looked around as if he didn't recognize the room.

"Dad, I —" Scott took a step toward his father.

"I can't believe this. I just can't believe Laurie won't be back. I just saw her this morning, before she left to go . . . I just saw her this morning," said Cameron

"Dad? Dad —"

"I have to make some calls. I have to call your brother and sister and tell them. I have to arrange her, her, her funeral." He began pulling out drawers and pushing them back as if he wanted to do something, but couldn't remember what it was. He stopped and looked around the room, a rat in a maze, lost and trying to find its way out.

"The funeral. What will, what will?" He stood up and walked around his desk.

"Dad? Dad?" asked Scott.

Cameron continued mumbling to himself. "She'll want to wear that dress that she loves so much. The one with the, with the . . ." tears began to course their way down his face . . . "with the red silk sash and the collar. She loved that black dress and it looks, looked nice on her, too." Suddenly he turned to face Scott. "Remember, Scott? The dress with the silk, with the red. Oh God!" He sat down in one of the chairs in front of his desk and tried to pull himself together. "Laurie's gone," he whispered. "Laurie's gone."

Scott saw that his father was not ready for a conversation about how his wife died and he probably wouldn't even remember the apology that Scott was about to give. He had to find a way to make things right, or as right as he could under the circumstances. "I'll call Becky and Jack, Dad. Okay? I'll call them."

Scott called his older sister Rebecca Kersey, who was now a doctor in a hospital in Pennsylvania, and told her about their mother. Becky said she would leave as soon as she could get a flight out. She promised to call so that Scott could pick her up. Then Scott called his brother Jackson Kersey and told him what happened. Jack told Scott that he would have his manager take over his computer technology company in New York and that he and his wife, Elaina, would be on the first plane back to Maryland.

Talking to both Becky and Jack, telling them about his mother, felt like punishment to Scott and he realized that his father was not the only one lost without her. Even though Rebecca and Jack lived in different cities, they kept in touch with their mother regularly. Both would have a hard time realizing that they would never see their mother or hear her speak to them again.

When he hung up, he went to the kitchen and spent the evening staring at a bottle of whiskey that sat on the kitchen table. He turned the cap on the bottle to loosen it, just a little. He got a glass out of the cabinet and set it down next to the bottle. What would it hurt to take one drink? He needed it so much, now, to mask his deceit, falsify the truth to himself and to prevent a white lie, something he always thought was innocuous, from ripping apart his family. He could stop at one drink; he knew that, he had proven it before. Just one little drink. He didn't have to fill the glass he could just pour it to about a half inch. One-half inch, how could that hurt him? But, it could be enough to take away his pain. Besides, he was an alcoholic. Drinking was expected of him; wasn't it?

Chapter 5
Scott

"Help, me. Help me."

"I can't find you, Mom. Where are you?" Scott ran down a long hallway that was lined with trees on both sides and that seemed to have no end. He heard his mother call out to him for help, but all he could see was more hallway.

"Scott, help me, please, please. I need you. Where are you?"

"Mom, Mom? I can't see you." He ran, or sailed or glided backward down the tree-lined hallway. "Mom, I can't find you. Please, mom, please."

"Mom? Mom? I want to help you. Where are you? Help me find you." He continued, frantically searching for his mother, now running down the hallway, between the trees, trying to breathe, running wildly. Then he came to an opening where the hallway led outside and the sun was so bright it blinded him and he still couldn't see his mother. "Mom, Mom? Where are you?" He walked out into the sunlight to a tree, the bark covered in red.

"Mom?" Scott walked closer to the tree where he saw the

tree dressed in his mother's favorite silk dress. The tree had a large dent that left it almost severed and caused it to bend to the side. The bark all around the dent was crumbled and on the ground. Something red, he thought was a scarf at first, poured from the dent. He couldn't see his mother's face, but gradually her faceless head came into view, a black sweatband holding back her hair. Suddenly he saw her huge feet with little sparkles around the edges of her running shoes and though she tried to run fast, she seemed to stay in place. Her huge feet that looked more like the feet of a cartoon character, wouldn't allow her to move fast enough. Then people he didn't recognize began to appear and one by one, they caught up to her and passed her. Some laughed at her and pointed to her feet, with the large rounded toes and smaller heel. Others scowled as if wondering how she thought she could run with such huge feet.

~~~~~~~~~~

With a jolt, Scott woke himself and sat up in the bed turning from side to side as if looking for his mother. He looked down at his clothes and found them wet from perspiration. He wiped his brow. "Mom," he whispered. He eased himself up out of bed — still looking around the room as if he thought the dream would return — and walked toward the walk-in closet. He needed a run to clear his head and he needed to find something that would lead him to the witness, the woman who saw the car that hit his mother. He threw on his running clothes and went down to the kitchen. The bottle of whiskey and glass that he'd gotten out the night before were not on the table. He stepped on the lever and looked in the trash. On top of the discarded food wrappings sat the empty bottle of whiskey.

After sitting at the kitchen table for more than an hour the night before, he thought about what his mother would have wanted him to do. He opened the whiskey bottle and poured it down the drain a little at a time at first; several times, he wanted to change his mind. He asked himself what throwing away good whiskey could accomplish. But he knew he had to do it and for the first time in almost three years, he poured liquor down something other than his throat. He threw the bottle in the trash and stood there for a while trying not to regret what he had done, and for a brief moment thought about buying another bottle. Instead, he went to his room, sat down in front of his computer and began re-writing a short story that he had begun about a year ago. He had shared it with his mother and she had wanted him to finish it, and try to get it published. When he thought he had finished it, he dedicated it to her.

Scott pulled into the parking lot and into the nearest parking space. When he got out and walked closer to where the bike and walk trail began, he noticed that the yellow tape from the day before was still around the parking space where his mother's car was parked and the chalk outline of where her body was found. It didn't seem fair; his mother was fragile and gone while the asphalt strong and durable remained. When he turned around he almost bumped into Kathryn, the lady from the day before; the woman who had the face of an angel, fine and delicate and alluring eyes that seemed to speak for her.

"Oh, sorry," said Scott. He stepped away from her to avoid a collision with her.

"No, I should have told you I was here. I just wasn't sure who you were."

"Scott Kersey," extending his hand.

"No. I mean I know who you are. I just didn't recognize you from behind. I'm Kathryn Milner, remember? You returned my ID? Thanks, again." She shook his hand again. "I'm sorry. I saw on the news and your mother's picture. I'm so sorry about your mother."

"Thank you."

He looked down at her ankle. "How's your ankle?" asked Scott.

"Much better. See no limping." She walked around in a small circle.

Scott noticed how well coordinated her rose color velour running suit with rose color around the soles of her shoes looked on her. She seemed more like she was modeling the clothes rather than using them. He looked down at his clothes that he had just thrown on and felt embarrassed.

"Is this where it happened?" She pointed to the tape and the space where his mother's life was taken.

"Yes. The police said that a woman saw the car that hit her. I was hoping I could find that person this morning."

"How?" asked Kathryn.

"Ask around. Didn't you run at the same time my mother ran?"

"Yes, sometimes."

"Well, you probably know who this woman is, this witness," said Scott.

"I remember your mother because she was usually going to her car when I was just coming in, although I would get here early sometimes, like today. I recognized your mother, but I didn't see her often and I didn't know who she was until I saw her picture on the news."

"The police didn't say whether the woman was coming or going at the time my, at the time," said Scott

"So, she could have been an earlier or a later runner. I see. What are you planning to do right this very moment?" asked Kathryn, a smile on her face.

"This is the time my mother usually took her run. I thought I would take a run myself and then see who was in the parking lot when I returned."

"Mind if I join you?" asked Kathryn.

"No, not at all." He smiled back at her. He liked that she wanted to run with him.

They took off down the trail. Scott wanted to get a look at everyone who jogged, or ran or walked during that time in the morning. When he was with his mother, like most runners, his mind was on running. He rarely looked at the scenery or other people exercising, mostly because he struggled so hard to get his breath and keep up with his mother. Now, he wanted to run differently. He wanted not only to see these people, but he also wanted to remember their faces as well. They passed an older couple walking their dog; a younger man running; a middle-aged man walking who seemed to have had too many beers judging from his mid section; a young girl running with earphones. He didn't know why but the girl looked familiar to him. As they passed her, he watched her as she ran along the edge of the trail.

When they had finished the four-mile run, they walked back to the car during the last quarter mile, remembering his mother's schedule and the fact that he could run no farther. They hung around the parking lot for the next forty-five minutes, and asked each person who drove up if they had witnessed the hit and run or knew who had witnessed the hit and run from the day before. None of the eight people to whom they collectively spoke knew anything and only two people even knew of the accident. Scott looked at his watch and realized that his mother's run would have ended by that time and she would have returned home.

Kathryn told him that because she only lived two blocks away, she ran to the park. He drove Kathryn to her house before he went home to change clothes. It felt nice having her run beside him, then sit in the seat beside him in the car. He felt her warmth, kindness and her sincerity; that pleasant something that hung in the air, something intangible, but definitely present. He was beginning to feel like she was a part of him and he was suddenly frightened by that fact. This is not what he needed at this time. Maybe it was just in his mind. After all, watching her - and he did - she didn't seem to be fazed by him one bit. He decided that he was making more of it than there was. But on the other hand, he couldn't ever remember feeling anything like that with Lisa, his girlfriend.

Scott looked at his watch again, and realized that he would have to hurry to pick up Rebecca at the airport. His sister's plane would be arriving shortly. Since the death of his mother, thinking about or even just the mention of his sister made his stomach contract into a tight ball.

Chapter 6
Scott

At the terminal, Scott stood with his father — the two of them peering through the wall-length glass window — and watched as the plane pulled into the airfield on the tarmac and navigate into the jet bridge. Overhead, a man's voice came on the loud speaker, and announced the arrival of the plane and gave other instructions. Outside, the empty trees allowed an unobstructed view of small buildings around the airport as well as the taller buildings off in the distance.

Scott looked up into the clear faded-blue sky with soft white clouds that gently bounced their way across the firmament, and for a moment thought about what heaven would be like. He wanted to think that his mother already knew what heaven was like because she was there and he tried to imagine his mother in a place like heaven where there was so much love and beauty. But he didn't want to, couldn't bring himself to think that. Then for a short moment, he gave in to the reality and thought about his mother in a land of beauty filled with happiness with love surrounding her and suddenly he wanted to cry. He turned away from his father, but kept himself from crying. His mother died a violent death. He was responsible for that. There was no way she was in a land of beauty. Wherever she was, he had put her there and that thought made him want a drink. He cleared his throat and turned toward the window again.

Scott saw his father's face through the glass and then looked over at him. The sun's short rays barely reflected through the heavy glass windows, but seemed to create a gold -lined passageway.

"Dad, I can meet Becky if you want." He felt a sudden stab of anxiety in his gut and as soon as he said it, he regretted it.

Scott dreaded the fact that both Becky and Jack would be in the same house with him again. He loved his sister and brother very much, but he thought that Cameron always compared him to Becky and Jack. Even though Cameron didn't outright say things like, "Why can't you be more like Becky or Jack." Or, "Look at how proud I am of Jack and Becky," Scott sensed it. Why else was he always saying things like, "Becky says her hospital is expanding its cardiology ward? She's a good doctor and her patients must love her." or "Jack's business is really flourishing. I saw in the paper where he's one of the few businesses that had maintained a steady growth over the past five years." With the two of them out of the house, Scott's underdeveloped aspirations weren't as prominent and he didn't feel the need to defend himself as much.

But, there were many times when Scott didn't feel like he was competing with his brother and sister. There was the year when the three of them were in high school at the same time; Jack was a senior, Becky a junior and Scott a freshman. That year Scott wanted to follow around behind his big brother, the dude every girl in high school tried to date. Jack was the one with the looks. He was 6'1", dark wavy hair he kept cropped close to show off his dimples the girls loved. Jack worked out a lot and always looked good in his clothes. He had taken care of his little brother and had tried not to let anybody bother Scott as the seniors did the other freshmen. Being stuffed in a locker after class or made to do something degrading in front of a hall full of your classmates in between classes was a freshman's worse nightmare.

Even though Jack did his best to keep Scott from hazing, he couldn't always be with his younger brother, especially since they didn't have many classes in the same part of the building. At that time in his life, there was just something about Scott that made the seniors want to taunt and bully him. These students always contented that given Scott's manner, he had asked for it. Maybe it was because he was a nerd, always writing articles for the school paper and didn't fight back that made him an easy target.

One afternoon during lunch, Jack didn't see Scott in the lunchroom. He went over to the table where Scott's friends usually sat and asked if they'd seen him. No one had. Jack looked up and saw four seniors, noted for bullying freshmen — the seniors Scott had had trouble with — entering the cafeteria laughing. One looked up, and saw Jack and nudged one of the others. They laughed again. Jack ran out of the cafeteria, up the stairs to the left and down the hall to Scott's locker. He saw Scott trying to extricate himself from his locker. Jack helped him out and then wanted to take on all four of the boys. Scott talked him out of it saying that it wasn't worth the trouble they would get into for the retribution.

During half time at the homecoming game that year, Scott had sat in the almost full stands with Jack and two of Jack's friends. Tara, a friend of Ellen, the girl that Scott was crazy about, but who hung out with the seniors, came to the stands to hand him a folded over note. The note said that Ellen wanted to see him. Scott didn't believe her at first. He didn't know Ellen's handwriting, and gave the note back to Tara. Ellen was also a friend of the seniors and even dated one of them. She wouldn't send him a note, he reasoned. But Tara insisted that the request was genuine and Scott went to meet her. Ellen led him to a secluded area behind the gym and in back of the school.

There, a group of four buffed seniors jumped him, tore off all of his clothes except his shorts, and spray painted his body with blue and yellow paint, the school colors. They put him in a grocery cart, two holding him down so he couldn't get out, and rolled him onto the football field right in front of the cheerleaders. As the seniors pushed him out onto the field, the cheerleaders, one by one slowed down as they watched, but they never stopped cheering. When the cart was out in plain view, the seniors took off running. They also ran because the principal and two assistant principals ran out onto the field to catch them. It took Scott a while before he was able to disentangle himself from the cart and he had to turn the cart over to free himself. He ripped his shorts in the process. The only thing that saved him from complete embarrassment was the fact that the seniors had painted him over so thoroughly, no one was able to recognize him.

When he was free, he ran off the field, behind the school and through the streets for almost a mile as fast as he could, holding his shorts closed. When he got to his house, Becky was coming out and saw him. She took him in the house and tried to get out of him what happened. But he was shaking and crying so badly she could hardly understand him. She took him to his room and made him get in the bathtub while she drove back to the school to get his clothes and to pick up body paint remover.

It wasn't until the game ended and he got home did Jack know that it was Scott who was "The Grocery Cart Boy," as the students dubbed him. Everyone found out later it was Scott when Cameron and Laurie had to meet with the principal about punishment for the students who did it and the repaying of medical expenses.

After it was all over, Becky encouraged Scott to write an article about what happened for the school's newspaper. The article was so good that the creative writing class wanted it to include in their school anthology. He also won a literary award for his artistic portrayal of bullying and hazing, which finally got the attention of the principal.

~~~~~~~~~~

"Dad? Dad? Are you sure? I can meet Becky if you want. You can wait in the car."

"I was just remembering . . ."

"Dad, you don't have to do this. I can meet Becky. Why don't you wait in the car?"

"You know, the first time I ever saw your mother was on a plane. She was getting off the plane that I was to board. I took one look at her and I knew that she was to be my wife."

"She was special." Scott had heard this all before, but he knew his father needed to say it and he let him.

"It took me a moment, but I followed her. I figured that I had a few minutes while they got the plane ready, but I knew that if I had to, I'd take another plane. I tried to catch her to talk to her. I didn't know what I was getting into and I didn't care. I just knew I had to meet her. I raced to stop her before she got to the busy part of the airport and into the crowd. When I finally reached her, I didn't know what to say, so I started blubbering and stuttering and then before I knew it, I was blabbing out the truth."

"The truth?"

"Well, and I don't know if I'd recommend this, you understand, I just told her I needed to get on the plane that she just got off of, but first I needed to know her name and how I could contact her. I think she thought I was some kind of half-crazed lunatic at first, but I told her my name, gave her my card, and told her that I just had to meet her, and wanted to take her out when I got back. Maybe she saw the seriousness on my face, or felt sorry for me, I don't know, but at the end of all that embarrassment, she told me her name. I asked where she was from and I told her that I was from Maryland. I begged her to call me at the hotel later that evening."

"Did she?"

"Yes. But, I think she was more curious than anything else."

"You won her over."

"Yes. I guess I did, didn't I?"

The door flew open and the passengers from the plane entered the waiting area just like race horses leaving the starting gate. Cameron and Scott looked for Becky who seemed to be the last passenger off. When she saw her father and, brother she ran to them and threw her arms around them.

That awful high school time flashed through his mind again and while he thought about it, he held onto Becky a little tighter. Maybe she wouldn't make him feel so guilty.

~~~~~~~~~~

When the three of them got back to the house, later on that evening, Jack and his wife were pulling into the driveway. By the next evening, everyone was there. Laurie's mother Sandra and her father, Michael, who had had a stroke and who was sometimes lucid, drove in from Virginia and they all stayed at the house. Laurie's two sisters, Ella and Julianne, with their husbands arrived from Texas and Canada. Their children also flew in from Texas and Canada and they all drove to a hotel. Cameron's parents, Barbara and Evan who were now divorced, drove in from North Carolina with their new spouses and they stayed at the house. His brother along with his sister and their spouses and children all stayed at a hotel.

After everyone settled themselves and shortly before dinner, one by one, they drifted to the great room and filled up the two large brown leather sofas that faced each other and the beige and ecru arm chairs as well as the tan striped silk wing chairs on each side of the credenza and table. The housekeepers had also added chairs earlier that morning. They left a tray of cocktails and glasses for those who wanted or needed it along with a pitcher of water.

Barbara's husband, Harry, asked about the weather. Scott thought that this was his way of trying to fit in. He really didn't understand why Harry would even bother to come, since he was not really a member of the family and never knew Laurie. As it turned out, no one really responded though there were a few mumblings that made its way around the room.

Laurie's mother, Sandra, asked Cameron, "How did this happen?"

"Oh, mother, we don't need to go through that again. We know how it happened," said Julianne, Laurie's sister.

Scott relaxed and let out a sigh of relief. He wouldn't have to face the family and tell them what he should have done. He knew that his father's philosophy was to protect the women. He had heard it enough times to know that's what he should have done.

"Who brought the carnations?" asked Laurie's father, Michael.

"Elaina and I did," said Jack. "They were her favorite."

"But, we brought her roses," said Julianne.

"I guess we'll just have to find a place for all these flowers," said Sandra, Laurie's mother.

Then there was quiet, an eerie stillness that filled the room.

Scott looked around the room. Everyone seemed to be in still motion. Laurie's sister, Julianne, with a glass in her hand at her lips, Michael, sitting forward in his chair eyes staring straight ahead, not blinking; Cameron standing turned to the window, looking out.

Cameron's stepfather, Harry, was the first one to break the discomfort by bringing up the weather again.

"What is the point with this weather?" began Jack. "I mean I don't get it. It's cold, so what? You happy?"

Barbara, Cameron's mother stood up for her husband. "He was just trying to make conversation. You don't have to get ugly."

Cameron's father, Evan, said, "I think he's just trying to make conversation."

"We don't need him to make conversation," said Sandra, Laurie's mother.

"I want to know what happened to my daughter," said Michael, Laurie's father.

"We already know what happened to her," said Julianne, Laurie's older sister. "Why do you keep bringing that up?"

"We don't know the particulars," said Ella, Laurie's younger sister.

"We do know the particulars. She was run over," said Laurie's mother. "What more do you need to know?"

"Where did all this happen? No one gave me the facts," said Evan.

"Yeah, was she alone when it happened?" asked Michael.

"What are the police doing?" asked Ella. "I want to know that."

"Are there any leads?" asked Michael. "Do they have any idea who did this terrible thing and why?"

"There was a witness," said Cameron.

"There was a witness?" asked Sandra. "No one said anything about a witness."

"Yes, what about the witness," began Evan. "I asked a friend of mine before coming here and he said —"

"What? He said what?" asked Cameron. He turned and took at step toward Evan, eyes crunched up, nostrils almost flaring. "Are you saying that the police haven't done enough? I haven't done enough? She's dead. My wife is dead. What other particulars do you need to know?"

"Dinner is served," announced the housekeeper.

Without another word, everyone except Cameron got up and followed the housekeeper to the dining room where they sat at different tables and according to their name cards.

Scott returned to the great room and saw his father standing at the window looking out.

"Dad?"

Scott heard Becky's voice behind him. He turned to her.

"Dad?" called out Jack.

Cameron turned from the window to face his children. "Go on and eat. I'll be there in a minute."

Jack and Becky moved toward their father who took a step toward them. They grabbed onto their father and held on tightly.

"Scott? Where's Scott?" asked Cameron.

Becky turned around and waved for Scott to join them. They held onto each other as tightly as they could. Scott felt the presence of his mother in that room.

"I can't believe that just a month ago Mom told us how she made all the food for the Christmas dinner," said Becky.

"We had her with us at Christmas," said Jack. "and we were all here the entire time."

"That was the first time in a long time we'd done anything like that," said Becky.

"I just got this feeling that I wanted to have everyone over for Christmas and have them stay as long as they could," said Cameron.

"I know it was an enormous job for Mom, but I'm glad you did it," said Jack, wiping his tears.

"Your mom has always gone along with everything I've wanted. Of course, at times, I've had to pay a price for that."

He chuckled. "But I've always loved that about her. This time she made Scott and me help her, too." He laughed again and wiped at his tears.

They were all quiet for a long moment, holding on to each other as firmly as they could as well as holding tight any memory they had of their mother and wife.

"I don't know what I'm gonna do, now."

"Dad, you're gonna be all right. Just give it time." Jack whispered.

"Besides, you have her teen project," said Becky.

"Yeah, that school and house for runaway teens that mom wanted. You have that to finish for her, Dad," said Jack.

"I can move back —" began Becky.

"Don't you dare," said Cameron. "You have your doctoring to do. I'll be okay. Like Jack said, I'll give it time. And you guys keep calling every week, okay?"

"She's ours, Dad. No matter what they think, she belongs to us," whispered Jack.

The four of them stood huddled in a circle, arms locked around each other, tears flowing and whispering, "She's ours, she's ours," again and, again.

~~~~~~~~~~

After the procession, when the service started, Scott looked around the church at the people in the pews. "I am the resurrection and the life. . . ." His girlfriend, Lisa, her black veil pushed up over her hat, stood next to him, a prayer book opened to the service for the burial of the dead. Scott, holding a prayer book, turned around and saw many of the women who ran with his mother. Near the back sat the older couple with the dog. He was surprised to see the girl with the earphones in a black suit. He remembered her now. His mother got her into the home. Laurie found her on the street and took her to the home. As he watched her, he remembered his mother saying she had re-enrolled in high school, graduated and entered college. His mother said she wanted to be a teacher.

"Please sit for the reading from the Old Testament. . ." He heard the priest say somewhere in the distance. Lisa pulled on his arm and Scott sat down. Across the aisle he recognized some of his mother's book club and coffee group ladies. Mrs. Edwards, always in her green hat with a black feather – according to his mother - wore a black hat today. Farther toward the back, he saw the women, men, and teens from the place where his mother volunteered, the house for runaway teens, and he even thought he recognized another teenager whom his mother had tried to help. Sitting behind them, he saw employees from his father's Real Estate Investments Planning and Development Agency. All around him he saw church members filling up the pews.

During the reading of the Gospel, Scott faced his mother's coffin wishing that his mother's death was all a mistake; or even that he was in some kind of dream. He had hoped with all his heart that she would jump up out of the coffin and say something like, "We fooled you, huh?" How he would have given anything to hear her say that. Instead, he heard prayers, words that spoke of dying and blessing the dead and words that asked for entrance into heaven.

When the service ended and the congregation began a hymn, Scott joined his father and brother as they walked behind the six pallbearers who carried his mother's body to the limo that was to take her to the cemetery. All his hopes dashed; he had nothing else to believe. He knew that this was no joke, no dream, and no mistake. His mother was never coming back. He would never get a second chance to show his mother that he could change.

They drove through the brick entrance of the cemetery and continued on the curving road to the open gravesite. He stood beside his mother's grave on a hill that overlooked the Potomac River, as he heard the priest say prayers over her coffin; prayers that asked God to receive her into His kingdom. He heard the family and friends, as they stood around the gravesite, saying The Lord's Prayer and he tried to say some of the words, but his heart was so full of sadness that the words stuck in his throat. Then he saw four workers lower the casket into the grave. He saw people throwing flowers on the casket and someone passed him a yellow carnation. He didn't want to at first as he held on to the stem and looked down on the casket, but Laurie's sister, Ella, whispered something to him, and he did as he had seen the others do. He heard the priest say other prayers and then an "Amen" chorused from the group.

Scott stayed behind with his father while others left. He remembered a poem by Edgar Allan Poe that he read to his mother one evening when she helped him prepare for a school assignment.

> How shall the burial rite be read?
> The solemn song be sung?
> The requiem for the loveliest dead,
> That ever died so young?

He remembered asking his mother if the poem was written about a child. His mother told him there were different kinds of dying. He didn't understand at the time, but now he understood her thought. He would not let his mother die. He would always carry her in his heart. He placed his hand on the coffin and promised his mother he would be okay, he would always remember her and he would lead his life the way she wanted. He told her he loved her and he would always love her and he asked her to look after his father.

On the way back to the car, he heard someone say it was a beautiful day, and Laurie would have loved her service. She would have wanted her funeral to be on a beautiful day. Scott looked up at the sky and saw that his mother would have loved it. The sun was out and the air was nippy, with a fresh, clean feel. His mother loved the chilly air and she always said the cold sterilized the earth and gave her a sensation of the world starting over again. Each day the world had another chance to get it all right.

Chapter 7
Scott

"Good morning, ma'am, this lady had an automobile accident here a few days ago. Did you see the accident or know anything about what happened to this lady?" Scott stood at the mouth of the trail. He held up Laurie's picture and stuck it in the face of a woman as he walked beside her. She pushed the picture away and took off running down the trail. Two other women had just finished their run and came to the end of the trail toward the parking lot. When the two women were a few steps away, Scott realized that he had already asked them. One woman looked at him and smiled.

"No luck?"

"No ma'am."

"You've been out here a while. How much longer?" asked the second woman. "You look a little tired."

"I think I'll give it another hour," said Scott.

"Good luck to you." The two women headed for their car.

Scott saw a man and woman approaching, both walking fast.

"Have you seen —"

"No," yelled out a man when Scott showed Laurie's picture. They quickly scooted away to the parking lot.

He saw a woman coming in the opposite direction. "Have you . . . , my . . . mother . . . ," began Scott.

The woman shook her head as she ran onto the trail.

A car pulled up into a space on the other side of the entrance and two women, one with a mixed breed and the other a terrier hopped out of the car. Before the woman could get the leash on him, the terrier took off running and headed for the trail. Scott managed to stop the dog by the collar just as it ran onto the trail. The woman ran up to retrieve her dog and thank Scott. Scott responded by thrusting Laurie's picture in her face.

"This is my mother. She was —" began Scott.

"Mister, thank you for my dog, but I don't want to buy anything. Besides, I didn't bring any money with me. Sorry," she said as she and her friend and their dogs jogged away.

After a few minutes, a woman and two men, came from the bend in the trail and walked toward the parking lot. "That's him," she said as she pointed to Scott still standing at the entrance to the trail. The woman passed by Scott giving him a look of disgust as she walked toward her car.

"Good morning, Mr. Kersey," said Haines.

Charles nodded at Scott. He unbuttoned his coat.

"Good morning. What brings you two here? You're not dressed for running," said Scott.

"No, we're not here for running, though I could use it," said Haines patting his belly.

"A complaint came into our office this morning," said Charles.

"A complaint? Is it something about my mother?" asked Scott.

"In a sense. Scott we got a complaint that someone was at this trail accosting people near the parking lot and blocking the entrance so that people couldn't get onto the trail. We're not the officers who would normally handle things like this, but when we heard it was at this trail, we thought we'd come and find out."

"Me? I'm not accosting people. I just want to find the person who saw what happened. I even brought along her picture so that people would recognize her." He showed them Laurie's picture.

The two detectives looked at the picture and then at each other. Haines cut his eyes away from Scott. Charles nodded his head several times.

"Scott, I know you want to help out, but you just can't do this. You can't stand here blocking the entrance to the trail and, preventing people from their exercise," said Charles.

"Oh, I'm not doing that. I am here at the entrance, but I'm not blocking anyone or stopping anyone.

"Go home, Scott."

He looked from one to the other. "I can't. I have to do something."

"I know. I know you do, but you have to go home and leave this to us," said Haines. "You just buried your mother this morning and that got you all upset. I understand that. Just go home. Let us finish this."

Scott looked down at himself. He was still in his black suit and tie. His mother was now in the ground and he hadn't a clue about who did it. He couldn't go home or think about his writing or work and leave his mother's killer unidentified. He should have been with her to pull her out of the way. He should have protected her, shielded her from harm. He should have stopped anything from happening. He should have called out to her, to the driver to stop. He should have stepped in front of the car himself. He should have . . . kept his mother alive.

At that moment, Cameron pulled into the parking lot. He got out of his car and ran to where the three men stood.

"Scott, what's going on? I got a call from these officers saying —" He pointed to Haines and Charles.

"We were just explaining things to him, Mr. Kersey. I think he understands now that he can't do this. Just leave it to us, okay?" said Charles.

The two detectives walked back down the trail.

"Dad, I have to do something. I just can't —" Scott began as he turned toward his father.

"I know, son. But we have to. This is police work."

"Don't you want to find out what happened to mom?"

"Of course, I do. But this is not the way," said Cameron.

"What is the way, Dad? Letting the police take their own good time about finding out who, who . . ." He turned his back and looked down the trail.

"Scott, we don't know what happened. There could be some maniac out there waiting to harm people. I don't want you harmed." He must have spoken louder than he expected and tried to quiet down at the end.

Exercisers coming on to the trail watched the two of them as they passed by.

Scott took a step left off the paved trail and Cameron followed. A man nodded to them as he went by.

Cameron must have seen the disappointment on Scott's face.

He didn't try to hide it.

"Scott, we may want to try to help later, but for now, we have no choice. Leave the police work to the police."

Scott reluctantly followed his father back to the parking lot. Cameron stopped at the yellow tape. He took a step closer and touched the tape.

"Dad, we have to find that person. You know we have to do it."

Cameron turned to him, reached out, and touched Scott's arm, then he walked toward his car.

The unrest that Scott felt from his mother's death settled in his chest and made him anxious. He felt so helpless at this point and he had to do something. But what? His father was right; they had no idea how to even begin to search for someone who didn't want to be caught. But he knew he had to do something. He thought finding the witness, the woman who saw everything was the place to start. He failed to protect his mother when she needed him. He allowed it to happen. He should have run with her that day. Had he been there, she would not have stopped to talk to anyone in the parking lot. Had he been there, they would have been home when the car pulled into the parking lot. Had he been there, his mother would not have been hit and would still be with them now.

Had he been there . . . .

Chapter 8
Scott

Later that evening, Scott went to Lisa's house to keep his date and, found her angry again, eyes blinking, foot tapping. She wouldn't let him in the house, mouth poked out just like a five-year-old child demanding her way. She complained about his tardiness once more. It was times like these when he wondered why he didn't just walk away and never return.

"What time did you say you would be here? What time is it now?" Lisa stood with her hands on her hips, driving home her point.

Scott stood in the doorway, hands stuffed in his pants pockets, humbling himself at first, as he usually did. Fatigue washed over him and it seemed to take an extraordinary effort for him to stand up, as he suddenly felt worn out. He struggled, but took his hands out of his pockets, straightened his back, looked at her and thought that it was not physical fatigue that he felt, he was just downright tired of the emotional drudgery. More than anything in the world, he needed someone to talk to, someone who understood what he was going through, someone to whom he didn't always have to explain things. Whenever he really needed anyone, he knew he could never depend on Lisa for anything. He didn't even understand why he went to her house. He had hoped that since she was with him when his mother was buried, that just once she would reach out to him, ask him what he needed, hold him and make him feel good about himself. He thought that she would understand and that just once she would listen to him, console him; help take some of his guilt away. He didn't think that was asking too much, especially considering the number of times he listened to her about her parents, her job, and virtually anything.

"You promised you'd start getting here on time, be more considerate, more thoughtful."

He had no one. He couldn't talk to his father; that would only make things worse for his father. He had done enough already.

"I just can't do this anymore, I just can't."

"Me either." Scott heard himself say as he turned and walked down the steps. He didn't look back.

"Where are you going? Scott? Scott? Aren't you going to tell me you're sorry?" Lisa started down the steps beside Scott; slow at first then she hurried her step when he did. "Scott, please, Scott?"

He heard the horror in her voice, but he never looked back. As he continued down the steps and walked to his car, he felt a burden, a sort of heaviness lifted from him. He looked up into the evening sky as if he could finally move from under his heavy weight. Saying good-bye to Lisa felt right; it felt final. As he drove away, he wondered why he had taken so long to let her go. He heard her yelling for him to come back and wondered if she ran after the car. She did that one time when they were splitting up about three months after they had met. Then, he turned around and went back to her. This time, Scott was through; he wanted no more of her.

Later, he found himself sitting in his car across the street from Kathryn's house trying to build the courage to knock on her door. When he left Lisa, he was in a fog and he drove around, no place in mind, until he ended up in front of Kathryn's house. He cut the motor and sat in his car, just staring out at the house. After a while, he realized that he didn't have the courage to go in, besides, she wasn't expecting him. He reached to start up his car when he noticed the car in front of him. Two people — a female and a male — making out in the front seat. Just what he needed now. The female raised her arms and the man slipped the woman's top off. Then he couldn't see them. Scott figured that they were about to take the next step. In a few minutes, Kathryn pulled up in front of her house. As she got out, she saw the car parked across the street. A woman's head popped up.

"Mary, Mary?" yelled Kathryn.

Scott saw the two people scrambling around in the car. The man got out at the same time he pulled his pants up and zipped up. Scott saw the lady put her top back on and then covered her face.

"This is not your concern," said the man.

Scott got out of his car, went to the other car, opened the passenger door.

"Do you live here?" asked Scott. He pointed to Kathryn's house.

Mary nodded.

"Why don't you get out and go on in your house?" He reached his hand out to her; she took it.

"Go on inside," he coaxed.

Mary walked toward Kathryn.

Scott walked over and stood between Kathryn and the man. "Do you need some help?" he asked Kathryn.

"Jake, this is not right. My sister is a minor," said Kathryn

"She's your step sister and she knows what she's doing," said Jake.

"Please leave before my father comes out."

"Not without Mary."

"Hi Jake. Scott. Why not just do what Kathryn asked?"

"Who the hell are you?"

"I'm Scott, Kathryn's friend."

"Why are you trying to tell me what to do?" asked Jake.

"You think she needs this? I know what you want, but give it up. It's not gonna happen tonight."

Jake looked at Mary. Kathryn turned to Mary. Mary stood head bowed, both hands clutching her shirt as if she thought it would open. She tried to wipe away her tears that left two black tracks running down her face. She smeared the tracks across her face, grabbed her shirt again.

"Damn" he said as he opened the door to get back in the car.

"I'll see you tomorrow," squealed out Mary.

"No you won't," said Jake and he sped off.

"Thank you. For a moment I didn't think he would leave," said Kathryn.

Mary looked long and hard at Scott as if she wanted to say something but didn't know what or how. She started away, but turned back to Scott again.

"Thank you," she finally said, then walked into the house, still clutching her shirt.

Kathryn turned to Scott, a questioning look on her face.
"What —"

"Would you care to have dinner with me?" asked Scott.

"Now? You mean now?"

"Yes, right now. We can go wherever you want. We can even drive in separate cars if that makes you more comfortable. But, I, I would like to have dinner with you."

Kathryn looked into his eyes and must have seen the heaviness that his heart carried; his paltriness. Perhaps she realized that he had just lost his mother, and still came to her rescue when she needed it. Whatever she felt, he was happy he asked.

"Okay. There's a little café near here that I like. Why don't you follow me?"

At that moment, Scott felt like a little boy opening a Christmas gift that he'd been wanting for a long time. He almost screamed out "Yes," but controlled himself and only let out a little smile.

At the café, Scott asked for a seat in the corner where he would have her full attention.

"I understand about your mother," she said.

"What do you mean?"

"I never knew my mother. She died when I was five."

"Oh, Kathryn, I'm sorry. That must have been hard."

"Yes. It was and is. Most people ask me if I miss her. Why didn't you ask me that?"

"I figured you did. She was your mother."

"People seem to think that if you never experience something you don't miss it. But I did miss my mother and still miss her so much. I really needed her when I was growing up."

"How did you get over the loss?"

"I don't think I ever did. I always wished I had someone to tell me how to dress, and do my hair, someone to confide in."

"My mother and I talked often. After college I moved back home and she and I did things together like running."

"What was she like?"

"Probably like your mother. She was a stable force in our home. Everything was always pleasant. No matter what any of us went through at school and college or even the work world, she always made everything seem okay. She was encouraging and she made me feel like what she was pushing me to do was something I wanted to do. I miss her so much. We talked often, but some things were personal."

"You guys. Women share all. You guys hold back. Why is that?" Kathryn laughed.

"It's how we are. How we're different."

He stopped and looked at her for a long moment in the glow of the candle light.

"What's the matter? Did I say something wrong?" she asked.

He leaned forward in his chair. "Absolutely not. I was just thinking how easy it is to talk to you."

"Funny, I was just thinking the same thing."

"Wow," he said and shook his head.

She smiled at him, a warm caring smile. She asked him about his job and where he worked and he dodged that question as much as he could saying that he worked for a real estate investment company.

He watched her as she talked and noticed the curl of her lip when she smiled, the way she held her fork just before taking a bite. She seemed free and she allowed him to feel free. He liked how she would just let loose and when she laughed, she gave a good hearty laugh. He saw what made her happy and to him she seemed to be happy over little things. He loved the smile that she gave him when he told her about his mother. He loved her thoughtfulness and the way she whispered "Oh, no," when he told her how he pulled a muscle running. Her body seemed to light up when he asked her about fashion designing. He asked her about her family and her job. She told him about her dream of becoming a fashion designer and about how hard it was to break into that world.

She told him that what people wore was a reflection of their personality. At that moment, he tried to apologize for his dress, but she told him that he looked okay and complimented him on his dress.

"You need to meet Frankie," she said.

"Frankie?"

"Yes, he's the designer I work for and a dear friend."

"I'd love to meet him."

She showed him the pictures of Frankie Sanchez and her father and Sylvia, Betty and Mary. He listened to her talk about fashion and marveled at her passion. He imagined her in one of her designs that she described, with her thin model-like body. He loved the way her clothes fell on her, not like Lisa who always looked like she had one French fry too many and, who tugged and pulled at her clothes all the time. He told her about Lisa, the break-up fight that they just had, how they had always fought and how Lisa didn't understand him. He liked her playful-like manner and he found himself smiling and laughing with her, something that he hadn't done in a long time.

He heard her talk about many things that night. He had

hoped he wasn't too overbearing, especially when he asked her many questions about why she loved the world of fashion. She smiled at him all night, and he thought that was a good sign. He saw how carried away she was with everything he said. He allowed her to talk, open up, express herself and she said she liked it; it was something new to her. She said she didn't even know she had that much to say about anything and that she was amazed at how he let her rant on and on. She told him about her best friend who moved away to a boarding school and how hard it was for her to make new friends. She told him about her first love, Steve, and the leukemia that took him away from her before they graduated from high school. She also told him about Harris Sweeney, the man she was seeing off and on and that she liked the distant relationship they had. She said that there was no commitment with either of them. Throughout, he nodded for her to continue. He seemed to need to know everything about her. He felt as if he was sinking, being pulled down into the swirl of her. He wanted to find the off button to his feelings. It was too soon, he knew, and watching her, she seemed to enjoy his company, but it didn't seem to him that she was falling for him — maybe this Harris Sweeney was stopping her — the way he seemed to be falling for her. The speed of his feelings for her frightened him.

Before they both realized it, the restaurant was closing and neither could believe how long they had been there talking or how much they had told each other. A warmth came over him when she told him that she didn't want to leave and it was then that he knew he wanted to be with her forever, but he also knew that they had just met and he was in a bad place.

Chapter 9
Scott

Scott raced to the door when he looked up and saw a flashing light coming from the family room on the main floor of his house. Cameron seated on the white leather horseshoe-style couch, family albums and loose pictures strewn about on the couch next to him and on the navy blue wool carpet in front of him. Home movies reflected on a screen in front of the entertainment center across the room, and the only light. Scott stood in the doorway watching. He hadn't seen home movies in quite a while and he realized that as he, Becky and Jack got older, his parents took less home movies or videos. More than likely, it was due to the fact that as teenagers they found doing things with their parents objectionable.

Scott fumbled for the chain light switch on the crystal lamp on the mahogany end table next to his father. He looked up at the screen and saw a movie of his mother, father, sister, brother, and him at the beach. He watched for a moment as he remembered years ago when his mother and father were younger and he was five. Then the pictures changed to his sister's tenth birthday party, with Becky blowing out the candles on her cake, and then a more recent one of his mother and father sitting in their backyard at a picnic table, Cameron's arms around Laurie. Scott remembered that afternoon and remembered the look that his parents gave to each other. At the time, Scott didn't know what that look meant, in fact, the three of them used to poke fun at that look when his parents weren't around. But seeing them now, he knew that it was the look of love. Kathryn's face briefly appeared in Scott's mind as he watched his father and mother on the screen.

He didn't think that he and Lisa had ever had that kind of love and as he stood there watching his father and mother, Scott knew that what he saw on that screen was what he wanted.

"Dad?"

No smile, his face empty, Cameron turned around to Scott who stood behind him.

Scott stared down at him not knowing what to say. Then he said with a vague confidence, "We're going to get through this, Dad. I know we are."

The movie ended and Scott turned off the video.

"I had to meet with the hotel people today, the hotel she picked for the home," said Cameron. "I can't stop thinking about her. I, I, I miss her so much. I miss us having coffee together in the morning. I miss talking to her about her day. I miss holding her at night while we sleep. I miss her waking me up through the night just to tell me one more thing."

Scott held himself straight. He didn't want his father to know just how guilty he felt. "That must have been hard." He picked up his mother's pictures, held them tightly, and sat down on the coffee table in front of Cameron.

"I kept forgetting, you know. I guess out of habit I wanted to call her, make sure we had the correct information and when I said that in the meeting suddenly everyone got quiet. They must have thought 'Poor Cameron Kersey. He can't understand his wife is dead.'" He looked around the room. "I never thought I'd have to go on without her."

They sat together in silence for a long few minutes.

Cameron looked at Scott and then looked away. He turned toward Scott.

"You know, it's all my fault," said Cameron, pushing back tears.

"Your fault? How is it your fault?" asked Scott hesitation in his voice.

Cameron gave his face a swipe with both hands and then sat back on the couch. "I should have gotten up. I didn't have to go back to sleep. I should have gotten up."

The last thing that Scott would have thought his father would have said was that he, Cameron, was to blame. Scott thought that his father would have pointed a finger at him. After all, Scott was the one who pretended to be asleep when his mother entered his room to ask him to run with her, even though he hadn't told that to his father yet. Scott was the one who ran with her when she wanted to run, most mornings, anyway.

"Dad, it's not your fault. It's the fault of the person who failed to do what was needed." Scott meant himself, but couldn't bring himself to saying that at that moment.

Cameron closed his eyes and then turned his head toward the ceiling.

"She was my wife and I promised to protect her. I promised to protect her and I couldn't do that."

"I think she would have said over and over again that you protected her always. You know that. And you know that it was not your fault."

"Why didn't she just run out of the way when she saw the car coming? When I think about what may have happened, I see your mother trying to call out to this person, explain to them that they were about to make a mistake. Why didn't she just run out of the way?"

Cameron turned away and picked up a picture of Laurie. He held it in his hands as if hoping that she had heard and that she had understood that it was not his fault.

"I can't blame her, can I?"

"Has the police talked to you since they were here last?" asked Scott needing to change the subject.

"Detective Haines said that they were waiting on the lab report. He said when they got it they would call and let us know."

Scott bent down to pick up the pictures and put them all back in the albums. Cameron joined him, stopping to look at the pictures as he did.

"We'll have to do this ourselves now. I let the housekeepers go and called the realtor."

Scott sat back, shaken by the thought of moving. He looked around the room. "Sell the house?"

"We have to. I have to."

"Are you sure, Dad? We've been here a long time. Remember when we moved in?"

"You were five years old then. Becky was seven and Jack, eight. Your mother and I waited a year for the builders to complete it. There was always something going wrong." He held up a picture of his family and their first day in the house.

Scott found a picture of a clown. "Remember when Becky had her seventh birthday party? We were all right here in this room. You and Mom hired a clown."

Cameron let out a loud laugh. "Who would have thought that she was afraid of clowns? She'd talked about them enough, even wanted to be one at one time."

"Yeah, Becky sure had us all fooled." Scott put the clown picture away. "I remember when Grandmother lost her glasses and Granddaddy stood guard at the door not letting anyone in or out until we helped her find them. I can't believe someone would take a picture of the glasses." Scott laughed and pointed to himself.

Your Grandfather can be a pretty stubborn man, as you know. I know; I had to grow up with him." Cameron stopped laughing. "Your mother and I, we tried to raise you kids differently from the way we were raised. She always said that it was a different time now, and we had to do things differently."

"You and mom did a good job with us, Dad."

Cameron continued to put the pictures away. Scott got up to put away the video camera and the screen.

"What's going on with you and Lisa?" asked Cameron.

"Why? Did she call?"

"Yes."

Scott sat down on the coffee table, again, thought for a moment.

"It's for the best."

"She seemed pretty angry. Something about being late all the time, and you walking off?" Cameron picked up a photo of Laurie and him from their wedding reception just when they were ready to slice the six tier white chocolate wedding cake.

Cameron ran his fingers across Laurie's face and her smile. He picked up another picture with Laurie and him on the dance floor, their first dance together as man and wife. He saw himself whisper something in Laurie's ear.

Cameron smiled a little at the photo and Scott watching his father, figured that Cameron remembered exactly what he had said to her. Cameron inhaled deeply and let it out. Then he put away all the pictures.

"What's with Lisa?" asked Cameron again, after he put away everything and sat down on the couch.

"I don't wanna see her anymore."

Cameron looked at Scott.

"Don't worry, Dad. It's going to be all right. I'm going to bed."

His dinner with Kathryn had filled him with exhilaration, an intense feeling of renewal. He felt like a man just out of confession, a man embarking on a new job that he'd always wanted. Her life had given him hope and an understanding about his mother. He knew that even though he was afraid and not ready to love, he had to see her. Besides, maybe he could help her the way she wanted to help him cope.

Scott wasn't ready to tell his father about Kathryn, and he just didn't care to go over how all the relationship problems he and Lisa had, and how things were his fault.

Chapter 10
Scott

After their first dinner, Scott couldn't wait to see Kathryn again which also left him very conflicted. On one hand, he loved being in her presence though he didn't think he did much for her. On the other hand, his mind told him to run for the hills; he was making a huge mistake, he wasn't ready. His selfish desire to be with her outweighed his ability to do anything for her so, he called her and asked her out to dinner. She surprised him by accepting which left him feeling good about himself.

This time they went to a swanky seafood restaurant about an hour's drive. The maitre d sat them in a small dimly lit, more intimate room where three other couples dined at tables for two. They watched as the waiter lit the candle on the table and handed them large menus bound in black leather. Scott placed his white linen napkin in his lap and then looked at Kathryn. He wanted so badly to please her.

They both ordered lobster and as they ate, she marveled about how tender it was. She handed him the butter for his baked potato when he asked.

"So what's your next story about?" asked Kathryn.

"I haven't decided yet. Maybe about a girl growing up with a step-mother." Scott chuckled.

"Well, be sure to include the loving father."

"You two get along okay?"

"My dad is my best friend. Sometimes I wish I didn't have to share him with my step family, but it gets better."

"I don't know if I can see myself being best friends with my dad."

"You will. Your father and mother are extensions of each other. If you love one, then you have to love the other. You will."

"I don't know."

"Try it. I'll bet that's what he wants."

"Kathryn—"

"Kat."

"What?"

"Kat. Call me Kat. Everybody else does."

"Kathryn fits you better. But since you asked, Kat, I think he does. I just can't take the demands."

"What do you mean?"

"My father thinks I can do better in everything. He says I don't try hard enough."

"Can you do better?"

"Whose side are you on?"

"Your side, of course. Scott, can you do better?"

He looked at her not sure how much he wanted to give away. "I don't know."

"Sure, you do."

Scott sat back in his chair, thought for a moment. How could she see this in him so quickly?

After dinner, on the walk back to his car, he slipped his hand in hers. She didn't pull it away. When he felt her hand in his, his heart raced and he wanted to take her in his arms and love every part of her. At the doorstep of her home, he asked to see her again. Again, she accepted.

The next evening, he took her to the history museum that had just opened up after a two-year refurbishment. He liked how she knew historical facts and the gleam in her eyes when she described what she thought a typical day in the life of a colonial family was like. They stayed until the museum closed. She wanted to go back to several exhibits and see them again. He was eager to return to those exhibits, postponing the end of the evening.

That following evening, he took her to a movie she was dying to see, and he wanted to put his arm around her, but restrained himself. They went to eat after and he told her more about his efforts to write. He didn't tell her that he spent his time at work writing his short stories since his father hadn't assigned him to a department and only asked him to help every now and then. He was too embarrassed to tell her that.

The next evening, they went to an opening night of a play that his friend wrote and invited them to a private cast party afterward.

"How would you like to go backstage?"

"Scott, can we do that? I mean do we have to let somebody know?"

"I think it'll be okay."

She followed him backstage.

"Dana? Dana Fisher," Scott called out when he saw his friend talking to three other people.

A man turned around.

"Dana Fisher? Aren't you the play write?" Kathryn looked from Scott to Dana, a look of confusion on her face.

Scott smiled, trying not to give anything away.

"Yes, I am." He looked at Scott, extended his hand. "Glad you could make it. This must be your friend, Kathryn?"

For the remainder of that week, they saw each other almost daily. He took her to one of his favorite places, the Marrakesh, an Indian restaurant, but he forgot about the fact that they had belly dancing. When the first course arrived, he tried to tell her that what she was about to put in her mouth was hot, but she ate it anyway. He gave her water and they laughed together. He couldn't help notice how she seemed to jump in without testing the water. He liked that about her. She didn't seem to be afraid. He liked a woman with an open mind, not judging people before hand. He wanted her to notice how hard he tried to attend to her rather than the scantily dressed belly dancers shaking and thrusting body parts.

One icy morning, the sky an ominous gray, Scott and Kathryn were finishing their six-mile run. His heart pounded ready to burst out of his chest, his body ached as he sliced his way through the thick cold air. When they reached the end of the trail and began walking, he heard Kathryn breathing and looked over at her.

"You okay?" he panted out.

"Yes," Kathryn coughed out to him. "I can't decide if it's harder to run when it's too cold or too hot."

He took her hand and led her to his car. After they got in, he reached behind in the backseat and pulled out a blanket. He tucked it around her.

She smiled at him as he drove her the two blocks to her house.

The following week he took her to a studio where his friend on a cable network taped a cooking show. His friend had Scott and Kathryn come from the audience to demonstrate how easy it was to make chocolate chip cookies. The two of them followed the special recipe given to them and for the next twenty minutes, they stirred the batter, put in sugar, and made the dough for the cookies. When the timer on the stove rang off, they took out the cookies. Kathryn's cookies were lopsided and very solid looking with dark brown edges. When the host tasted one, it was obvious she had left out an important ingredient, he said to everyone. Scott's cookies came out even and golden, and when the host tasted one, it melted in his mouth, he announced. The host finished that cookie and took another one.

After the show, Scott drove Kathryn home. He didn't get out to open the door for her. As usual, he had a hard time leaving her, but he noticed something was wrong.

"What's the matter? Did I do something?" He looked over and saw tears in her eyes.

"It's nothing." She tried not to look at him.

"Yes, it is. Tell me why you're crying." He took her hand, but he wanted to take her in his arms, keep her safe.

"It's silly, I know. But today at the show. Your cookies were better than mine."

Scott laughed.

"See. You think it's funny. I should be the one to make the best cookies." She started to wipe her tears, but he took her hand away and wiped a tear with his thumb.

"Why?"

"I'm the woman. We're supposed to be the cooks."

"Stop crying. Okay? I have a secret to tell you."

"What? You two planned that, didn't you?" She tried to smile.

"Now, why would I do anything like that? My mother taught me how to bake cookies. One weekend, she promised her teen center that she would bake the cookies for some reception or something they were having, but someone miss counted. Instead of two dozen cookies, she had to do twenty dozen cookies. She made us all help her. So, you see, I had plenty of practice." He laughed again.

"So it's okay that I don't know how to bake cookies?"

"It's okay. I would love to teach you."

He leaned over to kiss her at the very second she turned her head to open the door. He ended up kissing her on the back of her head. She turned around quickly. He was so embarrassed that he got out of the car to open her door.

To fill out the week, they went to a workshop for make-up and hair styling that Kathryn needed to attend. The workshop leader asked Scott if he would allow her to demonstrate the make-up using him. He agreed. He had to atone for the mess he made of the kiss.

He sat there in front of the women at the workshop and had his face cleansed, scrubbed, and had other things done to his face that he didn't understand. He even let the demonstrator put make-up and eye liner on him. He selected the shade of lipstick that he thought would look best on him, with Kathryn's approval. He saw how happy that made Kathryn and that made him feel good. He made the demonstrator and Kathryn promise to remove it all before they left and she kept her word. They made an early evening of it, and on the way home, he thought it best not to try to kiss her again, even though he would have given his right arm for it.

After he took her home, he heard the phone ringing as he was unlocking the front door to his house. It occurred to him that his father should have been there to answer the phone when he remembered that lately, his father was putting in long hours at the office. As he looked at his watch, he hurriedly opened the door and ran in to answer the phone.

"Scott, your father is having a heart attack and refuses to go to the hospital." June, Cameron's secretary, said before he got out a hello.

Scott rushed to the office and found his father with the paramedics trying hard to get him on the gurney and Cameron trying hard to talk them out of it.

"What happened?" asked Scott. He turned to June and the paramedics.

"Well, I came into his office and saw that your father wasn't looking well at all. His face had no color and he was just sitting behind his desk. I had a feeling something was wrong and, I tried to ask him something about the project he was working on but he didn't answer me. He turned around with his back to the door and for a minute, I thought he was deep in thought and didn't want to be disturbed. He didn't move, didn't say a word, didn't indicate to me that he heard me. When I walked in closer, I saw that he was holding his chest and the breathing. He was breathing so hard. I don't know why I didn't hear it from the door."

"Dad?" Scott moved closer to his father.

"I'm okay, Son. Everybody go home, please. I'm all right." He turned to June. "June, please send these paramedics away." He was as calm as a baby who had just been feed.

Scott looked at the papers on his father's desk and noticed the description of the hotel his mother wanted and a description of the home for teens. Working on Laurie's project was upsetting to his father and Scott tried to sound very casual, matter-of-fact, "Dad, I think you should go with them. You know, just to have them check things." He tried to be as delicate as he could even though knowing this frightened him.

"But, I don't need —" His voice held an even tone.

"Dad, please." Scott said it louder than he intended. Lowering his voice he said, "Please, Dad."

Cameron gave his son a long hard look, one that sought certainty. "Okay."

"I'm coming with you, Dad."

~~~~~~~~~~

"What happened?" asked the ER doctor taking Cameron's vital signs. A nurse came into the area, drew the curtain and stood beside the doctor.

"He couldn't get his breath," said Scott as quickly as he could so that Cameron wouldn't have a chance to alter what happened.

"Can you tell us what happened, Mr. Kersey?" asked the ER doctor looking directly at Cameron.

"It was nothing. I just felt a little light headed that's all."

"Can you tell me what happened before that?"

"I just felt a little weak, that's all. Maybe I haven't been eating right."

"Dad, June said that you were dizzy and that you couldn't get your breath. It is something," said Scott.

"Were you dizzy, Mr. Kersey?"

"A little."

"Anything else?"

"His secretary also said that he was perspiring some."

"Okay, get him ready for an EKG and let's get him on oxygen and some fluid in him." The doctor made notations on a form on a clipboard. He handed the clipboard to the nurse when he finished.

Later, the doctor came into the room with the news about Cameron's EKG. Cameron sat on the edge of the examining bed while Scott sat in a chair across from his father and near the window. Scott stood when the doctor entered.

"Everything looks good, Mr. Kersey," the doctor said to Cameron.

"What happened, doctor?" asked Scott.

"He probably had an anxiety attack which often looks like a heart attack. You have a bruise on your left leg," the doctor pointed to the bruise, "so I would like to keep you here overnight."

"But, I thought everything looked good," questioned Scott.

"Yes, the EKG looks good. Except I think Mr. Kersey has had the symptoms before, stumbling into things, and that's how he got that bruise. I just want to make sure that there's nothing serious. Can I see you for a minute?" He nodded to Scott.

The two men walked out beyond the drawn curtain and out of hearing range.

"Mr. Kersey, your father seems to be in shock and he seems a little depressed. Has he suffered a trauma recently?"

"Yes. He just lost his wife, my mother, she —"

"I see. Mr. Kersey, your father has suffered a serious trauma coupled with any other anxiety, say from a job, well he could end up back here."

"He's working on a project that my mother started before, before her accident. He has to finish it. For her."

"He needs the anxiety reduced. Is he seeing or both of you for that matter, seeing a counselor, therapist, or psychologist to help you both through this?"

"No. I didn't —"

"I think that's something you both need to consider. We want to keep him overnight, but whatever that project is, he's building up anxiety over it and could have a heart attack if he's not careful."

Scott went back into his father's room. "Dad, you heard the doctor. He's getting you a room." He held himself stiff, taut, and at the same time, not wanting his father to sense the seriousness.

~~~~~~~~~~

When Scott got to the hospital the next morning, the nurse told him that one of the doctor's other patients had an emergency that called him away. After a long wait, the doctor called again and said he would have to check Cameron out later that day.

On his way to the restaurant where he was to meet Kathryn, he thought about his father and began to shake. His father's attack gave him a huge scare. The thought of his father leaving him gripped him so that he felt like someone was squeezing the life out of him. He tore open his coat and undid the buttons on his shirt. He slammed on his brakes and threw the car in neutral.

His breathing came hard and fast and he felt a thousand knots tighten in his stomach. He tried to calm down, tried not to lose it, after all, his father would need to depend on him. Scott knew he was not reliable, couldn't carry things through. There was no way he could have his father depend on him. He would just fail his father. That's what has always happened. He didn't protect his mother and he let her die. If he didn't protect his father and show his father that he could depend on him, he could lose his father, too. And he would be responsible for both parents. What would it take for him to come to his senses? He missed the opportunity with his mother; he can't miss it with his father. He had to be a better person than that.

The man in the car behind him blew his horn. Scott tried to yell out to him, but he was still panting and breathing hard. He heard another car horn from behind him. He calmed down a little and opened his car door to get out; he needed air. Another man pulled up beside him.

"Hey mister, are you all right? Shall I call an ambulance or something?"

Scott looked at the man then looked at the man in the car behind him. "I'm fine. I don't need an ambulance," he said. He got in his car and drove to the restaurant.

When he pulled into the parking lot, he took several deep breaths so he wouldn't look so frazzled and wouldn't worry Kathryn. He sat there until he'd collected himself and the shaking subsided.

When he entered the restaurant and saw her already at a table, he smiled and at that moment, all he saw and thought about was Kathryn.

"How's your father?" she asked as Scott pulled out his chair to sit down.

"I think he'll be okay. The doctor said he was suffering from shock due to the trauma. And he's slightly depressed."

"Scott, I'm sorry." She watched him for a moment. "Don't think that."

"Why not? It's true, isn't it?"

"No, it's not true. Scott, it's not."

He reached over the table and squeezed her hand.

"I'll be okay." He smiled at her.

"Have you heard anymore from the police?"

The waiter came over, poured coffee in each cup, and handed them each a menu.

"No, not since they spoke to my father. They mentioned a lab report the last time he talked to them. I want to go see if it's ready. I'm not a police officer, but I think that report can be helpful to the investigation."

"Let's go then."

Scott looked down at the table setting in front of them both, confused by her comment. "Go where? Is there something wrong with the restaurant?" He looked around the room.

"To the police station. Do you remember the officer's name?"

"Are you always this wild and crazy?"

"Only when I need to be. Like now," said Kathryn.

"Let's have lunch first."

"I'm not hungry," said Kathryn. She folded her arms.

"Kat, I'll do it later. Let's have lunch now," said Scott.

"I'm not hungry."

He sighed. He thought that her insistence would make him anxious again, but for some reason it didn't.

"Let's go now. It's just going to worry you through lunch."

Kathryn was up out of her seat and headed toward the door.

She knew how to handle him. He stood up, took some money out of his pocket for the coffee, and tossed it down on the table. Kathryn waited for him at the door. Together they drove to the police station. He went in and she waited for him in the car.

~~~~~~~~~~

Scott found Detective Haines on the second floor in the Homicide Office sitting behind a desk in a busy open area where eight other detectives sat behind desks, some on the phone, some writing. On the front of each desk sat the nameplate of the officer.

"What brings you here this afternoon, Mr. Kersey?"

"We haven't heard from you for several days and I need to know how you're coming on the search for the person who ran over my mother?"

Detective Haines stared at Scott for a short moment as if he was trying to recall the incident.

"You remember, my mother, the car accident."

"Yes, I remember. Mr. Kersey, we don't have any leads, I'm sorry to say. We talked to the woman who thought she knew the woman runner who might have seen the car, but she didn't know the woman's name or where she lived and she said she hadn't seen her on the trail since the accident. We ran into a dead-end there. We're still waiting for the lab report and as soon as we hear about that we'll have more to go on."

"What is this lab report?"

"We took some paint and car samples from your mother's clothing and her car and we also got fingerprints."

"What will that tell you?"

"Well, that'll give us some information about the car that hit your mother and the motive."

"Motive?"

"Yes. Your mother was knocked down and backed over. We saw tread marks in two directions and we need to know if this was deliberate or an accident."

"How long does that normally take?"

"Mr. Kersey, I'm afraid I can't tell you anymore. When we get that report back we'll be in contact." Detective Haines stood up and extended his hand.

Scott stood and shook hands with the Detective. He had never been given the brush off so quickly and his suspicions about how Detective Haines handled his mother's case rose to an unanticipated height. That didn't matter to Scott. He knew he could get the lab report faster and he knew how. It wouldn't sit well with detective Haines, but that was just how it was.

~~~~~~~~~~

"Well, how'd it go?" asked Kathryn after Scott got in the car.

"Haines said the report wasn't back yet. I need to speed up the process. We need that lab report."

"How are you going to do that?"

"My father and I have a friend who could get us that report faster. From the conversation that I just had with Haines, I think I need to call in a favor. I'm going to take you back to work."

"I know you're going ahead alone, but will you let me know what happened?"

Scott studied her. He was dying to tell her that he loved her, especially now as he looked at her and saw the warmth and love in her big brown eyes. She comforted him and he liked that. He loved the way she made him feel good about himself, the way she made all the insignificant moments of his life seem important. The fact that she wanted to go with him to the police station made his heart fill up with love for her. She believed in him and he had a strong urge to show her he could be a better man. His body ached for her. He just wanted to kiss her, touch her hair, hold her in his arms. He loved how she always thought about him and how incredibly giving she was. He loved her smile when she was happy and the way her shoulders shook when she laughed hard. But he had to be strong because it just wasn't a good time for him right now. This was a vulnerable period for him and he was overly emotional with her in such a short time. He felt that she thought of him more like a friend than someone she would love. He realized that he was not someone she would want. He could see that and she made it clear to him during the past week. Kathryn wouldn't be happy with someone like him, a lost soul who drank and broke his promises. He wanted her, but in his current state, he wasn't sure he could be the man she wanted and needed.

"I will. I promise."

After Scott took Kathryn back to work, he called his father's secretary to get the number of the D.A.'s office.

Scott was well aware of the fact that the employees in his father's firm knew he held no authority, but no one treated him with disregard or questioned him in anyway and June gave him the phone number.

Scott called Cameron at the hospital and told him what he

wanted to do. Cameron liked the idea of expediting the lab report and asking his friend who was now the district attorney. Cameron said he felt better and wanted to meet Scott at the D.A.'s office. Scott told Cameron that he shouldn't do that and that the meeting could cause him to have a relapse. Scott explained to Cameron what the doctor told him about the stress and the anxiety he was under and that going to the D.A. could exacerbate his condition. Scott promised his father that he would let him know what happened and Cameron reluctantly and finally agreed to let Scott go talk to the D.A. without him. Besides, Scott said that based on his last conversation with Detective Haines, they needed to jump on this opportunity now. Cameron said he would call his friend to tell him that Scott was on his way to see him. A little nervous and feeling ebullient, Scott went to see the only man they knew who could put a rush on the lab report.

~~~~~~~~~~

The D.A.'s office was located on the top floor of a fourteen-story building and when Scott entered, he was amazed by the windows that spanned across the front of the office giving Steve Russell, the D.A. and Cameron's friend, the appearance of omnipotence.

"Scott, as I told your father, the only thing is that the accident is not in the hands of this office yet. You're asking me—" Steve sat back and rocked in his chair a bit. "Steve, I know. I just want a lab report given to the police and me. It's been two weeks. That's too long. I know that if it comes from you, then it'll get done. That's all I want; that lab report."

Steve fiddled with a pen on his desk, turning it up, then down, then up. He laid the pen down and sat forward in his chair, the obvious past between them hung in the air like wet wash on a rainy day. Steve rubbed his chin as if readying himself for Scott. But, all Scott wanted was the report about the car that hit his mother so he waited for Steve's response.

Steve had asked Scott and his father several favors in the past and both men did the favors no questions asked. As far as Scott knew, his father had never asked for a favor in return and Scott hoped that Steve knew that he would never bring up anything like that. Steve could either do it or not do it. Scott trusted him and whatever decision he made.

"First, you don't get a copy of the report. And, what you're asking means that all the people ahead of you will have to wait."

"I understand what I'm asking, but my mother was hit by a car and the car left something on her clothes and her car. I just want the lab to process that and do it quickly. Why does the report have to take so long?"

Steve sat back in his chair and rocked, again.

"I can see this is very important to you."

Scott knew what Steve meant except he wasn't there to bring up the past. He overlooked it. "I just need to find the car that hit her."

Scott could see sympathy in Steve's eyes and Steve's body sank as he gave in. Scott remembered that Steve had a brother, a police officer who was killed in the line of duty during a shoot out. The killer escaped, but not for very long. Steve didn't stop until he found the man who had shot his brother.

Steve sat forward in his chair, elbows on the edge of the

desk. "Okay, Scott. I'll do what I can. And if I can, I'll have them rush it."

Scott stood to hug him, kiss him, something, but he held out his hand instead.

"Thanks, man. I owe you one."

"No, Scott. You don't. Look, I'm sorry about your mother. I always admired her."

Scott stood in the elevator going down, a smile widening on his face. Finally, he felt movement, some progress in solving his mother's case. He now felt officially involved in his mother's case. He was more determined now to solve it. On his way back to the hospital, he hatched out a plan.

Chapter 11
Kathryn

When Kathryn arrived at the studio, Frankie Sanchez, sitting on his suitcase, told her to pack her bags and that she was going with him to France where they were to help get the Emeraude, a ladies' dress shop, back on its feet. He had worked it out with the owners of the shop and they had given him permission to take her with him.

"Oh Frankie, not now."

"Honey, I thought you'd be just as excited as I am."

"I am. It's just that this is coming at a most inopportune time."

"I thought you said that your father was doing better. Didn't you say that he went back to work?"

"Yes, but. . . ."

"Sweetheart, what IS the matter, then. Oh, I bet I know. That's right just throw that up in my face."

"Frankie. You know better than that. We've only been dating about two weeks."

"Kat, it's only for a week. We go there, straighten things up, and then come back. This could help you get your foot in the door with the owners if you want it."

"Just a week. I guess I could, just for a week, huh?"

"We'll do what we can. One week," said Frankie.

"Well, I guess I'd better go pack, then."

"You'd better hurry. Our plane leaves in three hours. Meet me in the airport in an hour."

"An hour? Frankie . . ."

"Honey, please. The company took care of everything. Just go home, pack a thing or two and then meet me in the airport. We can buy whatever you need that you didn't get to pack when we get to France."

Kathryn tried to call her father on the drive home, but for some reason she didn't get a signal. She drove as fast as she could given the fact that she was excited about the opportunity that she would be going to France.

At home, she left her father a note and then found a suitcase. She didn't stop to see what she packed; she just threw things in a bag and rushed out of the house.

She made good time on the side streets, but once on the interstate, the traffic slowed down considerably. Frustration mounted in her and she wondered why she would continue to live in the most congested area in the world. She loved the area; the hustle and bustle, but she couldn't understand why in this metropolitan area when time is of the essence, there is always an accident or some kind of obstacle that keeps commuters from their appointed destinations or causes them to be extremely late for everything. This day was no different and she hated this about the city. She turned on the radio and found the traffic channel. Due to a three-car accident at the juncture of 270 and interstate highway 495, that was beginning to clear up, traffic was at a crawl. Kathryn was beginning to think that she wouldn't make it to Dulles Airport before her plane took off.

She was anxious about meeting Frankie on time; she didn't want him to think that she had changed her mind, and she wanted to talk to Scott, too. She needed to let him know what happened and tell him that she would not be able to meet him for dinner. But, she was too nervous to take her attention off of driving, too afraid of being pulled over, and she inched toward the airport on the interstate in a line of cars some jumping from lane to lane hoping that would help them reach their destinations faster. She would have to call Scott from the airport. She wanted to talk to him when she had time to tell him everything that happened. She knew he would be just as excited as she was.

By the time she reached the airport and found Frankie, they discovered that they were late for the plane and had to run to catch it after she hurriedly checked in. Just before take -off, Kathryn frantically searched for her cell phone. She could call Scott now if she could find her cell phone. She couldn't have. She just couldn't have left her cell phone at home, yet it was not in her handbag, and she didn't remember using it after she tried to leave her father a message. She didn't know how to call him without her cell phone; she realized she hadn't memorized his number.

~~~~~~~~~~

At about the same time Kathryn and Frankie were running to catch their plane, Scott waited for Kathryn in the café near her house, her favorite restaurant, the place where they dined the first day he took her to dinner. He had called earlier after he left the hospital, and left her a message to confirm their dinner meeting that evening. He barely arrived on time himself, staying longer with his father than he anticipated. When he arrived, he asked to sit by the window facing out onto the street.

He looked at his watch again and saw that she was late, something that was not quite like the woman he had been seeing for the past two weeks. He was dying to see her and he called her cell, but to his surprise, he had to leave a message. A few minutes later, he left another message. He hung up; face sagging, disappointed that he couldn't reach her. He needed to tell her about the report and his meeting with the D.A.

Scott looked at his watch again. She was never late and since they had been dating; neither was he. She could need his help, Mary and Jake again, or her father was sick again. Maybe her car broke down and she was stuck on a deserted street somewhere without her cell phone. He opened his cell and called again, but this time the phone clicked and went to a forwarding number where he could only leave a message. He did. He wanted to call the hospitals in the area, but then he tried calling her work number thinking that maybe work held her up. He listened to a recording on the answering machine and Scott realized that the shop had closed. When the waiter came over, he ordered coffee and when he had finished and because she still had not arrived, he paid and left for home.

On the drive home, he thought about going back to the hospital, this time to ask about Kathryn, but for some reason his mind fought hard against doing that. He didn't want to think about why Kathryn didn't answer her phone or meet him at the restaurant.

Chapter 12
Kathryn

After the plane landed later in the morning, Kathryn and Frankie made their way to find the company limo that Frankie said would be waiting, ready to take them to the store. Outside the airport, Frankie looked at the line of cars, taxis and limos waiting for passengers and then again at Kathryn. She was barely awake; unable to sleep on the plane. She was in France, a place of her dreams. She absolutely would not let a little thing like being tired stand in the way of her enjoying Paris.

"I thought this was going to be easy," said Frankie looking at the horde of people standing on the sidewalk. He sat his suitcase down beside him and pulled his coat around him.

"Now what?" said Kathryn, irritation in her voice. "How could such a beautiful city be so cold?" She followed him and sat her suitcase down next to her, buttoned her coat, and stuffed her hands deep into her pockets. Two men came out, stood in front of her. She heard them speaking in English and looked at them thinking that it was nice to see Americans. Knowing that, she didn't feel so lost. Another man came out carrying two bags and joined the two men. She heard one of the English speaking men say something in French. They all began speaking in French and she turned back to Frankie.

"Okay, just give me a minute," he said. Frankie pulled out his cell phone.

"What are you doing?"

"I thought I'd call the store and let Michelle know we got here. But the cell phone doesn't work here."

"What about the time?"

"It hasn't changed over yet. I'll just call her from the store. It'll be okay; it's a business call."

Kathryn looked over at a group of limo drivers, one looking down at something in his hand and then up at the people coming out. The driver looked down and up again, relief spreading across his face as he waved his arm at Frankie and Kathryn.

"This way. That man is waving at us. The company must have given them a picture of one of us. Probably me." Frankie strutted over toward the limo driver sashaying and swaying from side to side and eager to get inside the limo that waited in front of him.

"Are you hailin us Darlin?" Frankie asked the driver who was a tall burly man who seemed to have outgrown his clothes.

"I'm to take you to Emeraude." He stepped aside to open the door.

Frankie bent down to get in followed by Kathryn. The limo driver put the luggage in the trunk first and then got in. He pulled away from the curb as they headed toward Paris and in the direction of the store.

"Brrr, can we get heat back here?"

"Frankie, can you wait a minute? Give the car a chance to get warm?" she said.

The driver must have turned up the heat. The warm air began to fill the car and settled on Kathryn, and she began to relax.

"We need a plan . . ."

Kathryn didn't want to hear anything about the store at this moment. She could hardly believe that she was in France. She felt all giddy inside. At that moment, she couldn't remember why she hesitated when, earlier, Frankie wanted her to come with him. Even though she didn't know how to speak French, she tried to remember the names of the streets they passed. From the Charles De Guelle airport, the limo driver headed south on the car-packed highway, people racing to their destinations. Another limo pulled up beside them with tinted glass windows and though she tried, she couldn't see inside. Big time celebrities, maybe. They must have been late for something, in a hurry because the limo passed them, going at a much higher speed. Looking around for signs, she wondered if they were going the speed limit. She had heard that there was no speed limit in France and most people drove fast. She was in no hurry to get to the store, nor was she prepared to move any faster than the limo was already going. It occurred to her that even if she saw a sign, she wouldn't recognize it. She chuckled to herself, looked over at Frankie and saw he was still talking.

"Remember that we'll . . ."

How could anybody tie up this beautiful moment with business? She turned toward the window again. They drove toward Rue de Turenne, according to the sign, where they passed the Centre National d art et de Culture Georges

Pompidou, a huge stone building that took up most of the street. They turned right on Rue Saint-Antoine, and continued on until the name changed to Rue de Rivoli. They passed by a park with a water fountain that ran almost the length of the park. She didn't know why but she was surprised to see the streets were crowded with bicycles and cars as well as people, especially given how cold it seemed to her. She looked at the people as the limo sped down the street and decided that she couldn't tell what the weather was like by watching the people on the streets. She didn't see anyone walking and holding a collar closed, or anyone holding a scarf around their neck, or anyone walking with their head down. She would stand out, show herself as a tourist, if she let the cold weather bother her.

Kathryn chuckled to herself thinking that perhaps Bethesda, Maryland wasn't the only place where people had little room to move around or drive. She looked up to a perfectly blue sky, the color she had never seen before.

"They are ready to wear clothing and sometimes people have a tendency to mistreat them . . . " said Frankie, voice trailing off.

Kathryn didn't respond. She still couldn't believe she had finally made it to the city of her dreams with its Romanesque and Gothic style buildings. She heard a car horn and turned in the direction of the sound. She saw a man behind the wheel, hand in the air, irritated with someone. She shook her head; she always thought that French people were very patient, very civil, and thoughtful to each other.

"Of course, we have to make sure that everything is there. You know, the clothes are there. I'm not saying that they won't be, but clothing can walk away, you know . . . ."

Kathryn continued watching the city and the people moving about, walking biking, driving. She saw people walking at a brisk pace as if late for an appointment somewhere. She noticed how the fast walkers maneuvered around the slower ones. She saw a woman holding the hand of a young boy trying to pull away. Kathryn wondered how she would be as a mother. She didn't want her children to pull away from her. She wanted her children to love her. She smiled to herself as she realized that when she thought of a family, she pictured Scott. She hesitated for a moment when she saw Scott as her husband. After all, she barely knew him.

They came to a three-way intersection and a big restaurant covered the corner of two streets. She didn't get a chance to see the names of the streets, the signs hidden behind a huge tree.

"Are you listening to me?"

The limo driver pulled up in front of Emeraude on Rue de Rivoli, a commercial street with other clothing stores and shops. When the limo stopped, Kathryn wished that she'd had time to learn some French. She knew that Frankie only spoke Spanish, and English, of course. She leaned forward and tapped on the window that separated the limo driver from them. The limo driver lowered the glass.

"Oui, Ma'dam?"

"Is there someone here who speaks English?" asked Kathryn.

"Oui, Ma'dam."

"Thank you."

She saw the limo driver push a button and the window rose up.

"How do you know he understood you?" asked Frankie.

"I guess we'll have to discover that when we get in the store." Kathryn smiled.

She realized she missed Scott and wanted him to be in France with her. The fact that she left her cell phone home and could think of no way to call him worried her. She made a promise to herself to try to use the store phone to call him if she could. She imagined him dropping everything and flying out to meet her when she told him she was in Paris. At the very least, she needed him to know she didn't just stand him up.

She knew she had strong feelings for Scott and worried that she was in love with him. Falling in love early in a relationship before really knowing a person was against everything she believed in, and though she changed her mind on many of her other beliefs, she couldn't face changing her mind on this principle.

They had only been seeing each other for about two weeks and he had not made any advances toward her. He only tried to kiss her once during the two-week period. She understood that under his circumstances, he would be distant, but she also had to consider the fact that he didn't see her as a romantic interest, only as a friend. Maybe he still cared for Lisa or maybe that kiss had something to do with it. It was a surprise to her. Could he believe that because she didn't encourage him to try again, she only thought of him as a friend? The truth is that she wanted him to try to kiss her again. The fact that he didn't, made her feel he really didn't like her enough. She didn't encourage him to kiss her again or hold her hand. She didn't like the feeling of rejection. No matter what, she had to admit that at that moment, she missed him.

When they stepped inside the store, Kathryn could see that it would take them longer than the week Frankie said to get the mess that she saw into shape, and as she looked around a wave of anxiety surged through her. Not only was the place a physical mess, but psychologically, it didn't capture a buyer's emotional need to purchase anything. No wonder sales lagged. She looked at Frankie, who actually could speak not one word. He stood beside her, mouth agape. After a while, he seemed to force himself to speak.

"Why? I can't believe this. Do they, how, what in hell, I mean how in hell do they expect to sell anything? Look at this mess."

The store's modern décor was hidden by the disarray of the clothing items as well as by six wooden horses that must have been left over from a merry-go-round, and was placed in the center of the store. Kathryn couldn't believe that no one thought these horses, though beautifully painted, were in the way. She could see her week's work would also include soothing Frankie, and she questioned how they would complete this project in a week's time. She saw that that was not the biggest problem when her eyes fell on the three store employees standing before them all lined up, and watching the two of them.

Frankie walked around the store as if he was on another planet and the clothing items were foreign to him. He picked up an unfolded shirt on a pile of shirts. Pants and shirts were left on top of the circular racks, clothes were hung on the doors of the three dressing rooms, and as she looked around, Kathryn saw clothes thrown or stuffed everywhere and in no general order. At least no order she could discern.

"Is this really what I see? How can people do this?" asked Frankie.

Kathryn walked to the table where the shirts lay and picked up one or two. They were different sizes but were in the same pile on the table. Then Frankie moved to a rack of assorted shirts, dresses, and pants that looked like they were on mark down. He saw that the sizes were not separated, and many of the items were hung, but jammed on the rack leaving them protruding out. Frankie pulled out a pair of pants half on and half off the hanger and held them up. "Where is the tag on these? Why are they all jammed up in here? They can get wrinkled like this . . ." His voice broke off as if he was about to cry. He held his hand over his heart, for dramatic effect, Kathryn always thought, and took a step back.

"Now, Frankie, we can fix this. We can clean it up this week," responded Kathryn.

They walked around the store while the employees, still standing in a row, turned to follow them.

The employees, three women who challenged the concept of fashion with their outlandish and ostentatious style of dress and multi-colored hairstyles, exchanged puzzled looks as they watched Frankie and Kathryn walk through the store.

Kathryn turned around to look at the three women. One who seemed about 5'9" had her long hair dyed orange, black, green, and yellow and wore huge hoop style earrings. She dressed in all black and had on so much silver jewelry that she seemed weighted down by the huge necklaces, bracelets, chokes, and chains around her waist. To top off her fashion faux pas, her skirt was hiked up almost to her waist. Her make-up, black eyeliner and fake lashes, made her look worn and old.

Standing next to her, a shorter woman, obviously in her 30s, who dressed like a teen, squeezed into low cut jeans with her close fitting shirt tucked in and her mid section spilling out all over her belt. Kathryn thought that she could use another size or two. Her blond hair combed back and clipped. Her make-up was less obvious than the first employee's and this lady wore a gold tone necklace that fell mid-chest.

As to the person standing on the end, Kathryn had to guess at what she was. She dressed like a young man, with trousers, white-collar shirt, sleeves rolled up to her elbows. Her hair cut short in a buzz on one side, and on the right side, longer, covering her ear. Her appearance seemed designed to send a message to the world. Kathryn hoped that none of what they wore came from the store. But then again, some people just don't do justice to clothes and three examples stood before her.

"Well, what daya think, darlin?" Frankie picked up another shirt that needed folding and then dropped it back on top of the messy pile. "Is this something or what?"

"We won't be here forever," said Kathryn running her finger along the counter and picking up dust. She tried to offer words of comfort, but she realized that under the circumstances, it was hard for her to do that.

"Doesn't anybody around here care?" asked Frankie. "These are clothes that someone took the time to design and cut out and, and, and, oh." At this point Frankie screamed out the words.

"Calm down, Frankie." Kathryn went over to help him. "Take deep breaths." She held on to his arm.

Frankie took several deep breaths as the three women watched.

"He gets like this when he sees people destroying fashion," said Kathryn, looking at the three women and knowing that they didn't understand.

The limo driver brought in the bags and spoke to the three employees in French. Then the limo driver introduced Frankie and Kathryn to the three store employees. He told Frankie that they could follow him up stairs to the apartment over the store where they would be staying for the week. He picked up their bags and started up the steps.

"I hope the apartment is in much better condition than those clothes," said Frankie as if he would not tolerate it and had planned to complain if it wasn't.

"I don't think we should count on that," responded Kathryn following behind the limo driver and Frankie as they climbed the stairs to the apartment.

They continued through the door and to a small hallway where they came to another door. The limo driver sat the bags down, unlocked the door, and stepped aside as he let them into the apartment. Frankie entered first and looked around the one large room. Kathryn entered and saw a neat little apartment with a dressing area and a sitting room. She looked at Frankie and let out a smile.

The limo driver handed Frankie the key and waited for them in the hallway. After they had had a chance to look around more, the limo driver took them to the bathroom, the only other door on that hallway. Kathryn wanted to say something, but remembered that they were in France and realized that going down the hall may not be so bad after all.

~~~~~~~~~~

By the middle of the first week at Emeraude, Kathryn had changed the mannequins to show the new line of clothing and to represent the styles for both the younger generation as well as the older. She selected one employee, the one who spoke the best English, the one with the dual hairstyle, and explained to her how to change the mannequins, when to change them and why. Kathryn rearranged the clothing in the store by colors that would attract the buyers. With the help of the limo driver, she explained the need to rearrange the clothing and showed them how to use colors and styles to draw customers. She asked all of the employees to continue to fold the sweaters, shirts, and smaller items even though customers would undo everything. She told them that keeping the shop neat enabled the customers to see items that they wanted to buy as well as all of the items in their immediate line of sight. This also encouraged customers to look further. She also showed the ladies how not to pounce on prospective buyers when they crossed the threshold of the store and that giving them a chance to browse a little and even allowing them to hold on to an item gave the customer a little more freedom and set a positive aura. She explained to the women that by doing that, a customer would feel less forced to buy something, would buy more, and would be less likely to run out of the store.

Frankie sent one of the employees out for cookies and coffee one day and cake, cookies and coffee after that. He said having a welcoming store made people want to buy. The thing she and Frankie found the most difficult to change was the attitude of the three employees. They didn't seem to care about the store and they were resentful of the two people whom they had never seen before coming in and from America, to boot, and telling them what to do about their store. The work at Emeraude had taken up all their time and they found that they had to spend more time on inventory and accounting if they wanted the store ready by the week's end.

As the days progressed, Kathryn and Frankie realized there were six employees when three new women showed up for work on that Thursday. They had to familiarize the new people with the new standards of the store including the dress code. The three new female employees had the same disrespectful attitude about the store as the others and Kathryn knew then, they had to call a meeting of all the employees of the store. With the help of the limo driver, who turned out to be a jack-of-all-trades, (he also fixed the leaky toilet and went and bought them extra blankets) they arranged a meeting of all six retail clerks to go over all of the new rules and care of the store. Kathryn and Frankie knew they had to get the employees to cooperate because they would be returning to the states after the weekend and they needed the store manager to be able to keep the store up after they left.

They didn't open the store until noon on Saturday even though they asked all the sales employees to come in at 10:00 a.m. for their meeting. Kathryn felt the meeting went pretty well. They asked the limo driver to translate as often as they needed and he straightened out two potential misunderstandings as well as helped tone down the negative attitudes two of the clerks had. When everyone seemed to accept the new rules and ideas and were clear about the new procedures, Frankie opened the doors to the public.

Kathryn was in the center of the store, bent down behind the counter putting away the box of price tags when she heard a voice familiar to her. She didn't think anything about it at first because she heard French. As the sound of the voice drew closer to her and then suddenly changed to English, she stood up.

"Kat? Is that you? What are you doing here?" asked Harris Sweeney. He turned in her direction when she popped up. When he saw her, he walked closer to the counter. "Hi Beautiful." He turned around and gave a wave to Frankie who was climbing into the display window.

"What are you doing here?" asked Kathryn. She looked at the beautiful tall, thin flat-chested Asian woman with long dark hair and who was glued to Harris's arm.

"Kat, this is Jenny Lee. She works with me."

"Hi," said Jenny extending her hand, a wide smile across her face.

"So, what are you doing here?" asked Kathryn again. She looked down at Jenny's hand, but she didn't extend hers.

"We're just taking a break. I'm working on the same project I told you about. I thought I'd take Jenny out to lunch and we just happened to stop here to look. Didn't we Jenny?"

Kathryn saw Jenny had wandered off to the lingerie table. She picked up a bra and looked at it and then she held up a pair of women's panties that looked more like something for a doll. "Look Harris, how do you like these?"

Harris turned to see the item Jenny held up. He blushed, took Kathryn by the elbow and the two of them walked to the rear of the store and stood by the empty dressing room.

"I know what this looks like —" he began, his voice low.

"What is that?"

"Okay, come on now. I know you're upset, but it's not what you think."

"What is it then, Harris? The last time I talked to you, you were in England. You said you would be there a few more days and that was over two weeks ago. I haven't heard from you since then. What is it, Harris? Tell me."

"We work together. That's all. Kat, when the company sends me somewhere I have to go. I was in England, then I went to Italy, and now I'm here. Alex is looking many places. I didn't call because I've been busy. That's it."

"You're right. That's it."

"What does that mean?"

"Harris, that's your girlfriend and you know it. You've probably had her and a string of others all along."

Harris paced back and forth in front of Kathryn. After a while, Kathryn started back to the other part of the store, but Harris blocked her path and stopped her from moving. "Kat, when I'm at work, I'm working. I know what you're thinking, but that's not true."

"Harris, what do you think I am? I can see that woman attached to your arm. Why would she do that if you two weren't in some kind of relationship, whatever kind you have?"

"I don't know. I can't answer that, but we don't have a relationship of any kind. We work together. She works in the office I'm assigned to while I'm here in France."

"How long have you been here?" asked Kathryn.

"Since last Thursday. Beautiful, why didn't you tell me you'd be here?"

"Harris, you promised to call me back." She felt herself giving in.

"Yeah, but you've called and left messages with me before." He took hold of her shoulders and looked directly into her eyes. "Beautiful, one reason why I didn't call was because I found out I would have to stay longer and I didn't want to tell you that."

"Your —"

"She's not my girlfriend. I just met her today when she came to work. She just wanted to take me to her favorite restaurant and we stopped in here on the way back."

He took a half step closer, his eyes fixed on hers. "Hey, Beautiful. You should have called me," said Harris so softly that he was barely audible. He leaned down to kiss Kathryn who closed her eyes as his lips touched hers. After the kiss he took her hands and kissed her again. "When will you finish here?"

"We close at six."

"Can I come by then? I want to take you to the restaurant I passed by last night."

"Harris, I don't think . . . ."

"Kat, have dinner with me and let's talk. I've been thinking a lot about our relationship, or whatever it is we have, and we need to talk."

"Okay." She could use the opportunity to tell him she'd met someone else, and that she wanted to end their relationship.

"So, I'll see you here about six, six fifteen?"

"That's good."

Harris leaned down and kissed Kathryn on the forehead. "See you then." He turned toward Jenny who was still holding the panties. "Get your clothes and let's go," he said as he walked past Jenny and continued out of the door.

Frankie turned to look at Kathryn when Harris left.

Kathryn had decided to meet Harris for dinner and discuss their, whatever it was they had. In the past, Harris was somebody she could depend on to go to parties and dinner and every now and then, he would take her to a play or a museum. They spent time together, but they both kept their distance. Once she thought about what she would say if he ever asked her to marry him, but then she decided that their relationship was too distant for that idea ever to become something real, and she didn't love him.

Chapter 13
Scott

Cameron had to promise Scott he would be careful and take things easy before Scott would agree for him to return to work. Cameron put up an argument with Scott about having to report to his son, but when he saw how important it was to Scott, he soon relented. The morning of his return, Cameron rushed into Scott's office carrying a large brown envelope that he said June had just given him. As he entered, the small bare office, Scott saw that his father looked more alive and cheerful than he had since the day he had to identify his wife's body.

"I got it," said Cameron waving the large brown envelope.

"What?" asked Scott. He got up to offer his father the only other chair in the austere office.

"I'm guessing this is the lab report that we've been waiting for." He pointed to the return address on the envelope. "I haven't opened it yet. I thought we'd do that together."

"Well, let's see what it says." Scott stood beside his father.

Cameron, as calmly as he could, given his anxiousness about the report, eased up the securely glued down flap without a rip and opened the envelope. He reached inside and took out three pages clipped together and tossed the envelope on Scott's desk. The two of them read the first page of the accident report including the coroner's report.

"What's this?" asked Scott.

"That looks like the car that hit her," said Cameron. He read: "A black metallic 1999 Mercedes-Benz C230.' It says here that the year and model were determined by the type of paint used during that time and the paint color code matched the color code on the website."

"I guess that means that if it's a match then the year and style are correct."

"Could be," said Cameron.

"The report confirms what Haines and Charles told me. Someone backed into her, knocked her down, and rolled over her twice."

They continued reading the three-page report until they got to the last three pages separated from the report.

"What is this list?" asked Scott.

"It looks like a list of people who own cars of this make and model."

"Were we supposed to get this list? When I asked for the list, Steve said that we wouldn't get it."

"I don't know, but we have it, perhaps thanks to some new person on the job who probably didn't know not to send it," said Cameron.

"Or maybe it was intentional, a gift from Steve."

"Never thought of that," said Cameron.

"Now, what?"

"They have the information that they need now. No more excuses. I want them to find the person who . . ." Cameron looked away.

Scott realized that his father still could not bring himself to saying the words, no more than he (Scott) could.

"I'll get a hold of Haines and Charles," said Cameron. He started out of the office.

"Dad," called out Scott.

Cameron turned around.

"Why tell them anything? They have their list, we have our list."

Cameron took a step back toward Scott.

"Maybe we should use it. I mean, we should use it. We should find the person."

"This is a police matter, son"

"I know," began Scott, "I want to do it. Haines and Charles talked about 'motive,' as if someone had it in for mom. I have to find out who would do anything like this to her."

"Absolutely not. I won't put you in any danger. I can't do that."

"Dad, I can handle it."

"Son, no. I think we should turn this over to the police. We don't have the expertise that they have. We wouldn't even know what questions to ask."

"I'll go. I'll take that list," he pointed to the list, "and knock on those doors until I find out the owner and driver of the car."

"What would you say to these people? Scott this is serious. You could get hurt."

Scott shrugged. "I'd just tell them that I'm looking to buy a car of that year and model."

When Cameron didn't respond, Scott began to think that using that ruse was not enough and that he had to come up with something better. "I know I could get hurt and believe me, I know how serious this is, but we should do it." He looked away, then turned back to his father. "I want to do it, Dad. I have to."

Cameron stood there a second as if he wanted to ask Scott something or say something, but instead, he gave Scott a hug and pat on the back. Then he turned around and headed out of the office.

"I'll make you a copy," he yelled back over his shoulder just before he rounded the corner.

Scott had convinced his father that he could look for the car. He had let his mother down when she really needed him. He couldn't do that to her again. He had to find the car and person and show his father that he was dependable, that in a pinch he would do whatever he could. He felt so helpless and ashamed of himself for the fatality that ended his mother's life. His father, by giving him the opportunity, believed he could do it. He had to believe the same.

Chapter 14
Scott

Once on the road, Scott looked at the list, saw the age of some of the cars, and wondered why some people would hold on to an old car for so long. He was nervous about searching for the car. He had never, in his life done anything like this before, but he tried not to think about what he was doing or how it could turn out. He drove all the way to Baltimore and pulled up in front of the first house, a brick semi-detached row house. Standing in front, he looked for a garage and saw one in the yard behind the house. The door to the garage was closed. Scott walked up the first set of steps to the second set and onto the porch. An elderly woman answered his knock. He let out a sigh of relief when he saw her, realizing his first contact would go smoothly. He asked her about the car and she told him that it was in the garage. She pointed the way and he walked back down the steps and to the back to the garage where he met the woman and helped her raise the door.

"See, it's been sitting here since my husband died. I don't believe it'll start."

"Have you thought about selling it?" He didn't have to ask

that because he could see that this was not the car or the driver, but he thought he'd still use the guise anyway. He didn't want the woman to think that he was some sort of scam artist and call the police. Besides, he needed the practice.

"Oh, I couldn't do that."

"Well, thank you very much, Ma'am." Scott pulled the door down and walked back to his car. He checked the name off the list and went to the next name. He had re-arranged the names on the list by area to make it easier on himself.

The rest of the afternoon was much like the morning until he got to the last name for the day.

"What's so important about my car?" asked a man who came to the door bare-chested and in old jeans. He had a scruffy beard and he smelled of alcohol.

"Well, I'm looking to buy a car. What do you mean?"

"The police were here about the car," said the man.

"When was that?" asked Scott.

"Earlier this morning."

"Where is the car?"

"My girlfriend ran it into a tree when she found me with her cousin?" He gave a wide grin that exposed two missing front teeth.

"When did that happen?"

"I'd say about two months ago."

"Where is the car now?"

"At the junk yard."

"Where?"

"Mister, you don't want that car. It was all torn up in the inside. I won it in a crap game about five years ago, and it wasn't in the best condition at that time. I can get you the address if you want it, but I don't think you do."

"Thanks, a lot." Scott turned and walked back to his car.

Just before his light changed so that he could make his right turn back onto the busy four-lane main street, he saw a black metallic Mercedes speed through the intersection. It was so fast and he wasn't paying attention that he didn't see who was driving. He turned onto the street, and sped to catch up to the black Mercedes. The Ford in the right lane in front of him, moved too slowly and he could see the Mercedes moving farther ahead. He was so close and wanted to blow his horn, ram through the car in front of him, something, but he knew none of that would do any good. He looked harder at the driver in front of him, and saw that someone was on the cell phone. Making a daring move, he jumped out of the right lane and into the left lane, still two cars behind the Mercedes. He looked ahead as far as he could and saw that the lights were all green and the cars now moved with increasing speed. The car in front of him slowed down to make a left turn. Scott jumped in the right lane and, again sped to catch up. He was now one car away and in the opposite lane. The Mercedes made a left turn at the green light. Scott tried to get back into the left lane but the car beside him wouldn't allow him. He raced to jump in front of the man who kept him out and made a U-turn in front of the street sign that read, "No U Turn." A police officer, sitting just behind the sign, put on his siren and pulled Scott over.

Scott ignored the siren at first. Maybe if the police followed him to the Mercedes, he could ask the officer to assist him. When he turned on to the street where the Mercedes made its left turn, the car was nowhere in sight. He lost him. If he had just stayed in the lane two cars behind, but no, he had to jump from lane to lane. He should have stayed in the lane behind the car, held back, see where the car was headed. Scott pulled his car close to the sidewalk and stopped. The first sign of hope and he couldn't catch the car. He always had to mess things up. The last thing he wanted to do was to take out his frustrations on the officer.

It was late; he was tired, so he drove back. He realized now, that the police had begun to look for the car and he felt an urgency to find the car before they did, especially given his car chase earlier. Though he didn't make any progress with the list, he felt like for the first time in his life he was doing something important, and his life was now beginning to have meaning. He knew that no matter what his father said he, Scott, would have to find the car and the person who drove it and be the one to put that person behind bars. He knew that he owed it to his mother and his sister. Maybe by doing this he would finally learn to forgive himself.

~~~~~~~~~~

On the drive back, Scott knew he had a stop to make before going home. He had to talk to Kathryn. He refused to accept the notion that she was through with him and decided that he needed to hear, however she felt, from her. He deserved an explanation. He drove to Kathryn's house and sat outside across the street first trying to decide what he would say to her and then whether or not he should bother. He had to come to grips with the fact that she was no longer interested. He cared about her and he felt betrayed by her, but for some reason he couldn't just walk away like anyone else would.

He sat back in the car. No matter how hard he tried to tell

himself otherwise, he had given his heart to Kathryn. He knew it the morning they first met. Even though he wasn't deserving of her on one hand, on the other, something inside him pushed him into not accepting the fact that she had betrayed him. That special person whom he met just wouldn't do anything like that to him. Now, he knew how betrayal felt; to need someone who didn't follow through. She'd made him feel that, and he understood how he made others feel. No one had ever done that to him. He recalled a conversation where she told him that she talked to her mother every day. She said it was encouraging to her and helped her get through each day. There were times when she just wanted to crawl under something and stay there. She told Scott that he couldn't let what happened to him stop his life. She told him that his mother wouldn't want that. She showed him that she believed in him and said that she could see that he had something else that bothered him. It was at that moment that he knew he needed her.

He sat and waited; his head swimming with his thoughts and the question of how long he had planned to sit in front of her house before deciding to either go in or drive away. Maybe he'd luck out like he did the last time and she'd drive up. But he had no such luck this time and after about twenty minutes of gathering up his nerve and with hope hidden deep in the crevices of his heart, he got out of his car, crossed the street and walked up the steps to the front door. He cleared his throat and then rang the doorbell.

Martin, still in his office suit and tie pulled loose at the neck, answered the door. "Can I help you?" He peered closer, almost as if he thought that the last person in the world he would see was the man standing on the other side of the door.

Scott let out a slight smile. Kathryn had described her father to him but she didn't say how much alike they looked. He stretched out his hand to Martin. "Hi, my name is Scott Kersey —"

"I know. Kat told me all about you. Won't you come in?" He stepped aside and Scott entered into the foyer, a brass chandelier hanging low from the ceiling. Martin closed the door and led Scott to the country-style living room with its beige and pink decor. Scott walked toward the living room looking around at the place where Kathryn lived, laughed, talked. Martin pointed him toward the pink, green and beige floral couch that sat across the room, as he pulled the chain to a table lamp. When the light came on, Scott sat down. Martin sat to Scott's right in a cushioned armchair with wooden arms. Jazz piano music played low in the background. The two men sat as the pianist ran up and down the scale and the smoothness of the high and low notes glided out of the speakers, settled in the air, and gently filled up the room.

"I'm Martin Milner, Kat's father." Martin cleared his throat, crossed his legs, uncrossed them, and finally clasped his hands together.

Mary walked into the living room. "Sorry," she said as she stood for a brief moment watching the two men before she left.

"You need something?" Martin called out to Mary. When he turned around, he saw she was gone.

Scott realized that Martin was just as uncomfortable as he was, but he was puzzled as to why he didn't tell Kathryn he was there to see her.

"Every month I make a check out to Kersey and Associates, any relationship?"

"My father. Kersey and Associates is my father's company. I work there."

"Does Kat know that?"

"I told her that I work at a real estate investment company."

"She told me about your mother. Sorry to hear that."

"Thank you." Scott wanted to ask for Kathryn, but something made him hold back. He tried to do something with his legs but he was afraid to move for fear he would kick the coffee table in front of him. He adjusted himself on the sofa — sat back, moved forward — until he finally moved up to the edge of the couch, ready to jump up and run away at a moment's notice. "Maybe I should go. I really don't know why I'm here."

"Stay there a second." Martin left the room and before Scott could even think of what to do next, Martin was back with a note in his hand. He handed the note to Scott.

"Kat is still in France right now. She left this for me. She never goes anywhere without telling me where she's going and when she'll be back, our rule. She knows how I worry about her."

Scott read the note that said that Kathryn was going with Frankie to France to Emeraude. After he read it, he handed it back. He was relieved to know that she wasn't ducking him, but not as relieved as he thought he would feel.

"She's been there for almost a week. I've tried to call her several times, but she never picks up when I call. She called the office once and left a message giving more details about where she was and why she had to leave so suddenly and more importantly for me, she said that she was fine."

"Thank you," said Scott, feeling like an intruder and rising to leave.

"Where are you going?"

"I don't think I should have come here. Thank you for your hospitality." Scott headed toward the door, feeling the way a man stumbling into a lady's bathroom would feel.

Martin opened the door.

"Nice to meet you. I hope we meet again." Martin stretched out his hand.

Scott looked down at Martin's hand and then into his half -smiling face, and shook his hand. "Thank you." Scott started out the door.

"I'll let her know you were here. I'm sure she would want to know." Martin called after him.

"Good night." With that, Scott went back to his car.

"Hey," called out someone just before he reached his car.

Scott turned around and saw Mary.

"Hello."

They stood just under the street light. He looked harder at her and saw that she was not wearing make-up. He remembered the last time he saw her, her dark make-up around her eyes ran down her face when she stood there crying as she watched her boyfriend drive off. "You okay?"

"Can I ask you something?"

"Sure."

She stared at him a long time as if she had planned to change her mind about what she wanted. "Do you think I'm a slut?"

He guessed Kathryn must have given her a good scolding and she used the word "slut" and Mary must have been thinking about what Kathryn said.

"No. I think you're a stunning, beautiful young woman who's turning herself into something she doesn't want to be. Someone she may be sorry about later."

"You really think I'm stunning and beautiful?" She gave a slight smile.

"Yes, I do," he said softly.

"You two are just alike."

"What does that mean? Who?" asked Scott.

"You're both sweet and kind hearted. Don't give up on her." And with that Mary turned toward the house and disappeared into the darkness.

~~~~~~~~~~

Later on that night, Scott, again, sat at the kitchen table staring at an unopened bottle of Scotch and an empty glass. Cameron walked in with the aromas of their dinner wafting from a brown paper bag that he sat on the kitchen table. He looked from the unopened bottle of Scotch to Scott.

"So you didn't have much luck, huh?" asked Cameron.

"Makes me appreciate the police more and I really think we need more laws about what people should do with their old cars."

They both laughed. Scott saw Cameron eye the bottle that sat before him.

"You know you never did tell me everything about you and Lisa. What happened between you two?" asked Cameron. "Why don't you tell me the whole story this time?"

Scott stared at the bottle, a statue in a park.

"Scott? What happened between you two? You know she keeps calling the office. It's only a matter of time before she comes here, if she hasn't already."

Cameron took the bottle off the table and sat it on the counter. "Son, talk to me. I want to know what happened."

Starring at the place where the bottle sat, Scott began, "Lisa and I are ancient history, Dad. It's been about three weeks since I saw her last and I hope to never see her again."

"Why's that?" asked Cameron as he opened the bag and took out two plates covered in foil.

"She just wasn't good for me. She complained about everything I did or said and I just got tired of it." He turned to look at Cameron.

"What did you say to her last?" He took the foil off one plate, steam rising with the aromas of the spaghetti, and placed it in front of Scott. Scott got up reached in the drawer and got out two knives and two forks, laid them on the table.

He stabbed a meatball with his fork, bit into it and dropped the uneaten half back on the plate.

"We got in another fight, she told me to leave and I did. I think she expected me to come crawling back like I usually do, but I didn't."

"So now what?"

"Now what? I'm in love with someone else. I've known this woman for about two weeks and I can't stop thinking about her. To make matters worse, she's not interested in me. But who could blame her."

"Who is she?" Cameron looked at Scott. The look on his face was one that said "I hate it when you talk like that." He took the foil off the second plate.

"Her name is Kathryn Milner and she went away to France for a week without telling me. She left a note for her loved one, her father, but I wasn't on that list."

"Scott, two weeks is hardly enough time to know anyone, much less love someone."

"How many times have you said that you knew from the

very first time you saw mom that she would be your wife?"

"I know. There are those times. You think that's happening to you?" He took his fork and placed it on the edge of his plate.

"Yes, I do," said Scott.

"Where did you meet her?" asked Cameron.

"You really want to hear it?"

"Yes, I think so."

Scott settled himself in his seat. "It was the day we had to go to the trail. Remember? After the accident? Coming out of the park I almost ran into her."

"Scott, you never mentioned that. That must have been, that —"

"She was so beautiful. Here I am, a mess, I know, and she wasn't afraid of me, wasn't cruel; didn't blame me for what happened. Her voice sounded so sweet, so kind, so determined. I knew the moment I heard her. She took a minute and looked at me. You know; really looked at me. I just knew." He took his fork and moved his pasta around into the sauce.

"I thought you didn't believe in love at first sight," said Cameron.

"For me, I didn't. For you, mom and someone else, I thought it probable."

"Why not for you?" Cameron took a forkful of his pasta.

"Well, you know. Lisa. She's not someone that you could fall in love with at first sight. You have to acquire a feeling for her, and that takes a while, and when I think about it, a long while."

"You two were together for what? A year? He got up to fill two glasses with ice and water from the refrigerator.

"Well, when you run into many "Lisas" in life you begin to believe that that's how love is for you and when you find someone you like even just a little you tend to try to make it work."

"You have to make it work when you find that person who is your other half," said Cameron. "What went wrong with your new lady, Kathryn?"

"I don't know. I thought we were doing fine. We were supposed to meet for dinner and then she didn't show up. I found out that she went to France to a store called Emeraude, in Paris."

Scott looked down at his dinner.

"Son, if you really want something, you have to go get it. You want her? Go get her." Cameron put a wad of spaghetti in his mouth, sucked up a string that refused to be twirled around his fork.

Scott watched his father suck up the string of spaghetti and smiled.

"I need you to help me tomorrow. With John out on maternity leave with his second child, I'm a little short handed. John wanted to come in and help, but I told him to stay home with his wife and new baby, and I would get help. We're acquiring new property and I want you, Eva and George to look over the plans, and land rights, and review the contracts. We'll need to start early, about 7:00 is good, I usually get there at 6:00, as you know. I meet with the potential clients at noon. I need everything ready for that meeting before noon. I need you to help, Scott. I want to be able to give some of my employees a salary increase. The success of this job will determine that."

Scott looked surprised that his father had asked him to

help. He seemed satisfied just letting him sit and take up office space. In the past, Scott had only done little things like rounding everyone up for meetings, making certain that everyone had copies of a portfolio, but nothing this serious. Reading plans and reviewing rental agreements were out of his league. He wasn't sure he could do that.

Scott was also afraid to "go and get her" as his father had just advised him. His father had never been in a situation where he wasn't worthy enough to have the best. Scott was in that situation and he had no idea how to go get something that he didn't deserve. Instead, he went to his room where he had another bottle stashed and drank himself to sleep.

Chapter 15
Scott

Scott overslept and when he arrived at the office late in the morning, he found a note on his desk from his father asking him to come to his office as soon as he got in. Scott stood in the doorway of Cameron's office waiting for his conversation with Eva and George, two employees, to end. As he turned away, June had just returned to her desk.

"Oh, Scott. Sorry I had to step away. He wants to see you, so don't go anywhere. They should be through in a few minutes."

Scott had hoped that the meeting would take longer. He wasn't in any hurry to talk to his father. He didn't mean to oversleep; he just did. Eva and George came out of the office, Eva smiled, George nodded at Scott on the way out. Scott, trying as hard as he could to keep his father from seeing how he was shaking, entered. Cameron didn't get up.

"Scott, have a seat." He got up and closed the door. "What happened? I thought you'd get here early." He took his chair behind his desk.

"I'm sorry, I overslept," said Scott.

"Son, I needed you this morning. I have a lot of money riding on these acquisitions, not to mention the fact that I had to pull two other people from their regular duties to help with what I asked you to do. Everyone in this office needed you this morning. When you didn't show up, at the last minute, I had to pull two other people to help me. I needed you here. Where were you?"

Scott could hear in his voice and see in him that he tried as hard as he could to keep calm.

"Dad, I said I was sorry. What else do you want?"

"Sorry is not enough. I need a good reason why you didn't show up and now you sit here and all you have is 'sorry'? We could have lost these accounts. Do you understand that? You could have cost me a good fortune."

"I know you need more, but I don't know what else to say. Get off my back."

Cameron stood, face red, fist flailing, voice loud. "Get off your back? For the past four years, you've just taken up office space. You've never come to me and asked to do anything; you've never even so much as tried to find out what we do around here. You drop in and out whenever you feel like it and you tell me to get off your back? Whether you care or not, I have to keep this company going; keep your mother's project alive. 'Get off your back?' Is that what I'm supposed to tell my employees? Is that how I'm supposed to handle your mother's project?"

Scott's eyes widened as his father yelled. He had never seen his father this angry. "You never came to me and asked to do anything." His father was waiting on him to ask. Is that how it worked? He always thought his father didn't give him anything to do because he didn't think he (Scott) could do anything right. His eyes filled with tears. "Dad, I don't know what to say. I'm so sorry, so sorry. Can I make it up? What can I do now?" His father was right. He had to care about his mother, what his father tried to do for his mother, and care about his father's business. He had to stop being a screw-up.

He looked at his son and lowered his voice. "I gave you this assignment because I thought you were ready. I guess I was wrong."

"No, let me make it up, please. What can I do?"

"Nothing; it's all done. Others did your work for you. I could count on them." He picked up some papers from his desk and began reading them.

Scott stood to leave. "Dad, I'm so sorry. I really am. I am ready, or I wanna be ready."

Cameron continued reading.

When Scott saw that Cameron wouldn't look up, he left and returned to his office.

Yet another time he'd let someone down. Again, he let his father see that he just couldn't depend on him. It was just as well, since he had no specific job at his father's firm, he wouldn't have known what to do, or how to read plans or a contract, for that matter. But his nonchalant attitude really didn't mask his feelings and he wanted to pound his fist against the wall. He sank in his chair. Maybe his parents should have named him, "Destroyer."

He needed something to do to make him happy, give him a sense of accomplishment so he turned on his computer and began rewriting for the third time, parts of the short story that he'd been trying to finish, something that his mother and sister had encouraged from his college days. He sat looking at the cursor on the screen. Even writing didn't take away the horrible feeling he had from letting his father down. If he could just talk to Kathryn she would lift his spirits, make him feel human, again. His father's words from the night before, "If you really want something go and get it," came to mind. He saved his story, closed out, sat back. He really hadn't intended to say anything about Kathryn to his father; it just came out. He'd been trying to forget her. His reality was that she deserved someone better than the man he was. He'd tried to tell himself that, but he had an overwhelming desire to see her. He really needed her now. He wanted to call her, go see her in France. How could he just leave like that? Wouldn't his father see his leaving as his running away again? He really goofed this time. He felt like the lowest form of any being, he had to make it up. He needed to search for that car, especially since he'd already started. He just couldn't stop now. He had to accomplish something to gain his father's respect. There was no way he could leave now. But he could call her, talk to her. What would that hurt? Just a conversation. He picked up the phone, called Emeraude.

He found out that Kathryn was away from the store having lunch and Scott spoke to one of the employees who told him that she had been there for a week, but her plans had changed. She would have to stay in Paris one more week. The employee didn't say why she would be there an extra week and Scott didn't ask. Since the accent was difficult, probably for both of them, Scott didn't ask anything of a personal nature, such as with whom she was having lunch. With the information he received, he was fairly satisfied, and before he realized it, he made a round trip reservation on the next flight to Paris, France leaving later that evening and returning on the next flight back. He also booked a hotel room for one night that the receptionist at the airline said was close to Emeraude. It just so happened that she knew Emeraude, she told him, and had stayed at the hotel she recommended for him.

When he hung up his body suddenly felt slushy like jello, he was so nervous. He left the office to go pack an overnight bag. Was he really going to do this? What would his father say? Maybe the get-away would do him good. Give him a chance to think things through and map out a new plan for himself.

He had never done anything this drastic with any of his relationships and he was beginning to enjoy the feeling; the adrenalin surging through his body. Treading new ground felt exhilarating, yet at the same time frightening. He had made it out of the building and to the parking lot when he heard Cameron's secretary, June.

"Mis-ter-Ker-sey."

Scott turned around and saw June running toward him. He started back to meet her.

"Whoo, I'm out of breath," said June breathing hard. She put her hand on her chest.

"Mr. Kersey needs you in the office now." She held up her hand to stop him from talking. "He wouldn't tell me what it's about. Whoa, I had to run all over the building to find you. I just happened to see you . . ."

"But I'm on my way to the airport." He held up his flight confirmation that he had just printed out.

"He just said it was important and to find you immediately."

Scott felt a little relieved, and a little disappointed. He went with the secretary back into the building and back to his father's office suite on the third floor. Cameron was walking out of the suite and on his way to the elevators just as Scott got off.

"Hold the elevator," yelled out Cameron.

"The police called and said that they needed to talk to us. I think they found the driver of that car or that witness who said they saw the driver," said Cameron punching the down button several times.

~~~~~~~~~~~

Detectives Haines and Charles were at their desks in the large open area of the Homicide Department. Detective Charles, seated facing the entrance, saw Scott and Cameron as they entered the room of busy officers moving about. The two officers stood when they saw the Kerseys enter.

"Thank you for coming in," said Haines with an outstretched hand to Cameron.

"We can talk back here," said Charles. He led the way to an interrogation room, opened the door, and ushered them in.

Haines and Charles entered and closed the door.

Cameron turned toward the door.

"Have a seat," said Charles to the two men, gesturing toward the two chairs opposite the observation window.

Scott walked to the wooden table, marred with gashes and stains, and two chairs on each side. He sat down beside his father and looked around the windowless room with its gray walls and floor and felt something unnerving, a strain, a certain uneasiness in the air and he stiffened his body, an attempt to ready himself for anything he might hear about his mother.

"Mr. Kersey, Scott," began Haines. "Is it okay to call you Scott?"

He cleared his throat. "Sure."

"What is it Detective Haines?" asked Cameron, irritation in his voice.

"Scott, you neglected to tell us about the altercation that you and your mother had with a man one morning when you were running. Care to tell us about that?"

"Altercation? I don't re —"

"We have witnesses that told us that you grabbed another runner and were making threats to him?"

Scott looked at his father. "Oh, yes, I do remember that, now. My mother and I had just gotten to the trail and I went over to the water fountain to get a drink of water before we started. I heard this man screaming and yelling, but I didn't pay attention."

At that moment, another officer opened the door, walked to the table, and whispered something to Detective Charles. Charles motioned to Haines and the three officers left the room. In a few minutes, Charles returned and sat down at the table.

"You were saying," said Charles.

Scott and Cameron looked at each other.

"Go ahead. You heard someone screaming and yelling, but you didn't pay attention, you didn't think it involved your mother. Go ahead."

"Well, the yelling continued so I turned around to see what was going on. I saw a man screaming at the top of his voice at my mother and she was cowering to him. I went over, grabbed him by the shirt, and began screaming and yelling back at him. I told him that this lady was my mother and nobody yelled and screamed at her. I said that if you have something to talk to her about in a dignified manner she'd be glad to hear it. But he couldn't scream at her. I told him that he needed to apologize. He did, asked me to let him go, I did and he ran away." Scott turned toward his father.

Cameron stared at Scott, eyes wide.

"Did you get his name or anything?"

"No, I didn't think to do that."

"Why was he yelling at your mother?" asked Charles.

"I don't know. He really shook her up. She said she really didn't hear much of what he said to her. But she thought he had mistaken her for someone else."

"What did you do?" asked Charles.

"Well." Scott looked at his father again. "She was very upset and she didn't want Dad to know. We just took our run. She made me promise not to tell Dad."

"Why is that?" asked Charles.

"My mom was afraid that Dad would go confront the man. She said he apologized and that was enough for her."

"So you never saw him again?"

"Not that I remember."

"Can you describe that man in any way?"

"Maybe, but it was a few months ago. If you had a picture, maybe I would recognize him, but —"

"We have a man we're interviewing right now. Will he tell us the same story?"

"What do you mean?" asked Scott.

"You just said that you stopped him from yelling at your mother. You didn't seek him out later and let him know how you really felt about that?"

"Detective Charles, that's enough. My son did not cause any of this. Someone just ran her down and drove away. That someone is who you need to interrogate, not us," said Cameron.

"Let me tell you two something. If I go next door and find out that Scott beat this man or humiliated him in any way, Scott could be looking at accessory to a murder."

"He did no such thing. I know my boy and he wouldn't do anything like that. You're saying that he had something to do with the murder of his mother and my wife."

"I did what I just told you, Detective Charles, nothing else," said Scott in a calm voice.

Haines opened the door, gave some sort of signal with his face.

"You two can go for now," Charles said, voice almost a whisper.

Scott and Cameron stepped passed Haines and into the hallway. A man flew out of a room. He stood in front of Scott, pointing and yelling.

"You little prick, you lied to these police officers. You told them I hit your mother? Huh? Huh? How could you lie like that? You goddamn sonofabitch . . . ."

Charles and Haines both grabbed the man on either side and pulled him away from Scott. The man struggled to get away, fist balled up, ready to hit Scott.

Haines took the man back into the interrogation room and left him, this time closed the door.

"Give him a chance to cool off," said Haines when he returned.

Scott turned to Haines, "You told him I said he hit my mother? You lied to that man?" Scott struggled to control himself in the police station. He couldn't continue looking for the car if he got himself locked up for assaulting a police officer. He jammed his fist in his pants pockets and took a step back.

"Why did you bring that man in here" Is he the driver?" asked Cameron.

"We don't know that yet," said Charles. He turned to Scott, "Your story checks out. You both said the same thing."

"I told you that."

"We picked him up because his car has a big dent in the rear and because the witnesses told us that he had an altercation with you and your mother. So he had motive." said Haines.

"Now, what? Are you going to question him further?' asked Cameron.

"Since we know he's a runner and uses the trail, he like anyone using that trail between 5:30 and 8:00 in the morning is a suspect and will be brought in for questioning. We will question him further, see what we can get out of him," said Charles.

"You need to explain to him that Scott didn't tell you that," said Cameron.

Charles nodded.

"Are we still suspects?" asked Scott.

"We've ruled you two out," said Charles.

"Thanks for coming in. You two understand that we have to do what we have to do in order to get at the truth," said Haines.

Cameron nodded and he and Scott walked out of the police station.

"What do you think?" asked Scott as the two of them walked to the parking lot.

"He didn't seem like the man to me, but like Charles said, maybe he knows something," responded Cameron.

Scott turned his head toward his father as they walked side by side to the car. His father earned a living by being able to read people and Cameron would know whether the police had the wrong man. Scott wanted the person caught, but he also wanted something to do with it. Scott was so sorry about letting his father down earlier and even so, his father had just stood up for him in front of the police. A warm feeling washed over Scott as he watched his father get into the car. His hand on the doorknob, Scott looked at his watch and then up at the noise he heard in the sky. The plane. He remembered. He had missed his plane.

Later that night Scott lay in his bed, arm under his head, thinking. He had become so involved with the interview that for a while he had forgotten about flying to Paris. He'd felt a momentary sadness, an emptiness and his heart stopped for a moment as he thought he might have missed his chance to go to her, missed that narrow window of opportunity. He could change his ticket; he still had time. But the truth was Scott didn't feel like he should go to Paris. He tried to think about what was keeping him back. The investigation was underway, he had the list of car owners, and had started his search for the car, and person who had taken his mother's life. He had to continue the search he started, and find the car before the police did. The police had the wrong man and Scott felt it. He knew his father knew it and soon the police would discover that the man knew nothing and had nothing to do with his mother. Meanwhile, this man would keep him ahead of the police. He couldn't leave the country right now; not until things were settled, not until he felt settled inside.

Chapter 16
Kathryn

Kathryn wished she were able to read minds. If she could, she would surely want to know what Harris Sweeney was thinking. She smiled as she sat across the table watching him take a sip of his Beaujolais vin and smiling back at her.

"This is a really nice restaurant, Harris, very upscale." Kathryn looked around the Pompidou Restaurant and noticed the white linen tablecloths on all the tables, the crystal chandelier in the center of the ceiling and the lit candles on the tables, the women in gowns and men in dark suits, bow ties, and neckties.

"Anything for you, Beautiful. How's your poulet? You need anything? "

"I'm fine. How's your steak?"

"This melts in your mouth, it's so good." He cut a piece and held it up to her. "Want a bite?"

She shook her head. It baffled her how he could eat steak with blood running out. "How'd you know about this place?"

Kathryn hadn't heard from Harris Sweeney since the last time he called her and told her he would be gone a few more days. A few more days; what did that mean? Harris was always saying things like that, things that had no real meaning. His ambiguity sometimes prevented her from making plans. When he did return, he would just show up at any time. She worried that he expected her to reschedule for him. There were just as many times when she had to do the very same thing. So they kept each other and the relationship in an indeterminate state, never moving toward the exclusive, the special.

One reason why she never bothered to talk to Harris about moving the relationship forward was due to his indiscriminate behavior. She always believed that while he was away, he saw other women and even when he returned, she felt he had someone else. She knew she didn't have to make a commitment to him, as long as he was seeing other women. She never demanded anything different of him.

"Alex brought me here the first night I arrived."

"Is Alex still in Paris?" Kathryn peeped around the waiter who brought more butter and was arranging it on the table.

"No. He waited for me here and left the next morning." He motioned for the waiter to replenish her wine glass.

She smiled and after the waiter poured her more, she took a sip.

"Do you need more bread, anything?"

"No. I'm fine. What's Alex's new line?"

"Now, Kat, you know I can't do that. Remember our promise." He cut off another piece of his rare steak.

"I know. I just thought I could trip you up."

"What about your design? Have you gotten it out yet?"

"Now, Harris, you know I can't do that. Remember our promise." She put a forkful of potatoes in her mouth.

Harris let out a loud laugh that continued for a few minutes. Kathryn didn't think what she said was that funny, but she guessed Harris needed to release his nervousness at this point, so when he looked at her, she laughed too.

When he stopped, Harris took his white linen napkin and dabbed at the corners of his mouth.

"Beautiful, I've been thinking about what we have, our relationship and I think, and I hope you'll agree with me, but I think we, we, well we need to get married."

Kathryn tried hard to keep the chicken in her mouth without choking on it. She didn't want to seem shocked, but marrying Harris never would have entered her mind. She wanted to ask him how he arrived at that conclusion. She never thought he would want to marry her, especially with all this running around and womanizing he was used to. Why her? She didn't know how to ask him that, and she had to bring this situation back into reality as best she could.

"Harris, are you sure we're ready for such a big step?" She tried not to sound incredulous, or that she questioned him.

"Oh, I don't mean right away. I thought we'd start by getting engaged and then going from there."

"Harris, I just never thought you'd think that way about me."

"Beautiful, I think it's time for us to reign in this relationship that we have and focus on each other."

"What will you do about all those other ladies you like to associate with?"

"What other ladies? You know you've been my one and only." He looked at her like he couldn't imagine her asking him that question.

Kathryn didn't know whether to laugh or cry. "You can't mean that." Was he making a joke or what?

"What?"

"Harris, you've always had other women."

"Maybe when we first met I was seeing someone else. And maybe I continued for a while, but I didn't do that for long."

Kathryn looked like she couldn't believe the prevarication; he continued.

"Don't look like that. I've tried to tell you that I really enjoy being with you. You make me feel good about myself and you make me happy. I've said that to you before, Beautiful, many times." He leaned forward.

"Yeah, but I always thought that was just something that you thought you should say."

"I said it because I feel it. I take it you don't feel the same way." He sat back in his chair, placed his knife and fork on his plate. His countenance dropped and she saw disappointment flash across his face.

She smiled. "I've always enjoyed being with you, you know that."

He let out a smile, relaxed a little. "I know you wanted to get back after your first week here. You told me that Frankie left over the weekend, and I know you're staying a week with me, but can I talk you into staying one more week? That way we can have two weeks together; no work, no other worries, just you and me."

"I have to get back. You've already talked me into staying a week beyond my original return date. The airline sent me another ticket too, by the way." She took another big sip of wine. She felt she needed it.

"Well if we just have one week, I want us to spend this entire week together. No work, no other people, just the two of us doing whatever we want together. We always seem to let other things interfere and I don't want that this week. This could be the beginning of our lifetime of being together. I'm looking forward to it."

"Me too, Harris Sweeney, me too." Kathryn smiled at Harris. She could hardly believe herself. It was days ago she missed Scott like nothing else and now she was promising another man a week with him in Paris and on top of that, she had promised him that they would have an exclusive relationship. She hadn't had a chance to contact Scott and explain things to him and by this time she was sure he had given up on her. Besides, she had been seeing Harris before she met Scott and now that Harris wanted to take their relationship to the next level, she felt she owed it to him to carry it to a finish point. She had only known Scott for two weeks, though she had to admit that in the time she had been seeing Harris, she had never felt about him the way she felt about Scott in such a short time.

Harris got them a hotel room at one of the swankiest hotels in Paris, so he said, and when Kathryn returned to the apartment to pack her things, she found a message from her father that one of the store employees left for her. She had to return his call no matter how costly, or he would worry. She used the phone that Frankie had brought in after they arrived when he discovered his cell phone didn't work in France. He had said that it was for business use only, but she used it to call her father.

"Hello, Dad."

"Kat! Hello, sweetheart. How is the store going?"

"It's okay."

"Oh, no. I know that tone. What's going on? You didn't have to actually fire anyone, did you?" He chuckled.

But she heard it as a fretful chortle.

"No. Frankie and I worked hard to get the store and the employees together before he left. You wouldn't believe the improvement we made. And the employees said they liked the new store." Kathryn forgot she was on the phone and did air quotes with her left hand for "new store."

"So what is this about Harris Sweeney? You ran into him in France? Is that why you're staying another week? I must admit I was rather surprised when you called and left that message."

Kathryn was silent for a few minutes before she responded.

"Dad, do you believe in love at first sight?"

Martin was quiet for a moment and Kathryn could hear him breathing in the phone. She was ready to take back the question when he answered.

"I guess it depends on the people involved." His voice was so low that Kathryn almost had to ask him to repeat. "Maybe for . . . Who is this about?" He asked a little louder.

"Nothing." She sat down on the bed, back against the headboard, legs crossed.

"Kat. What's wrong?"

"Harris wants me to marry him."

"Sweetheart. Marry? France is such a romantic place, you're not letting that influence you are you?"

She felt him squirming just the way he always did when he wanted to tell her something, but didn't want to say what she should do. "Why do you say that, Dad?"

"You've been telling me that you and Harris have a casual relationship. What prompted this? Is there something that you're leaving out?"

Again, Kathryn held a space of silence.

Finally, "Do you have to have love?" asked Kathryn in a quiet and serious voice.

"Most people start with that?" responded Martin, equally quiet and serious.

Kathryn didn't respond.

"Kat? Sweetheart, I didn't think Harris was the one you loved," said Martin.

"Harris is a good man, Dad."

"You don't sound so convinced."

"I don't?"

"Kat, I know you're thinking about Steve. Honey, Steve died because he had leukemia. Leukemia is not something that you can give to anyone. He had it for a long time. I know you two were in love in high school and you wanted to get married, but you have to realize that. You have to let go."

"I do realize it. I do. But Steve and I were very close, you know that. It was hard, really hard."

"Yes, but he was a high school romance. Who knows? Maybe after you two graduated, you would have gone your own ways. We don't know, except that it does happen. Maybe you would have outgrown him. Sweetheart, we've talked about this so much. You have to let Steve go and allow yourself to love again. You must allow yourself to love again. You owe that to yourself."

"Maybe I don't deserve it."

"Sweetheart, don't talk like that. Of course, you deserve it. If nothing else you're my daughter and my daughter deserves everything."

"You think so?"

"Of course, I do. Come home, Kat. Come home and let's work this out."

She could hear the desperation in his voice. "I'll be home by the end of the week. Don't forget to pick me up."

"Kat."

"Dad, I gotta go."

Kathryn sat up in the bed. She knew her father was trying to tell her to open her heart to Scott. She was shutting out Scott because of her high school love, Steve. As hard as she tried to tell herself that her father was wrong, she knew he was right. She thought about the time Scott took her to the play and introduced her to his friends. She thought about what her father did not say to her. Maybe she did agree to enter an exclusive relationship with Harris because she was afraid to be with Scott. She knew the pattern. She would give her heart to him and then he would leave her just like her mother, just like Steve and don't forget Edith who suddenly moved away. Edith promised to write her but she never did. Even after Kathryn wrote her several letters, she didn't bother to return them. Even her father gave her a titanic-size scare last year when he had his heart attack.

She stood up and went to the mirror, looked at herself – front, back, left, right side and back to the front. Everyone whom she ever cared about has left her except her father. He's the only one who has never gone away from her; she could rely on his love.

She picked up the dress she had worn to the play with Scott, held it up, and looked at it just before putting it in her suitcase. She smiled when she remembered that he bumped his hand against hers after the lights went down. She could feel him watching her and she remembered she wanted so badly to turn and look at him. Yet she didn't. She remembered how she wanted him to kiss her again and she flinched when she remembered the electricity she felt when his leg touched hers as he slid down in his seat.

If she forced herself to face facts, the fact was she loved Scott and wanted to spend her life with him. The fact also was she was deathly afraid of their relationship. It moved too quickly for her, this whirlwind and she had fallen for him too hard. If she lost him, she would never recover. Even though she hadn't called him all week, she knew she couldn't. It was best to just leave things like they were, however that was.

But Harris wanted to take their relationship into the serious category and while she was certain she didn't love him, he seemed sure that they could have a good relationship. A relationship with Sweeney was safe; she was convinced of that. After all, they had been dating for a year, she knew him; she wouldn't be hurt if she lost him.

Kathryn zipped up her bags, cut out the lights, and closed the door. Downstairs, she left the key in an envelope, placed it on the counter, and left for the hotel.

Chapter 17
Scott

Scott drove to east Rockville to the next house on his list. He walked up the three steps to the white frame house that sat close to the street. Absent a doorbell, he knocked on the door. An elderly man with white wild flyaway hair answered his knock. He looked like he was no longer in the driving age. When Scott asked for the owner of the car, the elderly man told him that two years ago, the owner took the car and moved to New Mexico.

The next house was harder to locate. The street was not really a residential street, but rundown-looking once-a-upon-a-time homes converted to small businesses. The house that Scott needed was between a variety store and a repair shop and had a huge sign over the front door that said "Pawn Shop." He didn't need to get out of his car thinking the store was too far away from the trail, coupled with the fact that it was a pawnshop. The third house was located in Silver Spring and even though a little far away, he wanted to check it out anyway. Maybe these people drove to the trail or had a friend who lived near the trail.

161

He located the apartment building first, and then drove several blocks beyond the building looking for the car. When he didn't see it, he turned around to park and went inside the apartment building. An older woman with too much make-up and dressed in a long flowing aqua-color evening gown opened the door. She held a drink in one hand and a cigarette in the other. When she opened the door, she took a step back.

"Well, you must be the answer to my prayers. Please come in."

"I don't want to take up a lot of your time. I can see that you're busy. I'm interested in your 1999 black metallic Mercedes."

"Well, honey, if you want me to tell you about the car you have to come in." She opened the door wider.

Leaving the door open, he stepped just inside, the messy apartment, with an odor he didn't recognize and clothes, papers, empty food containers strewn everywhere. A vicious looking pit bull jumped out barking and snarling. Scott took a step back until he was almost in the hall again. He noticed the dog chained to another door, but with the jumping and barking, he wasn't sure how long that chain or the door would hold.

"What about the car?' asked Scott.

"My boyfriend ran out on me and stole my car."

The barking dog was so loud Scott could hardly hear her. He hated to ask her again and drag this out any longer. Then he heard banging on the wall. Probably a neighbor upset over the barking dog.

"Are you the police?" she asked.

"No ma'am. I just want to buy the car if it's in good condition."

"I want my car back. Can you find my boyfriend and bring my car back?"

"I don't know . . . ."

She went into the next room. Scott wasn't sure what she had planned, so he took another step back until he was clearly in the hall and half faced in a direction where he could easily get out of there if he had to. The pit bull quieted down. The woman came back with a slip of paper and handed it to Scott. "Here, I think his new girlfriend lives here. I've tried to find the place, but I couldn't. Here's his name and address."

Scott took the slip of paper from her.

"Do you have a card or something?" she asked.

"No. I can give you my name and phone number." He wrote his name and cell phone down on another slip of paper that she handed him and gave it back to her. He thanked her and left.

He found the location of the woman's boyfriend who lived in a set of apartments off Twinbrook Parkway in Rockville, very close to the trail. Scott went to the apartment and knocked on the door. A young petite looking woman answered the door and when he asked for the boy friend, she called him to the door. Scott was a little surprised, but tried not to show it. The boyfriend was much younger than the woman in the evening gown, who didn't seem right for him.

Scott cleared his throat. "I'm looking for a 1999 black metallic Mercedes C class I was told you had. I'm interested in buying it, if it's in good shape."

"Who told you I had a Mercedes?" asked the man.

"I just came from the home of Bertha Kingsley. She said it was her car and you took it when you left."

"That bitch is crazy. I don't want to have anything to do

with her. Two months ago, I sold that piece of junk to a junk yard for cash. I wanted that thing and anything about that woman demolished. Who —"

Before Scott knew what happened, the pit bull rushed passed him and attacked the man. The man tried to get the dog off him and the two of them tumbled back into the man's apartment. The young petite looking woman screamed and yelled at the dog, trying to get the dog to unclench its teeth and free the man's arm. At this moment, the man's ex girlfriend came to the door. Scott's first instinct was to get out of there. He could see that the older woman had another motive and he fell right into her hands. He pulled out his phone to call 911.

"Lady, get your dog. I just called 911." Scott said to her several times.

"Thank you for finding him for me. I need to pay him back for what he did to me."

"Lady, if your dog hurts him, you can go to jail."

The boyfriend somehow managed to grab the back of the dog's neck and digging his hand in, was able to free his arm from the dog's mouth. He held on to the dog that was now helpless and with all his strength, threw the dog outside of the apartment. Scott could see the dog was angered and afraid and not wanting to give the dog anything more to attack, he went to his car.

The police soon arrived. They questioned the old girlfriend, new girlfriend and the boyfriend. The boyfriend said that his new girlfriend had nothing to do with what happened. The police called the dog pound and they took the dog away. An ambulance arrived to take the man to the hospital and the police took the old girlfriend, Bertha

Kingsley, and Scott to the police station to sort things out, so they said.

~~~~~~~~~~

During the interrogation, it became clear to the police that Scott had instigated the entire incident. It was just his luck that the man knew how to handle the dog. They handcuffed him and wanted to take him to a cell. Bertha told them that it was all her fault. All Scott wanted to do was buy a car. He had no idea that she wanted him to lead her to her boyfriend. She asked them to let Scott go. The look on the officers' faces was that they had better things to do than to straighten out a love triangle so they let them both go with a warning. Scott never mentioned the list that he had and told the police that he knew about the car through a friend. Bertha told the police that she let it be known that she was looking for her ex-boyfriend and the car.

~~~~~~~~~~

Later, in his office, Scott tried to put together what had happened. He realized he had made a horrible mistake and could have gotten that man and his girlfriend killed. He let Bertha Kingsley use him for her personal gain. Why didn't he see that coming? He saw how she had the dog tied up in the house and how the dog wouldn't stop barking. Why didn't he sense something wrong? As it was now, the man and his girlfriend may have to move. Bertha could return some day. Ever since he was a little boy, he had kept himself distant from people, from truths. This distance may be the cause of

Bertha's wreaking havoc on that family — something else he would have to face.

For now, he dreaded his father's "I knew you couldn't do it" look that would just crush him. He had no choice. He couldn't keep it from his father. He had to go in and tell his father what happened. Just once he wanted his father to look at him with an "I'm proud of you look." When he reached his father's office, Cameron looked up with a smile.

Chapter 18
Scott

In an overstuffed chair in his bedroom, Scott sat watching his cell phone as it rang, and rang, and danced around on the end table. He already knew it was Lisa and he already knew she would cry and plead until he agreed to go and see her. He couldn't believe even after all this time she continued to call. He thought about Kathryn how he wanted to see her. She must have known she would be going to France. Why didn't she tell him? The phone rang again and without giving it thought, he answered it.

"Scott. Can we talk this evening? I don't like how things ended with us. Can we meet somewhere and talk?"

Scott held a space of silence.

"Scott?"

"Where?"

"Here, so we can each say our peace."

"Okay," he sighed. His heart was so broken he was giving in.

Later that evening, Scott found himself once again lifting the leaf-shaped iron knocker on the front door of Lisa's house. He couldn't believe he had agreed to meet her. But, he was feeling very lonely and very vulnerable. He thought about it for a second and just as he had changed his mind and decided to leave, he looked up and saw Lisa opening one side of the double doors, a wide smile on her face.

"Hi, Scott," said Lisa. She seemed to bubble all over and at that moment, she reminded him of a little girl running after balloons rising skyward as she tried to catch them. She held out her hand, he took it and she led the way into her house through the formal eclectic antique-style living room and into the dining room. Lisa had the eight-person size table, with high back mahogany chairs set for what looked to him like a romantic candle-lit dinner for two. He noticed the crystal candleholders he had given her for Christmas. Her parents were never home and she had the house to herself again.

Watching her now, he saw there was something about her that made him curious. She seemed confident, as if she was the only one who knew the secret ingredient for apple pie. Then he realized they were not going to discuss anything but Lisa had planned for them to get back together. He shook his head slightly as he thought how she had done it to him again.

She directed him to his seat. As he pulled out the chair he, again, thought about leaving, thinking that there was no reason why he should be there. He even fantasized for a moment that Kathryn was trying desperately to get in touch with him and he needed to be by the phone just in case. Gathering his senses, he knew that Kathryn was not desperately trying to get in touch with him, that he would probably never see Kathryn again. He took his seat.

As Lisa walked to the kitchen, Scott could see she was as

happy as Mary Poppins, and he thought she would soon pull out her black umbrella. She just seemed a little too happy under the circumstances. In a few minutes, she re-appeared carrying a covered dish on a silver tray.

"I didn't think we were having dinner," said Scott, sounding a little peeved, irritated at her exploitation.

"I just thought you'd like something to eat." An obvious smile in her voice.

Scott settled himself in his chair.

"You can open the wine, if you like." She went back to the kitchen.

"Wine? We're having wine?" He said in a growl, loudly enough for Lisa to hear him in the kitchen.

"Well, I thought it would be nice. Is anything wrong with that?"

"I guess not." Scott squirmed a little, thought again about leaving, but then stood to open the wine. He poured her a glass and left his empty.

Lisa brought in two more dishes and positioned them on the table next to the chicken. She took a step back to admire her handy work, Scott thought.

"That's everything." She smiled at Scott and sat down at the head of the table.

Scott sat.

"I can serve you this." She began dishing out a chicken breast for him and then for herself. She looked over at him and gave him another smile. Then she dished out the mixed vegetables and the scalloped potatoes.

"I thought we were just going to talk," feeling uneasy and hesitant about being with her.

"But it's nice to have dinner while we talk, isn't it?" She

cut a tiny piece of chicken, put it on her fork, and eased it into her mouth.

Scott cut his chicken breast in half and moved it around on his plate. Ordinarily, he would have told her how nice it was for her to have gone to this much trouble and how good the food tasted. Under other circumstances, he would have noticed she made dishes that were not simple, that took time and care. Ordinarily. But, today she had angered him by telling him she just wanted to talk when she knew she wanted more than that. He had thought when he didn't return her calls she understood he didn't want to see her anymore.

"What did you want to talk about?" asked Scott. He pushed his plate away, impatient.

"Well, I didn't like the way, the way, you know the way we did the last time we were together."

"The way we did?"

"Yeah, you know. You were late . . . again . . . and I yelled . . . again." She gave a little chuckle.

"Oh, I see, so all of that was my fault. If I hadn't been late, then you wouldn't have yelled or gotten upset or whatever you do."

"Scott, I don't want us to get upset again, okay? Don't you see?"

"Have you ever thought that the reason why I'm always late is because I'm not happy in this relationship?"

"No, Scott, no. Don't you see?"

"I just can't belong to a one sided relationship anymore."

"Scott, it's not one sided. We both love each other. Don't you see?'

"We do nothing but argue. How could we be in love?"

"Scott, I know we do. That's part of our getting to know each other. I know you see it."

"We don't even like the same things. We don't like being with each other that's what I see."

"But, Scott you have to see it. It's so plain, you have to see."

"See what?"

"We belong together. We're a pair. Oh sure, we're having our difficulties, but that's just now. Once we work all this out, everything will be okay with us from now on."

"Do you really believe that?" He sat back in his chair.

"Of course, I do. You should, too."

"Lisa, I —"

"Scott, we really are. We really are." Lisa's eyes filled with tears.

He lowered his voice. "All we do is fight and argue. We don't agree on anything. You want your way and you get upset at times when I don't want what you want. I'm always uneasy and afraid that I'm going to make another mistake with you."

She reached over and held onto his arm. "But, I thought we could try again. Please, let's give it one more try. I'll do what you like and you can do some of the things I like," said Lisa.

"We'll end up arguing and fighting again. We always do. Can't you see that?"

"But, that's what I was trying to say. If we get that all out of the way, then we can be happy."

Scott put his napkin on the table and stood up. "Lisa, it just won't work. We have been trying for the last year and it just won't work. Let's stop fooling ourselves."

"Scott, I love you so much. You can't keep doing this to me."

Scott started out of the dining room and toward the door.

"Well, go then," yelled out Lisa behind him. "You always do that. You'll be back."

Scott heard Lisa slam the door behind him as he made his way to his car.

~~~~~~~~~~~

"Hit me again, Ben." Scott wobbled on the barstool.

"Scott, you've had enough to drink. I'm taking your keys," said Ben as he walked to Scott's end of the bar.

"Who the hell do you think you are? You can't take my keys."

"I don't have to. They will." He pointed to two huge men standing near the door.

Scott squinted to find the two bouncers in the dimly lit bar.

"Will you hand them over, or will I have to ask them to get them?"

A female came over to the bar and stood next to Scott.

"You wanna drink? Lemme buy you a drink?" Scott kept slipping off the stool.

"Pardon?"

"Ben, get the lady a drink," said Scott.

"Scott, I want those keys," said Ben.

"He thinks I'm drunk." Scott laughed.

"You are. You can't even sit on the stool."

"I'm not drunk. This stool is broken. You want a drink? I want another drink. Ben get us two drinks."

"Your keys, Scott, your keys."

Scott took out his flash drive on a small chain and put it on the bar.

"That'll fix 'em," Scott said, laughing again. When he laughed, he leaned into the woman and he almost laid his head on the counter.

A man seated at a table near the dance floor, called out to the woman, but Scott couldn't understand what he said. She shrugged her shoulders. Then the man got up from his seat and moved closer to the bar.

"Hey dude, you trying to hit on my girl?" asked the man approaching Scott. He turned to the woman. "Is he trying to hit on you?"

"No. Let's just go. He's stinking drunk. He doesn't know what he's doing."

"So, he is trying to hit on you." The man grabbed Scott by his shirt, and Scott attempted to hit the man in the face, but even being that close, the man pulled back and Scott missed. The man let go of his shirt and dropped him down on the barstool. The man turned to the woman, took her by the elbow, and attempted to walk away. Scott got up and this time, with better aim, gave the man a hard push forward. The man went sailing into a table of people. The table toppled over and beer bottles and glass dishes with nuts, along with the man crashed to the floor. One person at the table asked him if he was drunk, but the man didn't answer. The woman tried to help him up, but he pulled away from her.

"So you want to play that game, huh?' At this point, everyone at the table turned to face Scott who was wobbling, trying to stand up. The man got into a boxing stance and struck out at Scott at the very moment he had to bend over to remain on his feet. The man missed him, again. By this time, the man was angry. He raised his fist and began punching Scott in the face over, and over. Scott fell back onto the bar and the man reeled back to really let Scott have it again, when one of the bouncers grabbed his fist and pulled him off Scott.

Cameron walked into the bar and toward Ben who was standing at the end nearest the door. Ben pointed to Scott at the other end of the bar and holding his bloody face. One bouncer stood in front of Scott as a shield and the second bouncer escorted the man and his friend out of the door. Cameron made his way to Scott who was still trying to find his seat as he held his face. Scott looked up and saw his father. He wanted to be embarrassed, but was too drunk to care.

"How'd you know I was here?"

"Ben gave me a call. He still had the number."

"He took my keys. He thinks I'm drunk."

"He should have taken your keys. Come on." Cameron took Scott by the arm. Scott stood, but stumbled when he tried to take his first step.

"You are drunk. You can hardly walk."

"Don't forget to get my keys."

"Where?"

"There. Right there." He gestured somewhere near the bar. "Now, who's drunk?"

"Scott, that's your flash drive" He held it up in front of them. "That's not your car key. Come on, son." He grabbed Scott's coat from the other bar stool. "Let's get you home. We can pick up your car tomorrow." Cameron put his arm around his son, gave a "thank you" wave to Ben, and the two of them made it out of the bar and to Cameron's car without incident.

Just before he got into the car, Scott noticed it was snowing. He stuck out his hand to catch some of the flakes and to feel the iciness, but he couldn't feel anything. He gave off a slight smile as he got into the car.

At home, Cameron took Scott into the breakfast room, just off the kitchen and sat him in a cushiony chair. He cleaned his face, went to the freezer, got ice, and wrapped it in a dishtowel he found in a drawer. He handed the icepack to Scott. Cameron took the coffee out of the cupboard and made a big pot of strong coffee for his son. When it was ready, he poured it in two mugs and took them to the breakfast room. He sat next to Scott who was holding the icepack over his eye and cheek.

"Wanna tell me what happened?" Cameron took a sip of the coffee.

"I got drunk. What do you think happened?"

Cameron fingered his mug. "What happened, Scott?" He said in a soft voice.

"Something's wrong with me. I can't do anything right. I never know what to say to anyone."

"Who do you mean? Are you talking about Lisa?"

"Yeah. We had another fight, this evening."

"She called. Why did you go there? I thought the two of you were through?"

"I don't know. I just can't do anything right. I'm all wrong, Dad, and I can't get it right."

"Scott, you have lost your way —"

Scott got up, threw the ice wrap down on the table next to him, and started out of the breakfast room. "I don't think I want to hear how I'm a big failure. I see I'm a big failure. I found that out with Lisa and the jealous Bertha."

Cameron moved out of his chair, took Scott by the arm and stopped him. "Scott, what are you talking about?"

"Look, just leave me alone, okay?" Scott started out of the room, again.

Cameron stopped him, again. "What are you talking about?"

"Dad, I know you wanted me to be a better person, but, I'm not. I'm not the man you are and I'm not as good as Becky and Jack."

"What do you mean? I don't compare you with Becky and Jack. And I don't think you're a failure. What's bothering you?"

"You can't depend on me. Mom couldn't depend on me and Becky couldn't depend on me. I'm a lousy person, that's all."

"Tell me what happened with you and Becky, son." He led Scott back into the breakfast room and they sat down at the table.

Scott told his father about the time when he was nine, Becky ten, and the two of them were walking home from the library. On this afternoon, Becky talked him into staying a little longer at the library so they left later than they usually did. Two older middle school boys followed them as they walked home. The boys walked closely behind Scott and Becky and whistled at her, cajoled her and engaged in debauchery as they made perverted comments to Becky. Becky took Scott's hand. He was scared to death and hoped the boys would leave them alone. He remembered two boys both the same size as he was at the time. As soon as they rounded the corner, two blocks from their home, one boy grabbed Becky and pulled her away from Scott and into the bushes and trees. The other boy ran in behind them. Scott tried to stop them but one of the boys held him while one boy ran his hand over Becky's breast and tried to put his hand up her dress. She tried as best she could to fight back and slap him away. The boy fondling her, managed to get her pants down to her knees when Jack and two of his friends appeared. They must have heard Becky screaming. Jack ran the two boys away and got his sister together. Scott walked behind Jack and Becky on the way home.

"So, you see, Becky needed me and look at what happened. Mom, mom, mom, I couldn't, I couldn't . . . ."

Cameron got up and put his arms around his son. He waited for him to stop crying.

"Is that what you remember? Sit down, Son."

"I can't Dad. I can't. I just can't do this right now." Scott left the house and slammed the door behind him.

He had had enough. Enough of Lisa telling him he was the cause of all their relationship problems, enough of his guilt from his lie, enough of his father thinking he was a nothing or a nobody and enough of Kathryn dumping him for something better. He just couldn't listen to his father tell him another time how he should have helped his sister. He needed a turnaround; he needed a miracle. He needed more to drink, something that would wash it all away. But he couldn't take another drink. He had just broken his promise to his mother by getting drunk. He caved, first to Lisa, then to whiskey and he knew he couldn't do that again. He could feel himself falling and he had to stop himself somehow.

Chapter 19
Scott

Just before sun-up the next morning, Scott drove to the park. He pulled close to the space where his mother died, and got out. Looking around, he saw that there were only two other cars but parked on the opposite side of the lot. Sunrise is too early for people to run or walk, especially in the middle of winter and with a thin layer of snow on the ground. He climbed up and sat on the boulder that marked the entrance to the trail. As he looked around the parking lot, flashes of his mother ran through his mind. He saw her smile as the two of them talked and ran together, he out of breath, she running with ease. He saw her wave at one of the other runners coming in the opposite direction. He saw her stretching before her run and laughing and talking with others as they stopped for a breather. He saw her standing in the parking lot with a younger man asking him how his daughter, who had the flu, was recovering.

He looked up toward the sky and knew his mother was in heaven, now. He wanted his mother to forgive him for lying to her and for not helping her when she needed him.

He promised her, again, he wouldn't get drunk anymore, and he vowed to keep it this time. He knew that he would always tell his father the truth and stay on good terms with him because he didn't want his last words to his father to be a lie. He should not have pretended to be asleep when his mother came to his room. He should have told her that he didn't want to run that morning. He really could have gone and walked while she ran. The fact that he had pretended to be asleep many times before and he suspected that his mother knew about it didn't make it any more comforting to him. He had lied to her and he would have to live with it. What he did was something that, no matter how hard he tried, he would never be able to undo. Suddenly a feeling, a great relief washed over him. He felt light and easy, as if a heavy burden had just been lifted off him. He remembered feeling that way when he was a child and his mother had asked him not to worry about his grades, the report he found difficult to write, and the girl he liked who continued to ignore him. He knew his mother was watching over him and he felt the urge to give her a tight hug.

At that moment, a dark color car pulled into the parking lot. As it approached, he saw what he thought was the Mercedes emblem on the front hood. He stood up to get a better look and when he did, the car backed up, turned sharply, and raced out. He ran down to the entrance to see which way the car might have turned, but the car was gone. He stood there trying to remember any part of the license plate and realized he never saw it. There was not enough light. He ran back to his car and drove up and down a few of the streets near the park entrance, but couldn't find the car or anything that looked like it. Maybe he imagined it.

~~~~~~~~~~

Later that morning, Scott found Cameron in his office sitting behind his desk, busy reading. Before entering, he paused at the door. He knew he had to apologize, but wasn't sure how to explain his actions. Scott cleared his throat, but Cameron didn't move. Scott cleared his throat again as he walked farther into the office.

When Cameron looked up, he smiled. "Are you alright?"

"Yeah, Dad, I'm fine. I'm sorry I ran out last night. It's just . . . ." He stood in front of the desk.

"I know. It's okay."

"You're not stressing yourself out, are you? Remember, the doctor —"

"Scott, I've been thinking. I want to hire a private detective, give him that list so he can find the car and the owner."

Scott didn't want to show the anger he felt so he tried to keep a smile on his face. He actually thought his father had more faith and trust in him than he did in himself.

"Dad, this is rather complicated, I know that. For our own reasons, we both have a need to find the hit and run person. It's because of those reasons that I want to continue looking for the car. I've started it and I want to find the owner of the car." Scott tried to show his father confidence, especially after last night. Following through on this search would give him the strength and courage he needed.

Cameron stared at Scott for what seemed like an eternity.

He knew his father really believed he couldn't handle it, wasn't up to the mark. No matter what his father thought, he had to find the woman who took his mother's life. He expected his father to understand.

"This could be dangerous. We have to do this together."

He tried not to let his father see that he felt let down. He had to take it in stride and persevere. "The way I see it, we have two things. I know you're working on the hotel project. That's pretty demanding. I can look for the car."

"Scott, I think that this is a matter for the police. At least let's hire a private detective."

Scott didn't respond. He knew from the look on his father's face that his father questioned his ability to rely on him to follow through and he was concerned about Scott's safety, messing up could get him killed. Scott knew he needed to get back his self-respect and until he did, he would never stop drinking.

"Son, are you sure about this?"

Scott stood in front of his father, placed both hands on the desk as he bent down to speak.

"I've never been surer of anything in my life. I'll find the car and the owner and when I do that, I'll let you know and we can turn it over to the police. I promise."

Cameron held his stare.

When Scott saw his father's expression change, he knew that his father would give him one more chance.

Scott was not a hot head, but somehow he always ended up in a fight when he abused alcohol. He could never say whether he started those fights or not, but if he remained sober now and kept his head, he would find the car and its owner.

~~~~~~~~~~

As he went from house to house, Scott began to understand how tough it was for the police. Maybe Haines and Charles were doing all they could, though he held back from giving them too much credit. He discovered people gave their cars away to friends or relatives without signing the car over to them. One woman told him her car was used in a robbery three years ago after she gave it away to her niece. Some people just stopped using the car, let it sit and rot away, and in one case, the man had it junked but the records showed he still owned it.

Mid-way through the next week he had made it to the Ms and discovered a familiar name on the list. He knew he would have to treat that name just like any other and, at the end of the day, he pulled up in front of the house. He didn't want to think about it for fear he would turn back. So he walked up the steps and rang the doorbell just like he'd done his other searches. He froze for a moment when Martin answered the door and let him into the foyer.

"Hi," said Martin, with a questioning look on his face.

"I'm here on business."

"Oh? Business? What business?" He wrinkled his brow as if he tried to recall something.

"I'm interested in a car that you own."

Kathryn came to the front door.

"Hi, Sweetheart," said Martin as he turned toward his daughter.

Scott caught himself staring at Kathryn, as she came closer to them. His heart pumped faster and he felt himself shake. He didn't want to hurt her. During the time they dated, she helped him understand about loss. Now, he was beginning to feel like a traitor. How could one person have such a hold on another? All in all, he had to remember he was there for his mother and he would not be deterred from that.

"Sweetheart, Scott wants to know something about a car."

"Hi," said Kathryn as she looked down at the floor.

"Hello," he said in return.

"What car did you want to know about?" asked Martin. He seemed nervous.

Scott cleared his throat and tried with all his might to look at Martin. "You have, you have a 1999 metallic black Mercedes-Benz C class registered to you."

"Does Betty still have that car?" Martin turned to look at Kathryn.

Kathryn stared at her father. "I don't know."

"Are you interested in buying the car? Why are you asking?" asked Martin.

"Yes, I'm looking to buy the car. I've been following up on advertisements."

"Is Betty trying to sell that car? She never said anything to me about it."

"I don't know," said Kathryn, still looking at her father.

"I'm interested in a Mercedes and I like that style and model better than anything else I've seen." Scott did his best to sound business-like and convincing as he regretted the lie.

"Oh. Okay. Well, my step daughter, Betty, drives the car and she usually keeps it in the garage out back."

"Can I see the car?" asked Scott. He wanted to get outside from the stuffiness, the confinement.

"Sure." Martin seemed a little hesitant, but stepping aside, he led the way to the back of the house and the garage. When he realized he left the door opener inside, he sent Kathryn back into the house to get it.

Scott and Martin stood in silence, Scott wishing that Kathryn would hurry. He looked around at the large backyard. A patch of weeds took up the length of one side of the yard. A sagging badminton net barely tied to the two poles, was in the center of the yard, and had a series of holes. When Kathryn came back, she and Sylvia came out together. Kathryn used the door opener to open the door, but the garage was empty.

"What happened to Betty's car?" asked Martin.

"What do you need Betty's car for?" asked Sylvia.

"Mr. Kersey here is interested in it. Where's her car Sylvia?" Martin sounded forceful and Scott turned his head slightly in Martin's direction.

"Martin, I don't like all these questions. What is this for?" asked Sylvia.

"Mr. Kersey is interested in looking at the car. I guess he wants to buy it?" Martin looked at Scott.

Scott nodded in agreement.

"She came back from the university about a week ago and got it. I would have told you if you'd only asked," said Sylvia.

"She's away at school?" asked Scott.

"Yes. She attends a small college in Pennsylvania," said Martin, looking at Sylvia in disgust while emphasizing the word "college."

"The car must be in pretty good condition if she keeps it in the garage," said Scott. He realized that statement didn't make a lot of sense, but he couldn't think of any other way to draw out the information he needed.

"She usually keeps it on the street. I don't know why she started using the garage," said Sylvia.

"So then the car is in good condition?" asked Scott. He

tried not to give away the fact that the car could have a dent, provided it was the right car.

"I don't know. It's old sometimes she has trouble starting it. What are all these questions for?" asked Sylvia.

"I'd like to see the car. Where is her school?" asked Scott.

"How did you say you found out about the car?" asked Kathryn.

Scott saw Martin looking from Kathryn to him and from him to Kathryn. He saw the question forming in Martin's brain and on the edge of his lips. He hoped with all his heart that Martin would not ask the question that hung at the door of that garage where they stood.

"He told us that, Sweetheart. Sylvia you have that address for him?" asked Martin.

Scott handed her his notebook and pen as he quietly breathed a sigh of relief, and gave Martin a knowing glance.

"I didn't know Betty was selling that car. What will she use at school?" asked Sylvia taking the notebook and looking at Martin.

"Maybe she's found a better car. You said she had trouble starting that one," said Martin.

"She has to get enough money for it." Sylvia turned to look at Scott. She handed the notebook back to Scott and then she and Martin walked toward the house.

"Thank you," Scott yelled out to their backs. He quickly walked through the backyard out to the front. Kathryn followed him.

"Scott, wait."

Scott continued walking. He hadn't planned on Kathryn being present. Or maybe he wanted her to be there, but he just didn't think about how that meeting would turn out.

"Scott, wait, please." She caught up to him just as he reached his car.

Scott turned around. His heart ached for her. He just wanted to hold her. As he looked down at her, he saw a befuddled look on her face.

"That's not why you came here, is it?"

"I came because of the car."

"Tell the truth, Scott. Why did you come here tonight?" She shifted her weight.

"I just told you. I came because of the car."

"I don't believe you."

"I don't know what else to say." He looked away.

"Scott, I'm sorry —"

"You don't have to be sorry. We didn't have much. We really didn't know each other well enough to be sorry about anything." He turned toward his car.

"You don't understand —"

"You don't owe me an explanation. Really you don't." He said over his shoulder.

"Will you let me tell you?"

He turned around and saw her eyes filled with tears. He held strong and looked away.

"There's nothing to tell. It's okay. I really have to go."

Martin came out of the house and down to the sidewalk. "Is everything okay?"

"Yes, everything is fine," said Scott. He unlocked his car door and got in as Kathryn stood watching him.

Scott looked in his rear view mirror and saw Kathryn turn in the direction of the car as he drove off down the street. He couldn't turn the car around. As much as he wanted to go back, hold her, tell her that he forgave her, he couldn't. He was too afraid. He was terrified with the fact that her explanation would be that she never cared for him and that she hoped he understood. Even though he thought she did owe him an explanation, he didn't think he could bear hearing her say or imply that she didn't love him.

Chapter 20
Scott

Scott drove through the night and reached the town just before dawn. Everything closed, no 24-hour stores or gas stations; and the only lights were two streetlights at each end of Main Street. Being the only thing living and moving gave him a regal feeling, much like the town's owner. Yet the darkness also made him feel lonely. The fact that he was getting closer and closer to finding out who hit his mother kept him revved up, adrenalin pumping, but apprehensive. He drove through Main Street and looked for anything that could be a car repair shop. He spotted one in the center of town and continued driving down the streets parallel to Main Street until he came across another shop that advertised bodywork. Since there was no one around, not even a paperboy, he took the opportunity to drive down all the streets in the center of town to familiarize himself with the area. He remembered how unfriendly small town people were from the time he went with Lisa to visit her grandparents. They lived in a resort community, but to Scott that was close enough.

Once he'd found the garages, he drove to the school to see if the car was parked on a lot outside. If the car belonged to Betty, maybe she would park it in plain view thinking no one knew about her. He found three dorms, all identified with the word "dormitory," and combed the parking lots of each one. He didn't see the car. He drove to two larger parking garages that were three to four levels in height and required a ticket or pass. Since the arm was down on both parking garages, he got out of his car and walked to the first level of each. He could see that the parking garages were practically empty, so he went back to his car and drove back to one of the dorm lots and waited.

After a while, he heard the sound of a dog barking intermittently in the distance – the only other life in his kingdom. The semi-filled parking lot over flowed with the loneliness of the night, enveloped him and made him feel insignificant and slightly afraid. Deep down inside hidden at the edge of a small corner in his heart was fear that had been tugging at him since his mother's accident. Scott refused to let it surface. He scrunched down in his car, settled back, closed his eyes; and when he did that, all he could see was Kathryn's face. It finally came to him that she had a ring on her left hand, the ring finger. He saw it while he was standing there at the garage and as he watched her. It didn't register with him then. His mind was on the car and seeing her again. Maybe he didn't want it to register and he pushed it out of his mind and didn't want to believe it. He had certainly miscalculated everything about her. He had really believed she cared. And then, as if someone had slapped him awake, Scott had another thought. The car he wanted to look at belonged to Kathryn's stepsister. Still, he had to pursue this.

He had to find the person who ran down his mother and if it turned out to be Betty, then so be it. He was not pursuing this to get back at Kathryn. He was doing this for his mother. As badly as he wanted to find the person who hit his mother, he really didn't want it to be Betty. But his tenacity to find out was stronger than his determination to leave this unfinished.

~~~~~~~~~~

When it was daylight, Scott drove through the dorm lots again, but didn't find the car. Then he went over to the two parking garages and found the same few cars parked in the same places. He looked at his watch and saw it was shortly after 7:00 a.m., and drove back to the parking lots in front of the dorms. He didn't know when Betty had taken the car away. Sylvia said that she had come back to get it, so Betty came back to get the car sometime after the accident, but not immediately after. In that case, she had had enough time to get any damage repaired.

When he saw students coming out of the dorms and walking or getting into their cars, he knew people in this town were finally up and the day had begun. He drove back to the first car repair shop. The wooden structure resembled an old barn. Scott thought the area must have been a farm and the owner had probably turned the barn into the auto repair shop. The right side of the door was ajar. Looking around, he saw no other buildings nearby. He pushed the big barn-type door further in.

"Hi," he said to a man working under a truck as he walked into the rustic-looking shop.

"Hi," a voice came back from under the only truck in the

shop. He rolled himself out and sat up on the dolly. "Can I help you?" He looked behind Scott at Scott's car.

"I hope you can."

"Not if you need that thing repaired." He wiped his hands on his pants.

"You don't repair foreign cars?"

"No, sir. Most people around here drive old American cars or trucks."

Scott saw that he was only a boy. Perhaps he was one of those college students working his way through school.

"I'm looking for a car that a student might have brought in here. A 1999 metallic black Mercedes-Benz C class?"

"I don't remember no car like that."

"Do you attend the college a few miles over?"

"I've taken a class or two over there."

"You don't remember a girl, Betty Milner, who owns a car like that?"

"No sir." He scratched his head. "There was a Betty Gilbert, but no Betty Milner."

"Do you know if she still has the car?" Scott smiled.

"That's right. She did have a Mercedes. I ain't seen it lately."

"I want to buy that car, but I understand from her mother that she had an accident with the car. Where would she take it to get it fixed?" He took a step toward the man.

"I don't know, Sir. You can try out at Pete's farm. He has a lot of them foreign makes and he repairs 'em all hisself. He even does his own body work."

"Can you give me directions to Pete's farm?"

"Sure."

"Harry? Whacha doing?" asked a short older man who

was coming out of a structure that could have been an office. He pulled a long rag out of his back pocket.

"I'm just helping this gentleman right here. He needs to go to Pete's."

"Get back to work. He can git directions some other place, but this here is a repair shop." He wiped his hands on the rag then turned around to walk back to his office.

Scott thanked Harry and left the shop. He went to the nearest restaurant to order breakfast and if he played his cards right, he would also get directions to Pete's farm.

~~~~~~~~~~

Scott knew that his father worried about him snooping around alone so he called him to give him an update on his discovery so far. Cameron told Scott not to go to Pete's farm alone and to meet him at the airport because he was flying in. Scott couldn't decide what would be more stressful, having his father fly in or asking his father to wait until he returned with whatever news he discovered. Cameron wanted Scott to pick him up from the airport and Scott thought waiting on his father was a waste of time, besides Cameron wouldn't arrive until later and evening would be setting in by then. He could have been to Pete's farm in the time it took for his father to get to the airport.

Scott pulled out the directions and the hand-drawn map that the kind waitress had written out for him and started toward Pete's farm. He followed the written directions until he was well out of the town and then picked up the map when it was time for him to turn onto a narrow gravel road not identified. The waitress told him that the sign would be on the ground, so he looked for it. Going by the map, he now had to follow that road out for the next mile until he would come to a road branching off to the right. The road was lined with trees and Scott realized he was right in driving out to the farm in the daytime. After about a twenty- minute ride, but one that felt more like all day, Scott came to the right branch of the road exactly as the waitress had drawn for him on the map. He could tell she had been out to the farm several times. He turned down that road and soon came to a wide expanse on the right that led to a gate. Over the gate a huge wooden sign with the faded word "Pete's" loomed. Scott turned into the farm. The area in the front looked partly plowed, and a barn sat off to the left. Scott drove up to what he thought was the main house. A what-used- to-be a flower garden overrun with dried weeds covered most of the walkway and extended on to the front porch. As he got out, a dog barked from inside the house, the front door opened and a man dressed in coveralls, and wearing an old baseball-style hat, stepped out on the porch. Scott felt like he had stepped back in time.

"You must be lost."

"Hi, my name is Scott Kersey. I'm looking for Pete." Scott walked toward the house.

"I'm Pete. What can I do for you?" He came off the porch and walked to meet Scott.

"I'm looking to buy a car and I was told that you might have it."

"I ain't no car salesman." He pushed his cap up on top of his head.

"I know, but I was told that you had a lot of foreign makes."

"Who's been telling you all that?"

"The guy in the repair shop. I'm looking for a 1999 metallic black Mercedes-Benz C class. It's owned by Betty Gilbert. She attends the college in town. Her mother told me that she had an accident with it and I want to see it. I want to buy it."

Pete rubbed his chin. "I remember she had that car. But I don't remember the particulars 'bout it."

"So, she didn't have an accident with it?"

"She's my son's fiancée. Dunno nuthin' bout them want'n to sell that car."

Scott shifted his weight from one leg to the other. "I was hoping she would. I didn't know she was engaged."

Scott didn't remember Kathryn mentioning that Betty was engaged and he was sure Sylvia didn't say anything about it when they were standing in the back looking at the empty garage.

"My son, Edward said it. I ain't seen no ring, thankfully. He has a little apartment on the edge of town. You could talk to em if you like."

Scott took the information and headed in the direction of the airport. He had hoped he would have had something more solid to tell his father. On the drive to the airport, he looked around and felt enshrouded in the vastness of nature and for some reason he felt a part of the scene, a completeness of all creation. No high rises, condos or shopping malls, no hordes of people pushing and crowding, just those wonders that grow out of the ground and complement the blues, grays and cottony-like clouds of the sky. He marveled at the trees — fir and oak — the straw-like grass, and even the dried out weeds cast its dormant beauties as they overtook the flowers and bushes. The man-made, paved road, direct and straight seemed out of place as it lay against the fallen limbs in the pasture and the resting weeds and bushes in hues of brown, black , orange and green. He passed cows and horses grazing in a pasture, things that he'd almost forgotten existed in a world of technology, unfriendliness, and things moving too quickly. He felt a sense of belongingness to nature and its warmth and love.

A horse, brown in color, came up to the fence and trotted alongside him, a companion. He wondered if the horse wasn't asking to be freed of the easy, comfortable life-style. He rolled down his window, the cold air splashing and stinging his face and slowed down. "Friendly creature, aren't you?" Scott yelled out of the window. To his surprise, the horse whinnied back. Scott called out to him again, but the horse stopped at the fence line. He followed the road until it narrowed into a one-car bridge and noticed the stream below. He marveled at the splendor and peacefulness of the countryside and thought about his father, and how he knew his father would like to see buildings on the land, if he had a chance. His father said that buildings were a way of sharing the land and the beauty of the architecture. "Lines and form" his father's famous words as he would describe to Scott the different architectural styles and the type that America used. His father would also say that, "You have to appreciate Geometry and understand about line angles and how the lines come together to form a pattern." Scott learned not to argue with his father; he just listened. Though Scott understood what his father meant, it just didn't seem right to destroy nature to do it. His father was right about the sharing part. Man created things like poems, stories even buildings to share with others.

It was easy for Scott to find his father at the airport since it was so empty that Scott hardly saw the need to have an airport in that town except for the fact that it was certainly handy for him now. After he found Cameron, the two of them drove to Edward's apartment. They pulled into the parking lot of the four, four-level buildings each separated by grassy passageways that seemed to lead to a street behind them. They drove up to the third building, got out and walked up to the second level.

"My father said that you were coming to see me," said Edward standing in the doorway of his apartment, shirtless and shoeless. He opened the door before Scott or Cameron had a chance to knock.

"Can we see the car?" asked Cameron.

They stood at the door, an odor of fried food and damp air escaped and attacked Scott's nostrils.

"The problem is, is, well, the problem is that she, well she took off." He looked down toward the floor as he spoke.

"What do you mean son?" asked Cameron.

Edward looked up from Cameron to Scott.

"You mean you two aren't seeing each other anymore?" asked Scott, understanding Edward's predicament.

"Yeah. She just dumped me and took off. I don't remember her being in any car accident, though."

"How long has she been gone?" asked Scott.

"I dunno. For bout three to four weeks, I guess. I didn't tell my father."

"So, she's not in class at all?" asked Cameron.

"Naw. She hasn't been back," said Edward now leaning on the door.

"Where'd she go?" asked Scott.

"I dunno know. I call her to meet me after class one day and never could get her."

"Well, thanks, Son. And, I'm sorry . . ."

"That's okay."

Scott and Cameron left to head back to Maryland. Cameron wanted to check with the college first to see whether Betty had actually withdrawn, but Scott told him it was not likely she, being flighty in nature, would stay there after she dumped Edward, even if she hadn't officially withdrawn.

Cameron was worried they knew more than the police did and wanted to report what they knew so far to the police. On the drive back, Scott thought about a comment he had read in the newspaper about people who had less than he. They complained about the police being slow to help them and stated the police always moved faster for people who had money. Scott could see that statement just wasn't true.

They were driving back so they could turn what they had over to the police, the people who seemed to treat him and his father poorly because they had money. Turning over the information to the police was his father's idea, Scott didn't want to do that and if there was a way he didn't have to, he would have to find it. He was so close to finding the car and the person and he had to continue.

Chapter 21
Scott

"Mr. Kersey, I've asked you two in here because I've gotten some complaints about Scott. You followed up on a car with a woman, Bertha Kingsley, and endangered the lives of her ex-boyfriend and his wife." said Haines. His voice was loud and two other detectives turned toward him as they walked by his desk.

The precinct seemed rather busy with officers and detectives walking in and out. A man who seemed to need a question answered stood and waited, but turned to talk to someone else, when he heard Haines raise his voice.

"Detective Haines we have to remain civil here. My son —" began Cameron. He stood in front of Haines' desk. Haines stood on the other side.

Bending down, both hands on his desk, "Mr. Kersey, I know all about the incident you had with the woman and her dog. You're stepping in dangerous territory, and in light of your recent experience, I know you can see just how dangerous this is. You're interfering with an ongoing police investigation and if you continue to do that, I'll have to arrest you. I don't want to, but you'll force my hand," said Haines. "I hope you both understand that." He turned away from his desk to walk away.

"You've made absolutely no progress in trying to find that car. A little outside help shouldn't hurt," said Cameron, now his voice loud, hands waving.

"Mr. Kersey, the woman asked about the police officer which says to me you impersonated an officer. And, Mr. Kersey, that's a crime."

"Wait a minute," began Scott. "I never told anyone I was a police officer. I told her I was interested in buying the car."

"This isn't getting us anywhere," said Cameron.

"You're right, Mr. Kersey. Hurling accusations at each other will get us no where. Let's all sit down," said Charles.

Haines sat down. Scott and Cameron sat in the chairs opposite Haines's desk.

"Detective Haines, my son, and I have been waiting patiently to hear who ran down my wife. So, when we found car owners of that model we decided to move forward on this matter. You can't blame us for wanting to try to find that car. We've heard nothing from you and as far as I'm concerned you've been very uncooperative," said Cameron. He moved to the edge of his seat, closer to Haines.

"Well, I'm sorry that we have other cases and don't move fast enough for you on your case . . . ." Haines sat back in his chair and took several deep breaths as if he realized that he was getting out of control. Scott also thought he heard him mumbling something to himself.

"We realize," In a very loud voice, Charles interrupted Haines in an obvious attempt to cover up for the lack in diplomacy, "how you two feel," He lowered his voice, "but you have to understand what my partner is trying to say. We don't have much to go on. We haven't found the witness or the car owner. We've also been out to the trail to question anyone who uses it."

"I need to know who ran down my wife. Find leads. Do your job. If you two continue to drag your feet, you can bet everything you own that the public will know about this. I need to know who committed this heinous act, and I will find out with or without your help. I can't let this go, detective. I need answers and I need them now."

"Mr. Kersey, rest assured that we're not dragging our feet . . . ," began Charles.

"Show us. What do you have so far?"

They looked at each other. Haines took another deep breath before he spoke.

"As you have found out, we do have the list of automobile owners who all have that same year and model car. We have been tracking down people on that list to find the owner of one car used in the hit and run. That's where we are, so far and that's all I can tell you."

"What about the Milners?" asked Scott.

"Who?" asked Charles.

"Martin Milner and his stepdaughter, Betty."

Charles looked at Haines as if asking Haines to help him throw the two of them out.

"We're doing our job, Mr. Kersey. I know it seems slow going to you, but we're doing the best we can. Now we both know that Betty's last name is not Milner," said Haines. He was probably still angry that Scott went over his head and obtained the list.

"We haven't been able to find her, said Charles.

"Don't you think it's important to question her and get a look at the car?" asked Scott.

"Mr. Kersey —" began Haines.

"Where do you go from here?" asked Scott, not waiting for an answer.

"Mr. Kersey, why don't you just leave the investigation to us?" asked Haines, still a hint of anger.

"We've tried to do that and it's gotten us nowhere. We want to know what you will do next?" asked Cameron

They looked at each other again. Charles gave a slight nod to Haines.

"We will continue to try to track down Betty to get a look at the car, but her mother said she's been away at school all this time, so I don't think she hit anybody," said Charles.

"But you will follow up?" asked Scott.

"Yes," said Haines.

"What about the witness?" asked Cameron.

"We still need to find her. We understand that she hasn't been running since the accident."

"You sound like you know who she is," said Scott.

"We have leads and we'll follow them up. Look, I'm sorry, we're sorry this is taking so long, but it's just the slow pace that we're getting the clues. So far, no one's come forward to volunteer any information and that can make it harder for us. If you, either of you interfere with this investigation again, I'll have you arrested for interfering with an on-going investigation. Do you both understand that?" said Charles.

"Just do your job, so we won't have to do that," said Cameron.

They left.

~~~~~~~~~~

Scott had gotten in the habit of taking a run before work every day, the habit his mother tried hard to get him to form. He set out on the trail, a little later on this brisk morning; too brisk seeing as he only passed one other runner. Since he'd been running more frequently, his speed had increased and he ran in a more relaxed manner taking those slight inclines that he used to think of as steep hills with a little more ease. His thoughts went to Betty and the car. He had hoped the car would have been at Betty's school and he could have seen it was the wrong one. Nevertheless, he didn't like how this was shaping up and thought long and hard about the need to pursue this. Maybe his father was right, that this was a police matter and they should handle it. He couldn't help but feel that Haines and Charles were keeping something from them. They didn't become detectives fumbling through the way they were. Scott wondered what they were holding back and why.

His heart began to pound as he saw a figure running toward him, but too far away to recognize the face. As the figure got closer, he recognized the woman. She was one of his mother's friends; someone who used to run with her.

"Hi Scott," Ellen yelled out, somewhat out of breath. She ran up to him and ran in place.

"Hello, Mrs. Fisher." He ran in place.

She stopped running, stared at him for a moment as if she didn't know what to say, or how to form what she should say.

Scott stared back at her, turned away to cough.

"I, uh, I, I never got a chance to tell you, Scott. But I'm so sorry."

"Thank you, Mrs. Fisher. Thank you." He almost started

his run, but changed his mind. "The police said that there was a witness, but they can't find her. Do you know the woman who saw what happened?"

"I think I know who they may be talking about. She and your mother often stood in the parking lot talking. I only know her when I see her. I don't know her name, or where she lives. I haven't seen her since."

The surprise invigorated him, but he tried not to show her his eagerness. "Can you tell me what she looks like?"

"Tall, she always wears a bright yellow jacket and, I think, Nike shoes with yellow trim and yellow on the heels. I mean, when I see her, I always recognize her through her yellow jacket."

"Do you remember when she runs?" asked Scott.

"I think I see her when I'm finishing up, just before I get to the parking lot."

"About this time?" He looked at his watch.

She looked at her watch. "Yes, about this time, usually."

"Thank you, Mrs. Fisher. Have a nice run."

She started running in place, again. "A few of us want to try to improve this trail and I'm having a meeting at my house this evening. I wonder if you'd like to come."

"Improve the trail?" He looked around as if he had missed something.

"Yes. You know. We need to see to it that the weeds don't over run the trail, and we need parts of it repaved. Come on by; we could use your help. Eight o'clock. See you then."

They ran off in opposite directions.

~~~~~~~~~~

Scott arrived at the meeting a little late. Mrs. Fisher introduced him to the eight women and two men in the living room before she went to the next room to get a chair for him. He looked around the room at the guests seated on the couch and filling up the chairs, forming an oval in the living room. His eyes rested on Kathryn seated on the couch next to a man — probably the man she had told him about on their first date. He quickly turned his head away. At that same moment, a woman whose name he didn't quite remember asked him if he was a runner or walker. When he opened his mouth to respond, Mrs. Fisher brought him a chair and placed it directly across from Kathryn and the man. He glanced at Kathryn for a second and then noticed that there was no space between the two of them on that couch. He figured that he must be the man who gave her the ring he saw on her finger.

"Why don't we have some refreshments before we get started," said Ellen Fisher.

Embarrassed to sit across from Kathryn and the man, Scott jumped up right away to get a few vegetables and dip. He really didn't want to eat anything he just couldn't sit there in front of Kathryn. He noticed the bottle of wine on the table and thought about taking a drink or two or the entire bottle, even. If ever there was a time for him to take a drink, it was now. But he promised his mother and he didn't want to show Kathryn she still meant anything to him, so he passed up the wine. A woman reached across to the vegetables and Scott realized he needed to move out of the way. When he got back to his seat, he moved his chair back and slightly to the side so he wouldn't have to look directly into Kathryn's beautiful and intoxicating eyes. He heard Mrs. Fisher say from the other room something about getting the meeting started and the guests came back to their seats.

"Kathryn is that an engagement ring on your finger?" asked Margaret Jenkins who was juggling a hefty plate of food in one hand and a glass of wine in the other. She sat down across from Kathryn and the man and sat her wine glass on the table in front of them.

"Yes, it is," responded Kathryn. She slightly turned her head toward Scott and then held her hand out to Margaret.

"It's a beautiful ring," said Margaret with a forkful of food ready and headed toward her mouth. "How long have you two been engaged?"

"I'm Harris Sweeney." Harris held out his hand to Margaret Jenkins and Scott.

"We just recently got engaged," said Kathryn. She gave another sheepish look toward Scott who was pretending not to listen and stuffing broccoli with dip in his mouth.

"Have you set a date yet?" asked Margaret.

"No, nothing definite, but I really want to marry this woman soon."

Scott sat shocked and dumbfounded by the news, unable to move. He tried his best not to reveal to anyone that Kathryn's engagement mattered to him.

"Let's get this meeting started," said Mrs. Ames, an older woman who seemed to like to take over. She was the same woman who liked to tell everybody what side of the path a user could run or walk on.

Scott gave a quick glance over to Kathryn again and saw Harris taking her hand. He felt his heart beat faster and anger rose inside him until he thought he noticed her pulling her hand away from him and because he was so downhearted at this moment, this very tiny gesture gave him hope.

After the meeting was underway, Kathryn reached for her

glass of wine that sat on the coffee table closer to Scott. When Scott saw her struggling to grasp it, he picked up the wine glass and held it out to her. He couldn't decide what her facial expression meant, but he was sure from the half-smile that it was something positive or maybe that was what he wanted it to be.

Scott's cell phone rang and as he pretended to answer it, he announced that the call was an emergency and he had to leave. He asked Mrs. Fisher to keep him posted and let him know what he could do to help with her project. When he got outside, he breathed a sigh of relief and checked his phone. Lisa again? He didn't know what to think about what he'd just seen. For the time being, it was best for him to keep his mind on the car and the person who took his mother's life. He wanted to try and separate that from Kathryn as best he could.

Chapter 22
Kathryn

Kathryn opened the door to her bedroom and found Betty, standing in the middle of the room.

Betty turned around when she heard Kathryn enter. "I was, I just needed . . ." She held up Kathryn's suitcase. "I just needed to borrow a suitcase." She tried to make her way around Kathryn.

"But you have a suitcase. Why do you need mine?" She stepped aside to let Betty through the door.

"Kat, can you. Oh Kat, I can't stay here. I have to go. I'll return your suitcase."

"Betty, what's going on? Didn't you take everything when you left for school?"

"Yes."

"I don't understand. Betty, what's going on?" She saw tears well up in Betty's eyes.

"Nothing, Kat. I just needed another look at things, that's all." She held up the suitcase.

Kathryn stared at her for a moment as she tried to make some understanding of what Betty was doing. She thought she knew Betty, but now she seemed different somehow.

"Betty, something is wrong. Please tell me."

"Look Kat, I know we are only step sisters, but I've always felt like you were my real older sister. Just, don't. I needed another suitcase, just one last, well for my friend, but I wanted to do it before you got back. I have to go now." She gave Kathryn a long, tight hug. "I love you, Kat." Betty tried to leave.

Kathryn took her by the arm, wouldn't let go of her. "Betty, something is wrong. Please let me help you whatever it is."

Betty pulled away. "I'll be okay, Kat. I know I've always gotten into trouble and you've always helped me. But, this time I have to do this myself."

"What're you talking about? What kind of trouble are you in?"

"No, no. I'm not in trouble."

"What happened with your car? Did you have an accident with it?"

"What car?"

"You know. That old Mercedes. Someone was here looking for it."

"I sold that old thing some time ago." She gave a dismissive gesture. "Look, I gotta go." She started off toward the stairs. Then she turned around. "Kat, please don't tell anyone I was here."

"Betty, what's going on? This isn't like you. Tell me what's going on."

"Nothing. Just nothing. I gotta go now."

"Where are you going?" Kathryn followed her out of the bedroom door and to the stairs.

"Don't worry about me. I'll be okay." She stopped for a minute. "Kat, I love you. Thanks for everything."

Kathryn caught up to her and grabbed her by the arm. "No, Betty, no. Please don't go, please, let me help you whatever it is."

"I don't know how things got so out of hand. I wish I could just turn the clock back and start again, but I know I can't. You've always helped me and now I must help myself."

"Betty, please tell me what happened."

Betty pushed away from Kathryn and Kathryn fell on the steps. Betty stepped passed her and flew down the steps to the foyer and out the front door.

Kathryn got up, ran behind her, and stood out on the front porch to see where she had gone. Betty was nowhere to be found. Kathryn tried to remember if she had heard a car, but couldn't remember. She ran down the front steps and turned to the right. She didn't see Betty or a car. She turned and ran down the street in the opposite direction. Betty had disappeared. Kathryn wanted to find Betty, help her somehow. She could drive to Betty's school where she thought Betty had gone, talk to her, help her.

When she tried to steer herself in the direction of her car, she couldn't move. Maybe she didn't want to move or find Betty to help her. Maybe she just wanted to leave it alone. Kathryn had no idea where Betty went but from what she just saw, Betty was in serious trouble. Kathryn didn't want to know what trouble she was in or where she was going. Whatever it was Betty wanted to keep her out of it and Kathryn thought that was best. Kathryn turned around and walked back into the house.

Chapter 23
Scott

"How long has it been abandoned?" asked Scott. He pushed the button to let the window of the car down.

"Empty, but not abandoned," responded Cameron. He placed both hands on the steering wheel. Then he leaned over to look out of Scott's window.

"Can we go in?" asked Scott.

"Let's wait for the real estate man." Cameron turned around in the car craning in all directions to get a view of the circular driveway as he looked out for the real estate man.

"I can't believe this is really going to happen. This is a good neighborhood, too. The kids are going to love it." Scott looked around. "Well the hotel needs work, but the rest of the neighborhood is fine."

The hotel sat back about a half mile off the street. The shrubbery had turned into overrun weeds, crowding out the front parking lot. The building was not run down, more unused giving it that ghostly appearance.

"It's what your mother wanted. It's the one she picked out. I don't care what it looks like or the amount of work involved in making it livable. This is the hotel your mother asked me to buy for her." He took his hands off the steering wheel and sat back.

"I want to see if it's open." Scott got out of the car, walked up to the heavy-looking brass, and glass door and pushed in one side. He gave a wave to his father who was still sitting in the car.

Cameron looked around again, and seeing no one who resembled a real estate agent, got out and the two of them went into the empty hotel.

"I wonder why it's not locked?" asked Cameron.

"Maybe he left it open for us."

"Just be careful. You never know who or what could be lurking in the corners."

Cameron wanted Scott to see the hotel that through several meetings and skilled negotiating, he had finally purchased, Laurie's last project. The building was once a very upscale hotel, that catered to the rich people in the community and specialized in a week-end get-away, was left empty when the recession began and people could no longer afford the outrageous cost of a night's or a week-end's stay of pampering and self-indulgence. Before long, the hotel went out of business and the owner, whom Cameron knew, lost everything.

Scott and Cameron walked through what used to be the lobby — still with marble floors — and over to what once was the check-in marble counter. They entered one room off the huge lobby with chairs backed up to basins, the ones still attached to the wall, and shelves above the basins. In front, was a set of mirrors that stretched across the length of the wall. One mirror had a long diagonal crack. Scott stepped on an old towel that must have been used for hair coloring from the many hues of blonde, red, and brown that he noticed.

"A hair salon. This was a hair salon at one time," said Cameron, nodding several times.

~~~~~~~~~~

Scott remembered the time one Saturday morning when his Mother took him to a teen home where she volunteered. It was just an old house ready for demolition. Somehow, the two women who ran it got together and raised money to buy it. They refurbished it as best they could, and made it comfortable for run-away teens. They had ten to fifteen girls jammed into that old house, he heard his mother say. Laurie learned quickly that there were always problems in working with the needy and Scott always thought she gave as much as she could, sometimes even more.

"I'm glad you're here," said Melissa, one of the mothers, as Laurie and Scott entered. "Maybe you can help Sonya. She's not cooperating with me today." Melissa looked like she had had it.

Four of the girls doing homework sat at the dining room table, turned into a combination dining room and study hall. Scott heard dishes and kitchen things clinking and clanging and he could see several other girls moving about in the kitchen.

Laurie went into the living room where Sonya sat on the dark green second-hand couch with her arms folded across her chest. Scott stood between the dining room and living room facing Sonya and his mother.

"Hi Sonya," said Laurie. "Is everything okay?" She sat on

the edge of the couch next to Sonya and faced her as best she could.

Sonya didn't move. She stared at something straight ahead, her face with a far away look, tuning out Laurie and everything around her.

"Sonya? Can you answer me? I want to help if I can."

Sonya turned to Laurie and gave her a long hard stare. After a moment, she blurted out, "Well, you can't."

"What's the matter, Sonya?" She tried to touch Sonya, but changed her mind and brought her hand back.

Sonya looked at Laurie as if Laurie had done something to annoy her. "I'm tired of staying here. I'm leaving."

"Can you tell me why before you go?"

"Look, I know you people want to help, but I can't do this school work. I'm just not cut out for school work." With her arms still folded, she gave a big shrug as if to say, "They should have figured that out."

"Sonya you need a high school education. What trouble are you having?" Laurie folded her hands and held them in her lap.

"All I want to do is fix hair and I don't need to know how to write no paper to do that."

"What do you have to do Sonya?"

"Here." She picked up a paper that was in a ball and on the couch beside her and tossed the paper at Laurie. "We have to write some kind of paper. What the hell do I know about writing papers?"

Laurie took the paper, unfolded it. "That's no problem. This is my son, Scott. He's going to be a writer and knows a lot about writing."

Scott smiled at his mother and gave a slight wave to Sonya as he took a step toward them.

"Scott can help you with your paper. Can't you Scott?"

"Sure. Can I see what you have to do?"

Laurie handed the paper to Scott.

"This is not as hard as it seems. You just have to write a personal narrative. This is a paper about you. Can we use this table here?" He pointed to the dining room table where four of the other girls were sitting doing their homework.

The four girls made room for Sonya and Scott.

"Yeah, I guess so." Sonya reluctantly got up from the couch and plopped down at the table.

Scott found paper on the table and began asking her questions about her life.

~~~~~~~~~~

In the hotel salon, Scott felt something sacred about the school and everything his father did to shape it exactly as his mother envisioned it. He walked out of that room, turned down a hallway, and entered another room where a portable wall meant to separate or divide the room into two was off its track and falling down.

"Hello? Hello?" A male voice yelled from somewhere near the front. "I'm here, the real estate agent."

Cameron stepped out into the hallway and saw the real estate agent standing in the lobby. Scott and Cameron walked toward him.

"I'm sorry. When we spoke, I told you I had a closing this afternoon and my showing this morning ran way over. It's just one of those days. You can never time those things. Well, have you had a chance to look around? I'm Dewitt Howard, by the way." He extended his hand.

"Cameron Kersey. My son, Scott." Cameron extended his hand.

Scott nodded.

"We just got here," said Cameron.

"You know, this used to be one of the finest hotels in the area. Now, you're going to turn it into a home for run-away teens."

"A big undertaking, don't you think?" asked Cameron, looking around the room.

"How are you planning to do that?" asked Dewitt.

Before Cameron had a chance to answer, Dewitt Howard's cell phone rang. He took it out of his pocket, saw the lit-up face and pushed a button. "I have to take this. Good luck to you. Here are the keys." He handed Cameron a set of keys and walked out of the hotel.

Cameron took the keys, gently held them in his hand, a precious gem, a fragile newborn.

"It's Mom's dream," said Scott taking his father's hand and holding on to the keys, too.

~~~~~~~~~~

"I hear we can start work on this building," said Cameron as the architect, James Sparks and the contractor Max Henry came through the front door of the hotel.

"Yes, we can. I told you not to worry," said James, a smile on his face and carrying a thick roll of architectural drawings for the hotel.

Scott came in from what used to be the hallway and introduced himself.

"How long is this going to take?" asked Cameron. He tried

215

to position himself as best he could on the broken stool. He pulled it up to what used to be the information counter at the hotel.

"You've got a lot to do here, so it'll take some time," responded, James Sparks. He unrolled the drawings on the counter and each person found something to hold down the edges.

"I can give all my time to you right now. But even, let's see, electrician, plumber, inspection. . . This will take some time."

"Can you start tomorrow?"

"I can have my boys over here first thing tomorrow morning."

"That's good. I want this finished as soon as possible, but I don't want any short cuts," said Cameron.

"I know how important this is to you. We can do that, sir." He stood up. "I'm gonna take another walk through."

"I'll do that with you, if it's okay," said James.

Cameron, Scott, James, and Max stood to take another walk through the hotel. It took almost the entire afternoon as they went to every room on every floor looking at the plans and deciding on the size of the rooms and bathrooms. Cameron reminded them that he wanted as many rooms and bathrooms as he could get. The larger the number the more teens they would be able to house. When they finished with what used to be the guest rooms, the men went to the kitchen area, the dining room, what once was a bar, the spa, the pool and to all the other parts of the hotel. Cameron thought that they should keep the beauty salon, and have someone from the beauty school come and give the girls training. Then he got the idea to make the kitchen and dining room training areas, too. He said that should make it easier for the school system to accept it.

Scott was in a daze as he walked through the building. His mother's dream was coming to fruition. He remembered the times he went with his mother to that run down house where the overcrowding of kids became the norm. At the house three, four, sometimes five teens slept in one room. In the hotel, each teen would have his or her private room. His mother used to say that she would rather have them sleeping on floors and couches and in chairs some place where they were safe and cared for rather than on the streets. The house held too many teens, but it was warm with plenty of food, sometimes, and people who cared about them. Scott could hardly believe that the help that his mother always wanted to give to those kids would soon be a reality. His eyes welled up as he thought that his mother would never see the results of her hard work.

Chapter 24
Kathryn

Kathryn was a nervous wreck. She couldn't sleep; she had plenty on her mind. Frankie had offered her the opportunity to display a few of her designs during the last half hour of his upcoming fashion show. She tossed and turned, got up for water, came back to the bed and still could not get comfortable. So far, she had changed her mind three times about what she wanted to show, and she was still not sure about her last set of choices. And, there was something else bothering her, too. Tired of pacing across her bedroom floor, she rose and went to the studio. She knew how to get into the mall and store in the wee hours. Frankie showed her last year when she helped him prepare for his show.

She had been studying and preparing herself for this first step since she was fourteen years old, after she found out that her mother wanted to become a fashion designer before she died and certainly, well before Frankie promised it to her. The opportunity of her being a part of an established designer's show was the zenith for any novitiate and she was appreciative. Frankie told her that every designer had a certain style that "belonged to them" and she had to pick her style. He also told her to be careful about whatever she picked because she would have it for several years. Because Frankie had asked her to have her plan ready for him, she forced herself to concentrate and selected four different styles of ensembles.

After she began the next step, her mind went to Harris. On the drive home from the meeting with the walkers and runners, Harris had asked her to set a date. In fact, he seemed rather impatient and edgy, almost demanding that she set the date. Scott's presence for some reason he couldn't identify, made him uncomfortable, resentful. Harris seemed to have the feeling that there was something between the two of them. Could Harris tell what she really felt?

"Harris, I want to set a date, but the opportunity that Frankie's offering me has to come first. I have to wait until the show is over."

"Don't make up excuses. The show is coming up. You can set the date for later."

"You know that Frankie's offer is something I've wanted for a long time. I have to give all my time to that."

"I understand that. I can help, we can set the date for later, or we can get a planner. Your choice."

"Harris, I just can't do this right now. I can't even think about it. My mind is on the show, you know that."

"Does your wanting to push this back have anything to do with that guy?"

"What guy?"

"The man at the meeting who kept watching you? He seemed, he seemed, I don't know, like he wanted something, or wanted to say something to you."

"Harris?"

"You know who I'm talking about. Were you dating him or something? What's with you two? Is he someone I have to worry about?"

"Harris, what are you talking about? There was no man there watching me."

"Yes. He was. You pushed my hand away when he looked over at you."

Kathryn felt her heart race. She tried as hard as she could to keep Harris from seeing a change in her, but she had to admit that she was happy to hear that when Scott looked at her, it aroused jealousy in Harris. Not that she wanted men to fight over her, but the fact that Scott felt something for her seemed to make her smile inside. She breathed a sigh of relief when they'd reached her home. She didn't have to respond.

Now in the studio, she realized that she owed Scott an explanation, an apology for everything that she had done to him. Her father had tried to tell her that. But, it was so hard for her to think about Scott and face the fact that she really did owe him at least an explanation.

She turned to the window and watched a woman struggling with an arm full of packages and bags as she disappeared under the overhang of the building. Then, Kathryn looked at the clock and thought that some of the workers in the store would be coming in early and she had nothing done. She just couldn't concentrate.

She watched as a car drove up and a man got out. He went around to the passenger side and opened the door for the woman. He extended his hand to help her out and she took hold of it. She recognized Mr. and Mrs. Avery who owned the card shop on the first floor of the mall. The couple had owned that card shop ever since Kathryn could remember. She watched as Mr. Avery put his arm around his wife's waist directed her toward the entrance. She must have said something funny; they both laughed and he took the bag that she was carrying. Love was just too complicated for her. She thought about the day when Scott held her hand. They had just come from the theater and walking to his car, he took her hand. She remembered how nice and warm it felt, covering her entire hand, her hand in his. Kathryn thought about Harris. Would he carry her bag for her? Would he listen to her when she needed him, and laugh when she said something funny? Kathryn really didn't know whether Harris would do that or not. There was no doubt in her mind that Scott would.

She placed the sketches down on the table and sat back in her chair. Her mind was just too heavy with Scott, and though her show was important, she found that she couldn't work on her garments until she had at least resolved the issue with Scott. She had to find a way to make him want to listen to her, hear her out. She was unhappy with herself because she hadn't treated him fairly, especially during the meeting to improve the trail. She didn't understand how she let Harris talk her into going to that meeting. But she really couldn't blame Harris because she wanted to go. She'd thought it would be a chance for her to see Scott again. Nevertheless, she didn't want to hurt him. Scott seeing her with Harris was selfish and thoughtless. No good came out of it. She didn't bother to think what that would do to him. She had to find a way to undo that damage.

She could see that he really did care for her. She saw it when he came to her house to ask about Betty's car. She recognized it the minute she saw him and she felt something, too. Those feelings she had when they were together for those two weeks came rushing back to her the minute she saw him standing there at the door. She was wrong to agree to marry Harris when she still cared so much for Scott. Her father had tried so hard to help her get over her feelings of loss. Kathryn could see how her father was disappointed in himself, thinking that he had failed to help her. She was stronger now and no matter what her father thought, he had tried so hard to help her. She knew she had to show him that.

It came to her that she should make an appointment at Scott's office. She could talk to him there. It would be official and she would have to get right to the point. He would take her seriously and even if either one of them got angry with the other, the office environment would force them to conduct themselves respectfully. If he didn't want to touch her or kiss her, he wouldn't have to. His office was the best place. When she couldn't think of any other way, in her desperation, she called his office and made an appointment for that afternoon. When the secretary told her that he would be able to see her, she felt a wave of nerves surge through her body.

Through the window, she saw Frankie pull his car into a parking space marked "Reserve." He got out and opened the backdoor. Michelle got out of the passenger side and came around to his side. Kathryn watched Michelle take out a few garment bags from the backseat hanger and then walk toward the store. She and Frankie would be in soon and she, Kathryn, hadn't completed her work for the show. She had to be ready for the dressmaker.

After Frankie and Michelle dropped the clothes off at the

shop, they left and went to the Hyatt hotel, the place where the fashion show would be underway. Frankie made things seem easy, but he often worried about his shows.

After they left, Kathryn got herself ready for her appointment with Scott. In the dressing room, she went to the racks óf stored items and donned herself in a most sexy low cut red dress that emphasized the curves of her body and with a bolero-style jacket that covered her bodice. After looking in the full-length mirror, she quickly took it off, and put on something with a classic look, a royal blue A-line dress, round neck and fitted jacket, feminine and a tad bit sexy. She sat at the dressing table and fussed with her hair and make-up before she realized that she was over doing things. Her plan was simple. She would go to Scott's office and let him know that she was there to explain and apologize. She needed to assure herself, so she said aloud that if she went to his office he would see that she was serious. "I can do this. I have to do this. I can do this. I owe him this." With one last look in the mirror, she was satisfied with herself and left.

Kathryn pulled into the parking lot in front of the six-story glass front building off Water Street and sat there composing herself before she got out. She repeated her mantra, "I can do this. I have to do this. I can do this. I owe him this." She began to shake and wanted to turn back, thought it was a brainless idea, and almost started the car. Maybe given more time, she could come up with a much better idea. Maybe she could just write him a letter, send him a note or something that didn't demand this much backbone. Then she repeated her mantra and calmed herself. She pushed herself to continue with this, now stupid idea. At this point, she felt she had no choice but to continue, saying he deserved his apology face to face. She walked to the building that she discovered was a few blocks away from The Grove, the mall where her studio was located. When she attempted to push in the heavy glass door, a tall thin man in a guard's uniform helped her.

"Mornin' ma'am," said the guard, tipping his hat and smiling widely.

"Good morning, sir." Kathryn wanted to ask him about the floor and office, but she didn't want anyone to know where she was going. She headed toward the bank of elevators instead. She found the list of office numbers on the wall to the right of the elevators. Her heart beat faster when she saw the floor and office number for Scott Kersey. She noticed the name of the company and for a short moment realized Scott and his father must own the company, but at this moment, she was much too nervous to pay attention to that. A woman, whose perfume gave off the light scent of pears, came up behind her and pushed the button for an elevator and within seconds, the elevator door opened and Kathryn and the woman stepped inside. The woman reached over and pushed the button for the same floor that Kathryn needed, so Kathryn stepped back slightly behind the woman, the mild pear scent begging the nostrils to draw in its scent. Kathryn looked over at the woman out of the corner of her eyes. She realized that scent would drive some man crazy and she wondered why she didn't think of a spray of perfume. But she couldn't take her mind off what she had to do. In fact, she had hoped to get a chance to practice her speech on the elevator and now her stomach was beginning to churn. She saw the woman turn her head slightly in her direction. The churning in her stomach now felt like a big tight knot as the elevator inched its way up from floor to floor. She had refused to eat anything before she left and now she was thankful that she didn't. She felt her forehead wet and a wave went through her body making her weak at the knees as the elevator doors opened. The woman turned around and glanced at her before she stepped out. The woman turned to the right and Kathryn pushed herself off and turned to the left. As she walked down the hallway to the next two offices, she found that she should have turned right and went back the other way.

She passed the bank of elevators, and went down three doors on the right to the one that read: Kersey and Associates Real Estate Management and Development. Another wave went through her and she shook. This time she was ready to get rid of whatever she would have eaten, and she waited a moment before she pushed in the heavy steel door. Standing in the doorway looking around, she tried to move her legs — at the moment, seemed to be cast in cement blocks — and walk over to the male receptionist. He seemed so far away sitting behind a big curved counter in front of a wall-length window that looked out across the Potomac River. Still shaking, she somehow managed to force herself to take a few steps toward the receptionist. The sunlight streamed across the room casting a gold-like rainbow of light through the office. The male receptionist was on the phone and which was a good thing because Kathryn needed a second to compose herself. She took a deep breath. Just as she opened her mouth to speak, the woman on the elevator with her, jumped up from the guest seats along the sidewall. At the same time, Scott, carrying something, walked out of an entrance to the right of the male receptionist. Kathryn inhaled the pear scent and saw the woman walking toward Scott.

"Scott," the woman almost yelled out with a smile that seemed to light up her face.

The receptionist put down the phone and looked up at Scott.

She saw Scott walk toward the woman who held her arms open for him. She was ready to puke right then and she turned around to leave. When she reached the door, she tried to open it but for some reason she couldn't budge it; it was too heavy, or locked or something as she pulled and jerked it making it bang loudly. She felt like a caged lion, just caught, fear swelling up inside.

She heard Scott's voice from behind her, but she didn't stop trying to get the door open.

"Hi. Can I help you?"

She turned to him approaching her as she continued to shake and fumble with the door. She was frantic. She realized she'd made a mistake and she had to get out of there.

"Can I help you?" He stood next to her, took hold of the long metal door handle, his hand on hers.

She looked up at Scott, fear, devastation written across her face. "Wrong office," was all she could get out.

"Are you sure?" He asked, exuding an air of calmness that emanated from him and settled over her.

She slowly withdrew her hands from the door, looked up at him again, a scowl on her face this time. For a moment, she thought that the woman was a business interest but when she turned to look at the woman, she saw anger wrinkled across her face. "I think so. Yes." Kathryn said.

Eyes on her, he pushed open the door for her.

And as she wobbled out the door, she felt his eyes still on her as she headed toward the elevator.

She looked back at him when she got to the elevator. She wanted to go back. She had felt him, his confidence, sincerity. The bell rang and she stood there. Scott stood in the doorway, holding the door open, perhaps waiting on her to come back. Maybe the woman was there on business. The woman took another step forward.

"Are you getting on lady?" asked a man already on the elevator.

Kathryn stepped inside the elevator.

The elevator went down much faster then it escalated. She was out on the street and walking toward the parking lot before she knew it. She looked behind her several times and was disappointed when she didn't see him. She imagined that he ran to the bank of elevators and punched in the button. That woman yelled and screamed, pleaded for him to run back to her. She wanted to think that he didn't wait on the elevator, but ran down the stairs and to the underground parking where he thought her car was parked. When she didn't see him or hear him call out her name she wanted to believe that he ran down one level too many and missed her. She wanted to think that he continued running down the sidewalk to the nearest parking lot and stood at the gate looking for her, but he didn't see her anywhere. And even though she had waited for him, he missed her anyway. She wanted all this to happen to keep her from feeling foolish. She knew that it was only what she wanted and that it never happened.

Kathryn raced to the store as fast as she could and hid out in the one-person bathroom in the back of the studio. After locking the door, she took off her dress and threw it at the mirror. What was she thinking when she went to his work? If there was a prize for the biggest screw up, surely she should be the one to get it. She couldn't do anything else to mess up her life or his. All she wanted to do was to apologize to him. She could see that he had given up on her, moved on, and found someone else. She stood there stripped down to her bra and panties and looked at herself in the mirror. She was just asking for too much.

That's it. She was just asking for too much. Harris Sweeney was the man she needed. He was not too much. It was rather bigheaded of her to believe that she could have someone like Scott, anyway. She saw that the first day she met him and, certainly, she realized it during the two weeks that they were together. Besides, she had her show to think about. She wouldn't have the time for Scott.

She picked up her dress, held it up in front of her. Maybe this wasn't sexy enough. She slid the dress over her head and reached around to zip it in the back. She pulled the seat down on the toilet, sat down cross-legged, elbow on her leg, and cupped her chin. She couldn't help herself. Her tears came a little at a time at first, but then she took long, big sobs and her tears gushed down her face. She cried until she wasn't able to cry anymore and she no longer felt sorry for herself. Maybe the other woman was just what she needed.

Chapter 25
Scott

"You haven't started yet have you?" Scott stood in the doorway of Cameron's office.

Cameron looked up and saw Scott. "No, just getting things ready. Come on in." He motioned Scott to the table and held up the plans for the home for runaways.

Scott walked to a small table to the left of the desk and next to the window that overlooked River Road and parts of the towpath. He pulled out the chair and sat down; looked around the office. He recalled that he had only been in his father's office a few times — including the last disappointment — since he'd started working at the firm. Scott noticed that the office had much of his mother's taste, since it was furnished much like his home. It was safe to say that his mother had had a huge hand in the decorating. Scott could see his father sitting back letting her take over. He remembered hearing his mother talk about how she felt about being a stay-at-home-mom. She always said that Cameron's job was important and what she did was not. Scott now realized, that his father made every little job, no matter how minute, seem vital. Now, he could see why Cameron liked to spend time in his office. This was his father's way of keeping her memory alive. Every time he went to his office, he would feel her.

Cameron's desk was a remodeled antique desk with three drawers on each side, but also made to house a computer. The two chairs that sat in front of the desk, each with red and white striped silk seats and back with arms of mahogany wood were also what Scott thought of as "modern antiques". His mother loved antiques; Cameron always said he didn't care one way or another.

"What about some coffee before we get started?" asked Cameron.

"Sounds good."

Cameron left to get the coffee.

Scott rose from his seat, looked toward the open door, and went behind his father's desk, eyes on the chair. He swiveled the chair in both directions a few times then attempted to sit in it, but changed his mind. He ran his hand along the back feeling the smoothness of the leather and then across the seat of the chair. A chair made of leather that quality had to be comfortable, and he could almost see himself sinking into it. Quickly, he turned around and sat down in the chair, the chair of power. He looked over the desk, the command center, the place where his father made things happen. He turned to his left, to his right, pretended to talk on the phone and pretended to talk to June or someone like June. Maybe one day he could be the one sitting in this chair at this desk doing what his father did. Every time he tried to capture that picture of himself in his father's shoes, even making a call on his phone, or asking the secretary for something, the picture wouldn't stay in his mind and his face turned to a faceless mask, before it faded.

For a moment, he recalled the same thing happening to him when he was in college, but he thought that was because he was a faceless nobody. None of this felt right to him. Taking over his father's firm wasn't what he wanted to do with his life. He had kept that problem hidden all his life and for some reason, it was finally surfacing.

He swiveled around and noticed the painting that his father had in his office; the one directly behind his desk. He wondered how often his father looked at it. Scott remembered when they bought it.

~~~~~~~~~~

It was early fall and the three of them, his father and mother, were out shopping. Scott had come home from school to visit for the weekend since it was his mother's birthday. They were walking through Alexandria by the Torpedo Factory and his father got the urge to go inside. They went from one floor to the next, from artist to artist looking at jewelry, paintings, sculpture, clothes, and cards when Cameron stopped to watch an artist painting an oil picture of the monument and surrounding area.

"You like that Sweetheart?" Cameron asked.

"Oh, Cam, it looks just like Washington and the monument area."

"Is that what that tall building is?"

Laurie nudged Cameron in the ribs.

"Oooo," he pretended as he held his side.

"You know what I mean," said Laurie.

Cameron reached down and kissed Laurie on the top of her head. "You like it?"

"I love it," said Laurie.

"Why don't we look around? See what else this artist has?" asked Cameron.

The three of them walked into the artist's corner and looked around at paintings that he had completed, pulling back watercolors, pastels and other oils that he had stacked against the wall.

"What about this one?" asked Laurie as she held up another oil painting. It was a painting of downtown Washington, D.C. after a heavy snow in 1957, according to the title.

"Now, that's the picture," said Cameron. "Look, Scott. What do you think?"

Scott turned toward the picture. "I love it. You could get lost just looking at it, couldn't you?" He moved closer to the picture.

"Well, that settles it. This is the picture that I want to get for you, Cam, for my birthday."

"That's nice, but I thought we were getting something for you."

"Well we are." She started over to the artist. "You need something for your office to go behind your desk. Whenever you're in deep thought, you can turn around and look at the picture."

"Dad, do you really think that's fair?"

"No. But it's what your mother wants and I discovered a long time ago that there's no arguing with her when she wants something."

"We'll take this please," said Laurie, pointing to the picture Cameron held, a big smile on her face.

Cameron pulled out his credit card and paid for the painting. He carried it around until they finished their shopping. They went to the seafood restaurant where they ate by the window overlooking the water. When the cake came, Scott presented his mother with a handmade vase, a rose design that he managed to purchase when she wasn't looking. Cameron gave her a diamond and ruby necklace. She wouldn't let them sing "Happy Birthday." They told her.

"My guys." She waved at them as her eyes filled with tears.

Cameron took her hand.

~~~~~~~~~~

Scott slowly rose up out of his father's chair and took one of the red and white silk chairs in front of the desk. Cameron returned with the coffee.

"I heard that there was a little excitement here earlier. What happened?"

"Excitement? It was anything but that."

"What happened?"

"Lisa showed up out of the blue and on my way to talk to her, Kathryn was standing at the door."

"She's the one you really like, isn't she? Did you know she was coming?"

He looked at his father. He wasn't the scary man he once seemed. Instead, talking to him felt easy for Scott. His father's compassion was making him want to open up and tell him things. His father's kindheartedness was bringing Scott closer to him. "Well, yes. I guess. Yes, she's the one I really like. I didn't know she'd scheduled an appointment until after she left."

"They know about each other? Strange how they both showed up at the same time."

"I told Kathryn about Lisa on our first date, but Lisa doesn't know anything about Kathryn."

"What did you do?" He sipped his coffee.

"I think when Kathryn saw Lisa she changed her mind about whatever she came for."

"Whatever she came for? She came to see you."

"I don't know what I did to turn her away from me." Scott looked down, hands cupped around his coffee.

"Don't you want to know why she came? It could be about the car."

For the rest of the afternoon, Scott could hardly keep his mind on the plans for the home for runaway teens. He nodded to his father every now and then, as if he agreed or understood, but he couldn't get Kathryn, and the reason why she would come to the office, off his mind. Maybe she did have information about the car.

He looked over at his father again, busy explaining and rolling out the plans for the school. Scott smiled at his father and the afternoon at the Torpedo Factory fulgurated through his mind. Maybe he was changing, finally growing up, finally becoming someone even he could love.

Chapter 26
Scott

The next morning, Scott pulled in the parking lot of the walk-and-run-trail and parked across the lot on the opposite side. He got out and walked to where his mother's life was taken, and noticed the yellow tape half-down on the ground, half-torn off, but struggling to hold dear his mother's memory. He turned away, but turned back quickly. Flowers. Someone had placed flowers in the spot. Someone knew about the accident; possibly saw the car. The witness.

As he began his run, he felt a little different; more agile, flexible, legs moving in a lissome rhythm much resembling the stride of a racehorse at the Kentucky Derby. He felt himself folding into the scenery, feeling the hard, but giving asphalt through his shoes; his body bending to the curves of the trail; leaning into the inclines and hills, becoming one with the trail. He felt the increase in his speed, the strength in his legs and the length in his duration. Melting into the atmosphere as he whizzed by leafless trees and dried bushes sleeping for the winter, he ran a mile farther than his usual run — maybe he needed to get the kinks out — before he felt like turning around. He smiled as he realized that he was enjoying the run and now understood a little better why his mother had to have her morning run.

Before he knew it, he saw ahead of him a female dressed in yellow — yellow shoes, and outfit — just like Mrs. Fisher had said. He picked up his speed a little, as he saw the woman round a curve and in a few minutes, headed downhill. He knew that he needed to run faster when he saw that he was at the start of the hill she had just completed. If he didn't get to the top in good time, he would lose her. He made his brain tell his legs to move faster, push harder and used his arms to help propel himself forward.

His body began to respond, lungs hurting from expanding and contracting too rapidly, muscles in his legs and thighs aching, pressed to their maximum; his entire body begged him to slow down, stop the pain, rest, stop the horrible panting. As badly as he wanted to stop, he wanted to catch the lady in yellow just as badly, so he ran on, tried to push even harder, even beyond his limit to the point where "something else" took over his body.

When he rounded the curve and reached the top of the hill, he saw her running slowly on the downward slope. He looked ahead as much as he could given the hills and curves, and saw that the way ahead was almost flat. He wanted to maintain his speed coming down the hill, because if he didn't he wouldn't be able to run that fast again. But, that "something else" took over and he knew he would have to slow down as he began the down slope. When he finished the hill he pushed hard again, body still aching to stop, but still trying to catch the woman in yellow.

Then the woman stopped running and began her walk.

Scott knew that they were about a half mile from the parking lot and he had to get her before she got back to her car. This could be his only chance. From somewhere, he found the strength to move even faster and finally caught up to her. Walking beside her, he tried to catch his breath.

"Are you all right?" asked the woman in yellow.

"Yes, I . . . just . . . need . . . to . . .

"Take your time. Would you like to sit over here?" She pointed to a bench along side the trail.

He nodded several times, not able to speak right away. Finally, "Yes."

The two of them sat down on the bench. She sat facing him. He must have looked like he would soon need an ambulance or at the very least, oxygen.

"I've been trying to catch you."

"Oh, really?" The woman attempted to get up.

"No, no. Please, I need to talk to you. I'm not here to do you harm, I promise," still panting hard and forcing out each word.

"Okay. It must be important. You're so out of breath."

She must have realized that in his condition he wouldn't be able to do anything to her.

"It is." He waited until he was able to get it all out. "Uhh, that was tough. I understand that you witnessed a hit and run accident that killed a lady about three weeks ago."

"I don't know if I actually saw anything."

"Please, ma'am. The lady who was killed was my mother. I want to know what you saw."

"I'm so sorry. I thought I recognized you. You ran with her sometimes."

"Yes. My mother's name was Laura Kersey and I'm Scott."

"She was always so nice. She never failed to ask me about my mother and brought flowers over to my house when my mother died. I didn't even know she knew where I lived. Of all the people who I see out here running on a daily basis, she was the only one who took the time to do anything."

"So, you see why I want to catch whoever did this."

"Well. We were standing in the parking lot near the entrance to the trail winding up our conversation when this dark color, either blue or black older Mercedes-Benz pulled into the parking lot. It was a woman driving; a young girl. I thought I knew her, and waved to her. I thought she was going to get out and your mother and I stood watching her for a second. Then she backed up and pulled out toward the entrance. Laurie and I continued talking for a while longer and the young girl returned. We didn't know whether she was just learning to drive or what. In the evening sometimes, teens use the parking lot to learn how to drive. I thought she was trying to park. While I was there, she never got out of the car. We ended our conversation, and your mother went over to the water fountain to get a drink and I got into my car. I didn't know until several weeks later that someone was hit by a car and didn't know who it was until now."

"Did you get a look at the license plate?"

"No, not really. But, the car had Maryland plates. The funny thing is that I know I've seen that car before and the person who owns it ran in the morning or picked up someone."

"So, the person who was driving was a woman and she occasionally picked up another woman who ran regularly in the morning?"

"Yes. That's correct."

"And you don't know the names of either one of them."

"No, but I do know that no one who runs in the morning drives a Mercedes-Benz that old. She's more like a college student. I remember now; she's related to that young woman whose father had a heart attack about a year ago. Yes, I do remember now. I talked to her. She told me that her father was recuperating and I told her about my mother. What was her name? Katie? Carol? Kathryn? Carrie. I know it began with a "K or C."

"Did you tell this to the police?"

"No. They haven't tried to contact me. I felt sick the next day and the day after that. Then my husband came down with the flu. So, this is the first time I've been out running in about four or five weeks, maybe longer. I lost track of time.

"Thank you. You have been so helpful. You know, I didn't ask you your name."

"Janet Jefferies. I'm sorry I can't be more helpful."

"You've been very helpful."

"I live just up the street if you need to talk again. Go out here turn left and two houses down on the right." She pointed in the direction as she spoke.

"Thank you so much Mrs. Jefferies." Scott reached over and gave her a kiss on the cheek.

Mrs. Jefferies smiled as if she hadn't expected that. She got up and walked out to the parking lot.

Scott sat on the bench for a while longer going over everything Mrs. Jefferies had told him. It was just as he suspected. Betty, Kathryn's sister ran his mother down. That's why she can't be located. Kathryn knows she did it. That's why Kathryn left to go to France — to get away from it all. Maybe when she came to the office she had planned to tell him but got scared off. Scott knew he had to go back to the college. Police or no police, he had to find Betty. He had to know why she would do a thing like that to his mother, the same lady who took a stranger a bouquet of flowers when her mother died. How did Betty know his mother? What did his mother do to Betty that would cause Betty to take his mother's life? Even when his mother got angry at him or his brother or sister or even his father, no one wanted to lash back at her. If anything, everyone worried about making her angry and tried their best to do things to make her happy. What went on between his mother and Betty?

~~~~~~~~~~

"Dad, Dad?" Scott almost yelled as he burst into Cameron's office.

Cameron and the two other men, with whom he was meeting, looked up at Scott. At the same time, Scott stopped himself when he saw that his father was in a meeting.

"Just a minute," said Cameron, to the others. He got up and the two of them walked just outside the door.

"What's going on?" asked Cameron.

"Dad," Scott began, almost in a whisper. "I just came from my run and I found the woman in yellow. Remember? The witness? The lady that Mrs. Fisher told us about?"

"Yes. I do."

"I talked to her. She said or rather gave all indications, that the woman in the dark color car was Kathryn's sister, Betty."

Cameron gave his son a look that seemed filled with both compassion and sympathy. He opened his mouth to speak but nothing came out. Finally, "We have to call the police." Cameron was almost inaudible.

"I know, Dad, I know. But I want to take another ride out to Betty's school, talk to that boyfriend again."

"Son, I think it best if you step aside. Besides, I don't want you in any danger."

"I think that boyfriend knows more than he told us. I had a feeling at the time and I still think he's involved in some way."

"You think he's involved? Was he in the car, too?"

"No. Mrs. Jefferies —"

"Mrs. Jefferies? The woman who lost her mother?"

"Yes, the same one. Why?"

"Well, your mother said that she knew Mrs. Jefferies. They talked often. That makes sense."

"Mrs. Jefferies said that Betty was alone in the car when she, when it happened."

"What do you hope to accomplish by going back to her school? Are you thinking you could convince her to come back with you and give herself up?"

"Something like that. If she's not there, well I think the boyfriend knows where she is. I want to talk to her, ask her to turn herself in, but I have to find her first. I'll keep in contact and if things don't feel right, I'll call the police, but I have to do this."

Cameron stared at his son. He reached over and gave his son a big, long hug.

Scott grabbed onto his father but didn't expect to hold on to him as tightly as he did. He was finally making headway, and ending this burdensome ordeal. His father was right and he knew it. They should have turned it over to the police. The more time he spent on finding the person who took his mother's life, the more time he spent thinking about the ugliness that surrounded his mother's death. He had to admit that he needed to do that. He needed to understand what he did and how he left his mother vulnerable. Now, he wanted to think about all the good that his mother did and soon he would be able to.

Chapter 27
Scott

Scott knew he was taking a chance and possibly even arrested for interfering with an on-going police investigation. Haines and Charles made that very clear. But he had to. He drove back in the direction of Betty's school to her boyfriend, Edward's apartment. He was never totally convinced with the boyfriend's lie about Betty skipping out. If she truly did skip out on him, then he'd be a little more forthcoming with where she was. He probably held back to warn her first and maybe ask for another chance for them.

On the drive up, his thoughts went to Lisa and that she wanted him back, wanted another chance. When their fights began shortly after they started going out, she dragged him off to a relationship seminar where the topic was about making a change. Turns out some man, Scott didn't remember his name, was trying to sell his book, but he did have a few good points. He said something about in order to keep a relationship going in today's time the woman, especially, had to apply new relationship skills and that the old ones were no longer working. The author went on to say that for women, applying new relationship skills was extremely necessary if they wanted to get what they needed and wanted from men.

The thing about another chance that Lisa didn't quite understand was that when you got a chance, you had to make a change. You can't just do the same thing that caused that person to leave in the first place. He tried to tell Lisa that he wasn't getting what he needed from her and he really didn't believe that he was giving her what she needed either. He didn't know what either of them needed at the time, but now it's different for him. Somehow, Lisa thought that some kind of magic would take over and everything would work out. But life does not operate on magic. To make a change, a person has to desire it. He knew that the woman he really wanted he could never have now. Betty had fixed that for them. He didn't think he could be with anyone who was the stepsister to someone who would take a person's life and he didn't think that Kathryn would feel comfortable with him. He didn't see how he could make a change that huge. He didn't think he was that magnanimous.

Scott pulled up in the parking lot and parked beyond Edward's unit on the other end. No lights were on. He walked around to the back, which too, was dark. He parked his car beyond Edward's apartment on the other end, but where he could see anyone come and go. He waited. In about forty-five minutes, Scott saw Edward walking down the sidewalk beside the parking lot and go up to his apartment. He carried a bag from Burt's Burgers and Brewery according to the logo on the bag. He waited until Edward got inside and then got out and knocked on the apartment door. Edward answered the door. Scott saw that he wasn't taking their breakup well, hair disheveled, clothes wrinkled and stained with something Scott thought was food. He smelled as if he hadn't had a bath in a while.

"Hello Edward, remember me?"

"Yes, I remember you." Edward looked over Scott's shoulder as if he was expecting someone else.

"Who're you looking for? It's just me," said Scott.

"Nothing, nobody." He looked down at his feet.

Scott saw that he was wearing hiking boots and wondered if the poor man had other shoes.

"I need to know where Betty is."

"Man, I can't tell you that. I don't know."

"Yes, you do. Where is she?" Scott tried to look beyond him for signs of Betty inside the apartment.

Edward stared at Scott as if trying to decide. He looked so dejected, shoulders drooped, head held down, chest sunken in. Scott felt more like consoling him than hammering him about the lover who rejected him.

"She found someone else, didn't she? Where is she? Tell me where she is."

"She loves me, man I know she does," said Edward, hanging onto the door. He sounded like he needed to convince himself.

"I'm sure she does. Some women just don't realize what they want. Where is she?" Scott tried to say it as if he understood Edward.

"She's at her new dude's apartment. Two blocks from here. Come on in, I'll write down the apartment and directions for you." He opened the door wider and went to a room in the back.

Scott stepped just inside and looked around the college-like apartment with homemade furnishing, dirty clothing and food containers strewn about. He even thought he saw something crawling. Scott looked for a book, something that true college students should have, but didn't see one. Edward came out of the room with a piece of paper that he held out between them.

"You don't have to tell her that I said anything, do you?"

"I'll try to keep it quiet."

"Ah, what the hell. Here." He handed the paper to Scott.

Before he had a chance to change his mind, Scott took the paper.

"Thanks, man." When he got out on the landing, Scott turned around. "Hey, man. She messed up when she left you. She messed up." Scott turned around and started toward his car.

"Thanks, Dude."

Scott heard him say over his shoulder. He followed the directions on the paper that Edward had given him and drove the two rural blocks down to the apartment building marked with an "X." Scott saw lights on inside the apartment. His heart pounded so loud that he was certain that anyone for miles around could hear. Directly in front of him was the Mercedes-Benz that they had been looking for. The car. He quickly copied down the license number and wrote down a description of the dent in the rear of the car — as much as he could see — as well as took a picture with his phone. Then he called Haines and Charles.

Haines answered the phone and, commanded Scott to leave the area immediately. He notified Scott that the police would take over. Scott asked Haines what he planned to do and Haines informed him that he would contact the local police and have them tow the car back to Maryland and detain Betty until the morning when he and Charles would bring her back for questioning.

Scott called Cameron who must have been sitting by the phone waiting because he answered on the first ring.

"Are you all right, son?"

"I found her and the car."

"I'm coming right out."

"No, Dad. That's not necessary. Turns out she has a new boy friend who lives about two streets down. I'm sitting in front of his apartment now. The Mercedes is parked in the front and lights are on inside; somebody's home. I've already called Haines and Charles and they're sending the police out to take her in and have the car towed back to Maryland."

"How long will this take?"

"Haines said that the local police will hold her here overnight and when Haines and Charles get here in the morning, they will drive her back. I wish they could do this tonight."

"When are you coming home?"

"When they bring Betty back. I plan to stay here overnight."

"Son. "

"I'm fine, Dad. Really I am. I'll see you in the morning."

Scott sat and waited. Then the door to the apartment opened and two people came out. Scott sat up, cell phone ready, and put the key back in the ignition ready to follow them if he had to. When the two people came down the steps, he recognized the two women. He heard Mary and Sylvia argue about something that he couldn't make out. He heard Sylvia yelling at Mary, but couldn't make out what she said, either. He saw Mary start back in toward the apartment, but she turned around and looked out over the parking lot. Then she took one step down. Scott's heart stopped. He was sure she would see him. She knew his car; she had seen it before. Mary took another step down, now looking directly at Scott. He didn't move. It was dark where he was and too far away, he hoped. If he didn't move, didn't breathe, maybe she would think him a shadow in the dark. Then Mary came down the last step and held there looking in Scott's direction. She looked all around the parking lot, then turned and walked back up the steps. Scott let out a loud frantic sigh. She must have recognized his car. He couldn't come this far and mess up everything. That just couldn't be happening. He had a strong urge to get out of the car, grab Mary, stop her from going back into the apartment to warn Betty.

When Scott looked up at the apartment, he saw someone looking out of the window. Betty? Sylvia ran and grabbed Mary's arm and pulled her back toward the car. Mary screamed something at Sylvia. Sylvia let her go and yelled something back. She stormed off toward the car and Mary followed. Before either one opened the door, Scott scrambled to find a piece of paper to write down the license number of their car and the time. He took pictures with his cell phone, thinking he would need it later. He watched Sylvia and Mary drive off. Just before they pulled out of the lot, Scott saw Mary turn around.

Minutes later, two police cars entered the parking lot, one behind the other. Two officers got out of the first car, walked to the Benz. One officer looked inside the front and back of the car through the rolled up windows. One walked to the rear, checked the license number, and nodded to the other. Two officers got out of the second car, stood beside it.

Scott got out of his car and met the officers. He explained to them about the hit and run and that Haines and Charles were the officers assigned to his case. He also said that he had found out where Betty went to school and drove out to find her and the car. The officer in charge said that Detective Haines had already explained everything and asked Scott to keep out of the way.

Two officers went to the front door and knocked while two officers went around to the back of the apartment building. Scott watched and after a few minutes, the two officers brought Betty out in handcuffs. She squirmed and pulled away and finally broke loose. She ran down the steps onto the parking lot and headed directly toward the main street. Two officers ran after her and caught her as she got to the edge of the lot just before the jersey wall. They turned her around and headed her in the direction of the squad car where they placed her in the back seat. Betty's new boyfriend came out of the apartment and stood in the doorway watching.

The two officers who went in the back returned to the front and one called for a tow truck. Scott heard one officer ask another where to tow the car. In about twenty minutes, a tow truck came from the opposite end of the parking lot and pulled up behind Betty's car. A man got out and talked to the officer in charge who handed the truck driver a paper. The truck driver read it, stuck it in his jacket pocket, and hooked up Betty's car.

Betty's boyfriend again came out of the apartment, this time angry. He questioned the police and wanted them to take off the handcuffs until he had a chance to contact her parents. He had just tried to call them, but no one answered the cell phone. He told them that he was studying law and he knew that they couldn't do this to her. He demanded that they set her free and he especially wanted them to leave the car there. The officer who seemed to be in charge told him that they had orders to bring her in and that she was wanted for questioning in another state. He also told him that if he didn't back off they would let him sit beside her in the squad car where upon he calmed down and remained quiet.

By this time, the tow truck driver had the car on the bed and was ready to go. The truck driver led the way out of the parking lot and on to the main highway followed by the two police cars and then Scott. The officer in charge told Scott to go home, but there was no way he had planned to leave Betty. He followed the truck, and watched it head in the general direction of Maryland and trailed the two squad cars back to the police station where Betty would have to spend the night while waiting for Haines and Charles.

Just before dawn, Scott woke up and called his father again. He had actually slept in his car in the lot across the street from the police station. He thought that maybe they would be nice enough to let him stay there since they knew his story. The officer in charge didn't seem to be much older than he was. Scott wanted a cup of coffee from somewhere but was afraid to leave. He didn't know what time Haines and Charles would arrive, but based on what he knew about them, it could be afternoon before they did. Besides, all the businesses were still closed; too early for this sleepy town. He settled back to take his mind off his present situation. He didn't want to think about it. He didn't want to change his mind about Betty, about anything, so he didn't want to know what would happen next. He just wanted to feel good about finding the person who took his mother's life.

A knock on his window disturbed his thoughts. Scott rolled the window down.

"Thought I told you to go home," said the officer in charge. He handed Scott a cup of coffee and two donuts. "Our signature meal, if you know what I mean."

"Thanks. Just what I need." He took the breakfast.

"Detectives Charles and Haines called and said they should be here in about an hour. What are your plans?"

"Officer, I want to follow them back."

"Now, I'm not telling you that that's okay, you understand. But if I was to have to follow the police for any reason, I would stay far enough back so that they wouldn't pull me over for anything. You get my drift?"

"I do." Scott reached out the window to shake hands with the officer.

"If you need anything before they get here, there's a washroom around back. You head down that alleyway. It's marked, so you can't miss it." He pointed to the space between the police station and the coffee shop.

"Thanks, appreciate that."

"Good luck to you." The officer in charge whizzed back into the building just as quickly as he had appeared.

Scott settled back to drink his coffee and eat the donuts. He realized that for the first time in a long time he was hungry. He bit down into the sugar and buttery batter of the glazed donut and let it sink into his tongue, savoring its taste.

Chapter 28
Scott

Sylvia, Martin, Scott, and Cameron watched through a two-way mirror as Betty sat in the interrogation room staring down at the wooden table. She had asked to speak to Kathryn who was in another room where Haines and Charles, and Betty's attorney all prepped her. Betty's boy friend had called Sylvia and Martin who contacted a lawyer for Betty. As soon as the two officers brought Betty back to Maryland, the lawyer, Lyle Greene, appeared ready to protect the rights of his client. Yet Betty refused to talk to anyone, not even her lawyer, until she had had a chance to talk to Kathryn first.

When Kathryn was ready, she entered the observation room with the two-way mirror and sat beside Betty who never looked up.

"Are they watching us now?" asked Betty.

"Yes," said Kathryn.

"Can they hear everything we say?"

"Yes," said Kathryn.

Betty looked up at Kathryn, face tear stained. "Can we talk in private?" She looked like she was scared to death, like someone who had taken a fatal step only to realize that death was the only way out.

Kathryn got up and knocked on the door. Haines opened it and Kathryn stood outside in the hallway. The door of the observation room was open and Scott walked to the doorway. "Can you do that?" asked Kathryn.

"This is not a good idea," said Charles.

"We have to trust her," said Kathryn.

Charles looked at Haines, turned to Kathryn, and gave her a nod.

Kathryn opened the door walked back into the interrogation room and took her seat next to Betty at the wooden table.

"Wait a minute," Kathryn said.

In a few minutes, Martin opened the door and told them that everything was okay and that the speaker was turned off; they could talk freely. Martin closed the door and left.

Kathryn must have told Betty that even though the police turned off the intercom, they could still be seen because Betty looked up at the mirror. After a while, the two of them began to talk.

Before Kathryn went into the interrogation room with Betty, the two detectives tried to keep Scott and Cameron away from Martin and Sylvia, but Martin insisted that he and Sylvia needed to be in the observation room, the room with the one-way mirror, so that they would know what was going on with their daughter and step-daughter. Lyle Greene informed the two detectives that Martin was correct and thus, the room seemed to shrink in size as it held an air of uneasiness and tension lurking in the corners.

After about fifteen minutes, Kathryn got up and knocked

on the door again. An officer opened it and Kathryn entered the observation room. She told the group that Betty wanted to talk to Scott and Cameron. Sylvia objected and wanted to talk to her daughter, but Kathryn told her that Betty would not cooperate unless she had a chance to talk to Cameron and Scott first. Sylvia gave in. But, before he would allow that to happen, Lyle Greene asked to speak with Kathryn in private and they stepped outside the room into the hallway. When he re-entered the observation room, Lyle Green got everyone's attention to discuss the concern and the decision.

The detectives prepared the room. Charles brought in two more chairs and sat them at the table opposite Betty.

When they were ready, Scott and his father waited in the hallway between the observation room and the interrogation room. Scott took hold of Cameron's arm.

"You okay, Dad?" asked Scott as quietly as he could, stopping Cameron before they stepped inside the room. When Cameron turned to him, Scott felt something from his father. He couldn't decide whether it was anger, hatred, fear, or a combination. Scott realized that he kept his own feelings in a state of neutrality. Cameron didn't answer. They held a long stare, nervous and anxious. The fact that they were about to come face to face with and talk to the person who viciously ran down his mother and the person who had changed his father's life, almost caused him to break down in tears.

"Dad, if you want . . ." He wanted to spare his father of further heartache.

"It'll be rough, no doubt. You okay?" Cameron whisper back.

"I'll handle it. Dad, are you sure?"

"I have to do this, Son."

They smiled at each other, a smile that expressed love and togetherness. They walked into the interrogation room.

Kathryn sat on Betty's right, almost facing her. Betty looked up at Kathryn, wiped her hand on her pants, and then put a half-sweaty hand in Kathryn's hands. Scott and Cameron each took a chair across from Betty, their backs to the mirror. Scott gave a glance at Kathryn then at Betty. They all sat without talking for a few minutes. Scott could hear the hissing of the heating system and a cracking noise coming from the window behind Betty and Kathryn, the silence was so acute.

"Did you have something you wanted to tell us?" asked Cameron, breaking the silence. His voice sounded irritated, almost as if he couldn't take it anymore.

Scott watched his father. He was worried that his father would not be able to handle the interview. He wished Betty hadn't asked to speak to them.

"Betty has something that she wants to tell you both," responded Kathryn, looking at Betty who was still looking at the table. "Betty?"

"I just, I want . . . ." Betty began to cry as she struggled to get it out.

"Go ahead, Betty. Just like we talked about, remember? Go ahead," coaxed Kathryn.

Betty turned her head up and looked directly at Cameron, then Scott. "I just wanted you two to know what happened. It, it, it was an accident. We didn't get into a fight or anything. I didn't really know your mother, your wife." She nodded to each of them. "I went into the parking lot to look for Kat; sometimes I give her a ride home from her run when I want to talk to her. I was having trouble with my boyfriend and needed her advice. When I couldn't find her, I became frustrated and upset. I had to find her. I had to get her advice. When I discovered she wasn't there, I had to turn around so that I could drive out. My mind was on what I wanted to ask Kathryn. I wasn't paying attention. I tried to turn around. I didn't, please forgive me, please forgive me. I didn't know your mother was behind me. I wasn't paying attention and I thought I last saw her at the water fountain. When I backed up, I hit her car. I panicked and wanted to get out of there right away."

"But you backed into her, knocked her down, and rolled over her twice," said Cameron in a monotone voice that revealed the fact that he tried to control himself. He seemed to look clear of Betty.

"I didn't know she was behind me. I swear I didn't. I felt a bump, but I didn't know what that was. I thought it was something I'd hit on her car. I didn't think. I'm so sorry. Please forgive me, please. I didn't mean to hurt your mother, honest. If I could bring her back to you or exchange my life for hers, I would. Honest, I would."

Scott's eyes filled with tears as he listened to Betty describe what had happened. It infuriated him that she made the fact that she backed over his mother twice and took her life sound like an everyday occurrence like getting dressed, saying hello to someone, or eating, like nothing at all. "It's hard to forgive someone, who takes a life under careless circumstances."

Kathryn looked up at Scott with a surprise look on her face.

Scott looked at Cameron and saw that he was trying hard not to break down.

"I know, I don't deserve it. I know that. If you can't forgive me, I'll understand." She looked at Scott. "I know that Kathryn loves you and you love her and I've taken away your chances of being together...."

"Betty, that's enough. We didn't discuss this," said Kathryn.

"She's right. We didn't discuss this, but I feel like, not only have I taken away someone that you two loved and cherished, but I am also keeping you and Kathryn from being together. Please, don't blame her. She had no idea about any of this and I didn't tell her until she came in here earlier. I need you to understand that."

Cameron looked up at the ceiling then back down at Betty. "Thank you for telling us what happened. Forgiveness will take time." He stood to leave.

Scott stood.

"Please give Kathryn a chance," said Betty, reaching for Scott.

Scott pulled back. She took his mother's life, and in such a lackadaisical manner. Did she think that he would ignore this? Life with Kathryn would just continue to roll forward? Scott looked at Kathryn who had her eyes cast in her lap. He followed his father out of the room.

On the drive home, neither man spoke, each in his own cocoon. In fact, Scott was so engaged in his thoughts that he wasn't aware of the drive home. Betty's confession was puzzling to him. She had just told him that Kathryn had no idea what she'd done. Scott couldn't decide whether his not knowing that fact made things easier or harder. Now, that he knew the truth, that Kathryn was not involved, what's next? He was tired of thinking about it. His body and mind were so exhausted with this nightmare. He couldn't let Betty off the hook; she had taken his mother's life and she had to pay for that. He couldn't just excuse her because he was in love with Kathryn. What would that do to his father? For now, it was better for him to think about the upcoming school board meeting, something pleasant, something that took his mind away from the cruelty that surrounded his mother. He turned his head slightly to glimpse his father. He saw that his father had chosen to do the same thing. After all, his father was in the same interrogation and heard what Betty said, as he did.

Chapter 29
Scott

When Scott began his preparation for the meeting with the school board, he realized that he needed to do more research on the school board members and the superintendent. Then, he and Cameron set up a meeting in the school board office to discuss their hotel for teens. Scott convinced his father that if he could give the board members a better idea of how things would work, then they would be more eager to approve their plans. Scott and Cameron stood together before the ten-member board as they presented Laurie's vision of the school and her plans for implementing her vision. The board members all seemed to sit back in their high back thickly cushioned executive-style chairs, seemingly looking down on the two of them.

Sweat emerged on Scott's palms and beads formed on his forehead. The dim overhead fluorescent panel lights made the board members seem even farther away and Scott was reminded of the time that he and his father were standing on the beach in front of their beach home. The neighbor had his raft tied to his dock, but Scott pulled up the tether and the raft began to move. The water took him farther and farther out and Scott called out to his father. Scott remembered feeling smaller and smaller and almost gave up hope of his father saving him when he saw his father dive in the water and swim toward him. Scott looked at the board members sitting at the long horse shoe-style table. He gave off a light smile and swiped at his brow as he felt his father coming to save them again.

Cameron, speaking on behalf of his wife, saw the hotel as part of the school curriculum for students who wanted non-academic careers. Thinking about the times he went with his mother to the first teen home, Scott discussed using the hotel as a training facility. He had outlined their plans to have a beauty salon with a curriculum for hair and nails, a barber shop for men, a hotel management program, housekeeping, plumbing, heating, air conditioning; physical management training, cooking and chef programs for the students. The students who lived there would attend the neighborhood school, and would take the required classes of English, science, math and social studies. Students from the nearby high schools who were interested in the non-academic careers could also take training classes at the hotel. Cameron wanted the board to know that this would be an exchange of students and that he was not asking the board to allow only the kids from his hotel to participate. He emphasized that point when one of the board members, Brian Hodge, raised a question about that intent. The two requirements of the school board were to provide a bus to take the students back and forth and the qualified teachers for the subject areas.

When Brian Hodge, with the support of the superintendent, asked him about including a requirement to contact their parents letting the parents know that their run away teens were safe and living at the home, Cameron said that one of the requirements for a teenager staying in his home, as his wife required, would be that they would have to contact their parents. He also said that those who had parents or parents' who cared would want to know where their teen was and that they were safe.

Scott's nervousness held him back. Perspiration rolled down his face. He looked like he had just dunked his head underwater. He shook uncontrollably. He feared he would make a mess of things. Before he sat down and let his father handle the presentation, he stuttered, repeating things again, and again, and finally managed to inform the committee that many teens actually were kicked out of their homes and no one wanted them back. Cameron said that his wife wanted to show them that someone cared and he wanted to carry that out for her. Cameron also said that these teens had the right to a future and if they could establish this teen home, teens wouldn't have to sleep on the streets or get mixed up with drugs and prostitution. He pointed out that someone might even want to become a superintendent of schools. That seemed to generate a chuckle from some of the board members.

It seemed as though the superintendent and most of the board members were in favor of the proposal, especially since everything would be physically located in one place. The board said they needed to contact the parents and students in the county to find out how many students were interested in a program such as the one they were proposing, and they would need to look into hiring teachers. After a few moments of the board members huddling together and murmuring, they concluded that they needed further discussion on the matter. Scott didn't think that was a good sign, but he decided to keep it to himself, especially when he saw his father smile.

When Cameron and Scott left the meeting, they were convinced that the superintendent and board members would seriously consider their offer. At the very least, they all needed to display a positive front. After all, Cameron had invested all of the money and he was taking all the risks. All he wanted was for the diplomas to indicate that these kids had finished a program in a regular high school. Cameron said he thought that was a start for these students. Just before they left, the president of the school board told them that they would have an answer soon.

Cameron picked up his portfolio, other papers and put them in his satchel.

"I'm sorry," whispered Scott still seated. The look on his face was a combination of shame, fear, and fright, like the moment someone died unexpectedly, much like the look on his mother's face.

When Cameron turned around and saw the look on his son's face, he sat down beside him, took hold of his arm, held on to it as tightly as he could. He cleared his throat. "Maybe you tried to take on too much too soon."

"I wanted to —"

"I know, Scott. I know."

"You did it, Dad. Mom was always so proud of you." He searched his father's face, eyes for approval. "I don't know how you did it. I got so nervous, I couldn't speak."

"I've had practice, Scott. It takes a lot of practice to do something like that, keep your mind of what you want to say, as well as knowing how much time you have. If you want to know a secret, I was nervous, too. You stood up with me, supported me and you said something. I think you did okay."

Scott looked at Cameron and almost didn't recognize this change, this "new father." Then, maybe it was Scott who had changed, who was the new person.

Scott and Cameron returned to the office building where the employees crowded into Cameron's office throwing out one question after the other about the meeting. Scott looked up and saw not only June, Cameron's secretary, but Cameron's department heads, assistants, one man whose job was to seek out property. Scott never knew his name. He looked around and saw that every employee had come to work on that day. Cameron came around to the front of his desk and sat on the edge. Scott stood at the side of the desk facing the group.

"I don't know what to say," began Cameron. He looked over at Scott. "I think we're making improvement, but we don't have them yet. What do you say, Scott?"

"I'd say that's pretty much right on target. We have a little more convincing to do."

"Maybe we need Jason. He can convince the IRS to give him two income tax refunds."

The employees laughed, remembering the joke that spread throughout the office. Scott laughed, too, even though he really didn't know why.

The telephone rang and Cameron turned to his desk to answer it.

After they had spoken last, Max stayed up all night organizing and arranging the work. He brought in all of his workers and asked both the plumbing and electrical companies with whom he subcontracted to send in as many of their workers as they could spare. Scott heard Cameron say he and Scott would stop by the hotel to see the renovation so far.

The next afternoon, they pulled up into the hotel parking lot. Cameron couldn't understand why there were so many cars, and why they had to search for a parking space. As soon as they entered the lobby, they were surprised to see so many workers. Two men were painting the lobby walls a beige color, one man was using a machine on the floors on the other side, and one man was on an extended rolling ladder doing something to the ceiling while another man stood below yelling out orders. As they moved through the hotel, they saw other people who weren't wearing uniforms, men and women, cleaning and scraping walls and floors and painting. Cameron sought out Max who was on the second level handing out orders. Max looked up and saw Cameron and Scott.

"Isn't it something?" asked Max.

"What's going on? There are over a hundred people here," said Cameron.

"Two hundred and one, to be exact," said Max, a big smile on his face.

"Cameron, you won't believe what's happening. Somehow, the community got word of your project and they've come out to help. Isn't this amazing? In all the years that I've been a contractor, I've never seen anything like this."

Just then, a man wearing old clothes and a white baseball cap, interrupted. "We're finished with our room. What do we do next?"

Cameron extended his hand to the man. "Hello. I'm Cameron Kersey. This is my son, Scott. We want to thank you so much for donating your help to us. I don't know when I've seen anything like this before. We appreciate your every effort."

He took Cameron's hand. "You're welcome. It's time someone tackled that school system and offered a program more suitable for the students. My son always wanted to be a mechanic, but the schools didn't offer enough courses for him to do that."

Max pointed him in the direction to one of the professional workers.

"Thanks, again," yelled out Scott as the man left.

Cameron and Scott watched the volunteers and workers scurry around, moving from job to job and asking how to do things.

"This is amazing," said Scott.

Max walked Cameron and Scott back down to the entrance. "You just leave things to us," Max said. "Oh, and I brought in all my crew, but the price tag is the same. It's nice to know that somebody will be looking after our children. I have three teenagers and if they ever decided to leave home, I would hope that they would come to a place like this."

"If they ever decide to leave home, you tell them to come here. We'll take good care of them," said Cameron. On the way back to his car, he took out his cell phone and ordered lunch and snacks for two hundred and two people.

Chapter 30
Kathryn

The sewing machine buzzed and stopped buzzed and stopped and Kathryn having a time concentrating, looked up at the seamstress each time the machine stopped annoyed by the distracting noise. She looked at Kathryn and smiled at her and Kathryn feigned a smile back. The shop grew smaller each time they had a show to do and Kathryn needed space to think. She finally decided to put her patterns away in her portfolio with the hope she would have another opportunity to display her line.

She saw that she had no other choice. She would have to tell Frankie when he came in, that she couldn't spoil things for him, and that she would have to bow out. The picture of Betty in the interrogation room along with Scott's face as he sat across the table, plagued her and no matter how hard she tried, she couldn't remove either picture from her mind. As much as she wanted to be a part of Frankie's show, she couldn't defame him. Surely, the news about Betty would be in the newspapers. Since they were stepsisters, people would always look at her as if she had something to do with Betty's crime. Someone was bound to connect her with Betty and then Frankie would be caught up in the chaos. Kathryn had hoped that one day she would be famous, watch the models wear her styles down the runway, people clapping and murmuring to each other about how beautiful her clothes were. She didn't see how that could happen now.

"Day dreaming about your stardom?" asked Frankie, carrying an armful of bags.

Kathryn jumped when she saw Frankie standing in front of her. "Frankie. I didn't hear you come in."

He looked at her as he put the bags down on a nearby table. "What's wrong?"

"Nothing, why?"

"You look like you just saw a ghost," said Frankie letting out a little chuckle.

Kathryn held a space of silence.

His face became serious. "There is something wrong," he said.

"Frankie, I can't do the show on Saturday." Kathryn saw no need to beat around the bush.

"Why? I know I'm not giving you enough time or help. Look girl, I forgot that this was your first time. Tell me what you want me to do."

"No, it's not that. Something's happened," said Kathryn.

"Girl, one minute you're worrying the hell out of me —"

"My sister is in jail," blurted out Kathryn, tears easing down her face. The person who ran down Scott's mother was my step-sister, Betty."

"Oh, honey. What happened?" He sat down beside her.

Kathryn filled Frankie in on everything including what Scott said in the interrogation room. She cried harder when she told Frankie about Scott and where that left them.

"How can I show my face to either of those two men? I have to pull out of the show. I have no choice. I can't do this to you."

Frankie reached over and gave her a long hug.

"It's also hard trying to face my father who had so much faith and trust in me," said Kathryn after her tears subsided.

"Why? I'm sure he wouldn't have expected you to know how to fix Betty."

"Frankie, I still have to quit the show. Once people find out about Betty and that I work here, that'll be the end of you. I love you too much to let something like that happen to you."

"First, I'll decide that, if you don't mind. Besides, I'm pretty well established. Sure I want to climb a little higher and I will."

"And you thought that I could help with that as well as get myself out there," Kathryn suggested.

"Kat, this show Saturday is a door opener for you. I think if you don't do this now you never will. Besides, you really don't know about Betty. It could be that no one will find out, connect Betty to you, or me, or even care about that for that matter."

"I don't think I should take that chance."

"I think you're worrying over nothing, but, Kat, I love you for thinking about me. You just do the show for now and we'll deal with what's to come later, if anything comes of this."

When Michelle came in later, Frankie asked her to help Kathryn select the outfits that would represent her and that would keep up with Frankie's quality. Kathryn wanted her name changed, just in case. She insisted on it. Michelle called the printer and had Kathryn's name changed on all the programs.

"Darlin' you're doing it, now," said Frankie when he saw the things that Kathryn and Michelle selected.

The ringing phone startled her and she sat looking at it as if she couldn't believe it was actually ringing. Holding her breath, Kathryn picked it up.

"Hi, Sweetheart," said Martin.

She slowly exhaled. "Daddy. Is everything okay? What's going on? You don't often call in the middle of the day like this."

"Everything is okay. I just wanted to know how you're holding up."

"I'm okay."

"Sweetheart, whatever happens, I want you to go ahead with your show and stick with fashion designing."

"You think so? Even now?"

"Yes, without a doubt. Kat, honey, don't take that on. I know you and I know you feel like you're in the middle of all this and that you should drop out of the show. But, I don't want you to do that, okay?"

Kathryn didn't answer.

"Kat? Promise me you won't drop out or give up fashion."

"Daddy. I love you. I promise."

"Wow! I love you too, Sweetheart." Martin was quiet for a while.

"If I'm going to stay in the show, I have work to do, okay?"

Martin didn't answer.

"Daddy?"

"Sweetheart, I moved out of the house. I told Sylvia that we would move all of our things out sometime this week after your show. I'll drop the key off and the address to the townhouse later today. I know you're busy now."

"No, you can't do this."

"Yes, I can and I have."

"Are you sure? I know you care for Sylvia. Don't do this. If you love her don't do this."

Martin didn't respond.

"Are you sure?"

"Yes, I am sweetheart. We're not careless people."

"I see you're bothered by that, too."

"Sweetheart, I hope that had that been you, you would have had the decency to get out of your car and see what you might have hit. To back into something and pull away without checking is so much more than careless."

"I know. You're right. I would have gotten out of the car to see what I hit and tried to help. I love you Daddy. You're the best father in the world."

"Finish your work. See you sweetheart."

Chapter 31
Scott

Scott finally made himself call his sister, Becky and asked to see her. He was surprised that she was eager to see him, which made him nervous. Maybe she thought that it was time for him to own up about her and their mother and she intended to give him a piece of her mind. He drove up to Pennsylvania and took a cab to her hospital. He hadn't been to her hospital since she was a resident, but the hospital had made a few changes since that time. As he entered the stately building, he supposed that Becky was a much-needed surgeon now or at least on her way to being one. He tried to remember what he had heard his father say about her being in demand.

When he arrived at her floor, a nurse told him that Dr. Kersey was called into surgery earlier that morning and she had requested that Scott wait on her in the hospital waiting room. She said she didn't know how long he would have to wait. He whiled away the time sitting in the waiting area trying to work on a short story, but ended up watching the nurses. He listened to one nurse who was on the phone and seemed to be trying to calm down someone on the other end. He heard the nurse say that the patient was no longer in the hospital. That must have sent off an alarm.

About the time she hung up, two other nurses carrying plastic food containers and one with a lunch bag, walked through the door, both laughing. He tried to guess why three older women and two older men in the waiting area needed to see a doctor. His sister was a heart surgeon and this was the heart wing so, he reasoned that they were waiting because they had some kind of heart problem. He picked up a magazine, flipped through a few pages, and placed the magazine back on the table. He was too nervous to concentrate on one thing and when he tried to think about how he would start the discussion, he couldn't think of anything to say. He put away his short story and began to think that Becky would think him silly for coming all this way to talk about something that he couldn't express. Scott knew how important this was to him, a step he had to take. So, he stayed and he had hoped that Becky would understand and would help him through this. After all, she was a doctor. It was her job to help people. In about an hour, the phone at the nurse's reception desk rang. The nurse told Scott that Dr. Kersey would be out in a few minutes.

When Becky came out she was wearing scrubs and Scott gave his sister a smile that extended across his face as he stretched out his arms, all apprehension vanished now. She introduced Scott to the nurses letting them know he was single. They walked down to the doctor's lounge where she changed clothes. When they entered the lounge, Becky went to her locker to get her street clothes. She smiled at him as she took her clothes and went behind a portable screen where she changed. Scott guessed that there was no men's or women's room. Just as he was about to pick up an article of clothing, sitting on a table in the middle of the room, Becky called out to him from behind the portable screen. "Don't touch anything in here. People get grouchy about their stuff."

Scott pulled his hand back and looked around the room as if he thought he someone was watching him. Maybe Becky saw him through the screen. He looked toward her and saw that she was still behind the heavy screen. He never thought about a break room for doctors. He thought they were always working. He imagined the half-filled coffee pot and pictured doctors entering the lounge, filling in around the table and drinking coffee while people outside bled to death. He shook his head to get rid of that picture and his sister came out from behind the portable door all dressed and ready to go.

"I have to say that this is a really nice surprise," Becky said leading the way out of the room. Just when he thought he was calming down, her comment made him nervous all over again.

~~~~~~~~~~

Becky opened the door to her townhouse and Scott followed her to the living room, which didn't seem to fit the lively Becky he knew. The living room and connecting dining room were plain, lacking life, out-of-date rental furniture. She went to her phone to take down messages while Scott walked through the dining area to the sliding glass doors that led to the yard. Scott watched two boys in the yard next door throwing a ball back and forth until one boy dropped the ball. Beyond the yard a sidewalk where several mothers, dressed in coats and jackets, pushing baby carriages walking and taking their babies for air. Scott saw mothers on the sidewalk with heavy coats, headscarves, and mittens and he suddenly realized the winter they were having was a cold bitter one. He hadn't noticed, and for a few minutes, he couldn't remember whether he'd worn his coat each time he'd gone out into the cold air. He touched his coat and saw that he had worn one this day. Winter would soon be gone and taken over by the colors of spring, where all the dried out old weeds would be forgotten and new healthy flowers and greenery would suddenly appear. For a moment, he was frightened. He didn't want to forget his mother. He would allow himself to forget the ugly thing that happened to his mother, but he would never forget her.

"How about a pizza?" asked Becky.

"Fine," said Scott turning to face Becky.

"Good. I ordered one while we were at the hospital. Give me your coat and have a seat. We can catch up."

"You like living in Pennsylvania?" He handed her his coat and took a seat on the couch.

"Sure. I have to say that I spend most of my time at the hospital." She hung up his coat in the closet. Then she walked to the kitchen.

Scott could see part of the kitchen from where he sat in the living room and he saw her open the cabinet, take out a bottle of wine and then put it back. He got up and walked to the kitchen. "Could I get a glass of water? For some reason, I'm really thirsty."

"I think I'll have some too." Becky filled two tall glasses with ice and tap water.

Scott walked back to the living room and sat down on the couch again.

Becky brought the two glasses of water and took a seat in the wing chair to his right. "I thought James would come by for a few minutes. I wanted you two to meet."

"Tell me all about James. Who is he? When did you meet? Where did you meet? How long have you two been an item?" He chuckled.

"Scott. Geeze. You came here to talk. I don't want to take up the time about me."

"I know, but I want to know about James. Tell me about James."

"Okay, if you don't mind. I'll start from the beginning. James is an anesthesiologist. He works in the hospital with me. He's been working at the hospital for about ten years. He was married for eight years and got divorced about two years ago. We met about a year ago when his supervisor took a job at another hospital. She was very popular and the entire hospital threw her a huge party. We met at the party, and we've been dating for about a year." Becky's mood changed from happy and playful to something more serious. "He still has his apartment, and sometimes he wants to stay with me for a while. I allow it, but I'm not sure if I should or not. I don't want to push him into anything. He has to make up his own mind and I understand that he wouldn't want to rush into anything after his divorce." She looked up at Scott. "I'm going on and on about myself. I'm sorry. You're just too easy to talk to."

"That's okay. Go ahead," said Scott.

"Well, his divorce was hard on him. He said that he hadn't planned on a divorce, but he caught his wife with someone else. She couldn't get used to the idea that he worked in a hospital, I guess. Anyway, according to him, he never dated after his divorce until he met me."

"What do you think? Is he still in love with his wife?" asked Scott.

"You know, I think about that often and I feel hurt when I do." She paused for a moment as she looked down at her feet. "I don't know for sure. He doesn't talk about her or his marriage and I won't bring it up. Sometimes I think that he still loves her. Other times I think he's just afraid he'll get hurt again. What do you think?"

"It's hard to 'unlove' someone even when something that serious happens. Once we get hurt we tend to pull out the armor, shield ourselves from the pain."

"So, he keeps going back and forth. That's his armor," said Becky.

"It sounds like you're in love. Since you know his history, I'd say proceed with caution. It looks like you're doing that. Just don't expect what he's not willing to give. The more he sees he can trust you, the more he'll give. Patience, my dear, patience."

"And that's spelled, p-a-t-i-e-n-c-e, not p-a-t-i-e-n-t-s."

They laughed.

"Oh, funny," said Scott. "I'm the comedian, remember?"

"You're right, baby brother. But you came here to talk. Tell me what you want to talk about."

He took a sip of water. "I'm finding it hard to begin. So, I just want to jump right in."

There was a knock on the door and Becky, held up one finger motioning for Scott to give her a minute to answer the door.

Scott stood up to stop her and pulled out some money for the pizza.

Becky smiled at him and paid the pizza man. She closed

the door and the two sat down again. Becky looked up at him, another smile on her face. "Continue," she said.

"I came here to apologize to you. I really wish I could take the day back, start all over again."

"What day are you talking about?" She reached in the box and took a slice of pizza, pulling a string of cheese.

He took her question as a caution sign and he drew his body in, stiffened. "You were twelve and I was ten and we were coming from the library. We walked along the street about two blocks from home and ran into two boys from the middle school. We were trying to get home and they, and they . . . ."

"Grabbed me and pushed me into the bushes." Becky finished his statement, but she sounded so mechanical and her smile was gone.

"Yes. You remember then?" He reached in the box and took a slice of pizza.

"Yes, Scott. I remember. What about that day?" She took a sip of water.

Scott placed his pizza back in the box, looked down in his lap. He thought he heard caution in her voice, again. "Yes. They, anyway, I just want to say I am so sorry for letting you down. I should have done more to protect you. I was so scared that I let my fear stop me from helping you."

"Scott, look at me."

Scott looked over at his sister.

"It was because of you that nothing happened. You kicked, and screamed, and did everything humanly possible. Don't you remember?"

Scott's face formed a question.

"Two boys held you, they were fourteen and fifteen, high

school, not middle school boys and you were only nine not ten, almost ten, but still nine. You kicked the hell out of one of the boys. He was so bad off, he couldn't run. I think you might have fractured his leg or something. They beat you all in the face and stomach when you wouldn't stop screaming for help. You tried to get loose and sprained your arm very badly in the process. We thought it might have been broken. When I looked over and saw how badly your face looked all bloody and all, I tried to yell for you to shut up so that they would leave you alone. One of them had his hand over my mouth. It was because of your yelling and screaming that brought Jack and his friends. I really don't think they would have found us if you hadn't. What do you have to apologize for?"

"Becky, no. I did nothing. They were two middle school boys. One was, was with you and the other with me. I just stood there and let it all happen. You did the yelling."

"Don't you remember that you couldn't go to school for almost a week because of your eye? Mom and Dad took you to the eye doctor and you had to wear a patch for a week."

"I remember the eye patch, but that was from something else," Scott paused for a moment, searching, thinking back. He took a bite of the pizza and put the remainder in the box.

Becky got up and sat beside Scott on the couch took his hands.

He relaxed.

"Let's see if you still have that scar under your lip." She looked hard until she saw something. "Here is where that scar used to be under your lip. Don't you remember how I put medicine on it for you and had you keep ice on it?"

"Yes, but wasn't that from . . . ."

Becky shook her head. "Scott, I was the one scared. I was so scared that those boys would rape me. But you saved me. I was so proud of you and so thankful to you. Don't you remember how I nursed you back to health? Remember how I used to say that all the time?"

"All these years and I remembered it wrong?"

"I think you thought that since they were holding you that you couldn't do anything and imagined that you weren't helping. Scott there were four high school boys."

They each bit into their pizza, lost in their reminiscence.

"Do you remember what dad did? Jack knew the boys and told Dad what happened. Don't you remember, Scott?"

"No. I guess not."

"When we got home, mom was horrified when she saw you. She drove you to the hospital and made Jack and me come too. While we were there, she called Dad. He came rushing over and when he saw your face, he became enraged. 'Who would do anything like that to my children?' He kept yelling in the hospital. Even Mom couldn't calm him down. After the doctor saw you, Dad made Jack tell him everything. I was embarrassed and wanted to keep it quiet. But Dad saw it differently. He found out the boy that put his hand that, well, he and Jack went to the boy's house. His father answered the door and dad said that he wanted to speak to his son. Dad saw the boy inside the house coming to the door. He pushed passed the father and walked up to the boy. Before anyone knew what had happened, he had the boy's pants down, grabbed hold of his crotch, and didn't let it go.

"That boy stood still and let him do that?" asked Scott.

"That's what Jack said. The boy was scared to death. Jack said that his eyes almost bulged out of his head when he looked down and saw Dad holding on to him. Dad asked the boy how it felt to have someone violate him. He turned to the father and said, 'Your son touched my daughter, stuck his hand up her dress. Then he turned back to the boy and said, 'You weren't going to try to stick this thing in my daughter were you?' Jack said he told the father not to do anything to make the situation worse, so the father stood still. Dad told the man that if his son ever came near his daughter again that he would take him to court and have him labeled as a serious sex offender. Then Dad and Jack walked out of the man's house. We never heard from the family of the boy you kicked. Dad said later that the families must have gotten together and decided not to do anything. Dad told us that he was proud of us and how we all stood together, during that time. He told me not to be ashamed and that it wasn't my fault. He told you that you had protected me. Don't you remember? That's when I stopped calling you my baby brother. You actually saved me from a life time of therapy and maybe a personality disorder."

"A personality disorder? Really, Becky?"

They laughed.

"Dad kicked butt?"

"Dad really kicked some butt that day," said Becky.

Scott fell silent. He sat back on the couch lost in thought, recalling the past.

"Is that what's been bothering you?"

He nodded. "It's been on my mind a long time. What happened to them?"

"Scott, you don't remember any of this?"

"I guess not. Not this version anyway."

"Dad wanted to drop everything. After he came from that boy's house, he and mom told me that they decided not to press charges or anything like that. Dad was afraid that I'd carry a mental scar from the experience. Mom wanted me to forget the whole ordeal. Just as things were getting back to normal, dad got a phone call from a lawyer. It seemed as though the boys had done it to another girl, but this girl wasn't fortunate enough to have two brothers to fight for her. They raped her. Her parents pressed charges and somehow they found out about me. They wanted me to testify on behalf of the girl."

"I remember that. I remember you had to go to court for something."

"I agreed to testify but only if they would leave you out of it."

"Why Becky? Why would you take that on yourself?"

"I thought you'd been through enough. Scott, you got the worse of everything. The only thing that happened to me was that a boy pulled my pants down. They beat you, brutally. If anyone should feel guilty, it should be me. I was scared I didn't think you'd ever see again out of your eye."

"Oh, Becky."

"I went and testified. The boys went to jail. You know, there's a memory from that day that just won't leave me. It was after the trial, dad pulled the car to the front, and we got into our car. The father, of the boy who dad confronted, the one with his pants down, stood in front of the courthouse just looking at dad. I was in the back seat and when I peeped out on the driver's side, I saw dad just standing there looking back at him. It was like some unspoken message that these two men secretly passed back and forth at that time. I can imagine that he was thanking dad for giving his son a chance and sad by the fact that his son didn't take the chance."

"I should have been there."

"No. I just wanted to give back to you, to spare you."

Scott looked around the room. "I miss mom so much."

"Me too, Scott. I called her every week no matter what and after I called, you know, I forgot."

"Yes, I know. Several times I've gone to her room or in the great room to look for her."

"Dad answered the phone on those times just as I remembered she wasn't there anymore and I wanted to hang up. I hated myself for making him think about her. Somehow, he sensed it and told me that it was okay for me to call. He said he wanted me to call him every week."

"Dad is really hurting. He means it," said Scott.

"When we were young, and even up to the time I was in high school, I used to think that if you told mom something that she wouldn't share it with dad. I see now that they told each other everything, especially anything about us. I guess that's why I always felt close to dad even when he couldn't be with us," said Becky.

"That's true, isn't it?" said Scott. "I remember something about Dad going to that boy's house and pulling down his pants, but I only overheard parts of the conversation. Everyone got quiet when I came in the room. When I asked about it, Mom always said 'Nothing'. Maybe that's why I felt like I'd let you down." He looked at her as if her face had alerted him to something new. "You know, we never talked about this. How are you about all this?"

"At first I was embarrassed, ashamed I had led those boys on some kind of way. When Dad went to that boy's house, I realized that I didn't do anything. They were looking for trouble that day and thought we were easy prey."

They fell silent.

Scott couldn't understand what happened, why he didn't remember. He pressed his mind to recollect what happened and little by little, some of the facts, though scattered, began to come back to him. Becky got up and refilled their water glasses. Scott took his glass when she returned. He took another bite of his pizza slice.

"What does this have to do with mom?" She took another slice of pizza, sat back and crossed her legs.

Scott looked up at her with a start. "How did you know?"

"I didn't until now."

Scott looked at Becky, outside beyond the yard at the people walking, and around the room. "She came in my room on that morning and tried to wake me up to run with her. I pretended like I was asleep." He looked at her for a moment, then at the pizza, at the people on the street outside again and back at Becky. He cleared his throat. His eyes filled with tears. "See, I let that happen, too."

"No you didn't. You can only be responsible for yourself. You can't beat yourself up for something that you couldn't help. You can't make something happen to someone else and you can't stop something from happening to someone else. That's just the way the world is. You have always been the best little brother a sister could ask for and what I needed that day was just beyond your scope. Still, you did what you were able to do and that's all anyone could ever ask. As far as mom is concerned, how could you stop a car from hitting her? You could have gone running with her, stepped away for some reason, maybe to get water and the car still could have hit her. Scott you can't blame yourself. You could not have stopped that any more than you could have stopped those boys. Mom always saw good in people. Maybe she saw the accident coming, but still thought the driver had everything under control. You can't beat yourself up about that. You can't drink to make something that never happened, go away."

They were silent for a while before Becky asked, "What would you have done if you had been there?"

He looked at her, now realizing that what he held in his mind no longer made sense, but he needed to say it out-loud as if saying it out-loud would sanction the thought. "If I'd been there, we would have left right away. She wouldn't have talked to anyone in the parking lot and she wouldn't have been there for anyone to back into her." He nodded as if to say "that's it" that's what would have happened and there was no way that could change.

"Now, Scott. Have long have you known Mom? Do you mean to say that Mom never stopped to talk to anyone in the parking lot after her run, and especially with you?"

"Becky, don't —"

"No, Scott. You have to face things. You just can't do that to yourself. You wanted to make yourself believe that, didn't you? Think about it. Mom was a social person, someone who cared about people. Do you really believe that she didn't always ask people how they were doing and ask how she could help? I know when I ran with her she talked to everybody all the time. I was always ready to go and she wanted to talk."

Scott looked at Becky as if she'd snatched his soul right out from him. He crossed his arms, hugged himself; he was feeling so vulnerable. He realized that his mother always had to talk to someone in the parking lot or at the entrance, or even on the trail. Even if he had been there, he couldn't have stopped what happened. He remembered that in order to get her to wind up her conversation, he would get in the car and he would hear her tell her friend that her son was ready to head back.

Scott sat back on the couch. He remembered the poem by Edgar Allan Poe and the last line "that ever died so young." He realized that Becky had gone on with her life. When his mother told him that there were different kinds of dying, he realized now that she didn't mean burial was the only kind of death. People die every day over a loss job, a loss love, a loss of something. He saw that dying meant destroying yourself, giving up, giving up on yourself and on life. Becky hadn't done that. She became a doctor, and a good one at that. Scott had given up. He promised his mother that he would take care of himself and he had to start keeping his promise. He had to be alive to do that; the kind of alive that meant living a good life, having a career, falling in love, having children, being a part of the world.

~~~~~~~~~~

On the drive back, he tried to recall everything that Becky said that happened and realized he had tried to help. He remembered the swollen eye and lip and the entire side of his face. He remembered how Becky nursed him every day. Thinking back now, she must have felt guilty thinking it was her fault he was so badly hurt. He tried so hard to keep his sister safe and in the process, thought he wasn't doing enough. He thought he had allowed those boys to take advantage of her because he was too afraid to stop them.

Becky was right. He took a brutal beating from those boys for trying to help his sister and the more he tried to help her, the more they beat him. He didn't let her down or let his father down. All these years, he thought he'd let down his sister and his father who felt strongly that the men in the family had to protect the women. Becky was also right about his mother. He didn't let her down either. He realized he was already the man he thought he wasn't. His father had been trying to tell him all along. He had spent so many years fighting against himself thinking he was not reliable and pushing people away from him. It was time now for him to begin believing in himself. It was time for him to start living.

~~~~~~~~~~

When he pulled into the driveway, he saw the "For Sale" sign looming in the yard. He noticed the lights on in the front on two floors. As he entered, he saw the realtor showing the house to a young couple in their early 30s. The woman looked happy and he overheard her say how beautiful the kitchen was and how convenient it was to have a family room right off the kitchen. Scott felt resentment as he realized this woman or some woman would take the place of his mother – the woman who designed the kitchen and family room and the entire house – in this house and that woman would change things around. Then there would be no physical effects left of his mother.

Chapter 32
Kathryn

Of all the regrets that Kathryn had about herself none was larger than the regret she had of not taking that final sewing class, the one that would have given her pointers on how to sew a straight seam and make the dress look like there was no seam. Frankie had hired only one dressmaker and she was busy with last minute changes to his clothes. Kathryn knew she needed to be as far ahead as possible, but up until now, all she had succeeded in doing was stabbing herself with the needle as she hand sewed the tiny fasteners. She did take the class that suggested doing something by hand and liked that idea. She could see that hand sewing the fasteners gave it that special personal touch. She knew she had to work more rapidly, kept telling herself to move faster and tried to keep pace with the clock on the wall, but no matter how hard she tried she wasn't able to pick up her speed.

In the past, when she had helped Frankie get his shows ready, there were always needed changes to the dresses. Frankie's show during Kathryn's first year with him surprised her. She had always thought from the time she was a little girl that each model had such a perfect body that surely those bodies would fit any dress. During her first year with Frankie, Kathryn soon discovered that no one's body was perfect even though it was supposed to look that way when the model walked down that runway. So actually, a size two had many different sizes.

"Okay, you won't get that done by daydreaming," she heard from behind her.

"Frankie, you have to stop doing that. How long have you been standing there?"

"You're moving a little slow, aren't you?" said Frankie. He walked over to a rack of clothes, pulled off the plastic clothes bag that covered the rack, let it drop to the floor. He slid each dress, blouse, pants, and jacket across the bar so that he could look at each of them individually.

"Are those the things you're showing?" asked Kathryn.

"Yes. How're you coming with yours?" He looked over his shoulder at her, head bowed and looking out of the tops of his eyes as he pushed the clothes along the rack.

"I'll be ready. Theresa," she pointed to the dressmaker in the corner, whizzing away on the sewing machine, "finished most of them." She held up the pants. "See, I'm working on them now, adding final touches." She laid the pants in her lap.

"Kat . . . ." began Frankie. He turned to her.

Just then, the phone rang and Frankie got up to answer it. "Hi, Harris. . . . Yes, she's right here. Just a minute."

Frankie handed the phone to Kathryn, made a funny face, shook his head. He left the studio.

Kathryn took the phone and took a deep breath.

"Hi Harris. . . Dinner? . . . Tonight? . . . Sure. . . . What time? . . . See you then."

Kathryn sat back in her chair. She needed to get the dressmaker to finish making the last item, and they worked until almost time for her dinner date with Harris. When she held up her dress, pants and jacket she was even amazed at the quality of her designs, the material that she picked for each because it would wear well, the color, the pattern, the stitching, and her signature label. She hung them and looked at the three items completed so far. She realized that they were really good, like the clothes created by well known designers. She's going to be a "real" designer one day soon.

~~~~~~~~~~

Kathryn was outside the store, and on her way to the sidewalk, when she saw Harris pull up. He got out and met her just before she reached the curb.

"Hi Harris," Kathryn greeted him. Out of habit she kissed him on the cheek and then wrinkled her face; she didn't want to do that.

"Hi Beautiful," said Harris. "You ready?"

Kathryn looked into his eyes. He always asked her that even when it was obvious that she was ready. This time the question was a door opener for her. "Actually, Harris, can we just sit and talk for a minute?" She walked toward the car; he followed.

"Sure." He opened the car door for her and helped her in.

She watched him walk around to the other side and get in. Her stomach began to tighten as he pushed his seat back, crossed his arms, and rested his head against the headrest.

"What's up?" He kept his eyes toward the car ceiling.

"I . . ." She looked over at him. When she saw that he

wouldn't look at her, she lost all confidence. It was always so hard to tell someone unpleasant news when they expected to hear it. She almost hated the fact that he expected the conversation. She tried to think of something else, but she couldn't. Maybe another way to say what she had to tell him; anything but what he expected. Before she could get anything out, he spoke.

"I know. You're gonna say that you're tired and you want to just go home and rest. If that's what you want that'll be okay."

She felt as if he was giving her that to say, a way out because he didn't want to hear it. "Really, what —"

"No, if you want to do this tomorrow, we can. In fact," he sat up, pulled his seat forward, and started the car, "where's your car. I'll take you to your car and we can just do this tomorrow, or sometime next week. Okay?"

"Harris, stop. I have to tell you something and you're not making it easy for me." She held onto the door handle.

"I know."

"Harris, I'm not ready to get married. I liked what we had before, where we just saw each other every now and then, no commitment, no expectation. I liked that. What we're doing, now, well, I don't think I can continue the commitment. I'm not ready and I'm not the girl for you. The fashion world may be opening up for me and I don't want it to pass me by. I have a chance and I want to take that chance."

Harris sat silent for a few minutes.

"You knew, didn't you?" asked Kathryn.

"I suspected it when you said that Frankie was letting you show some of your things in his show."

"I'm sorry, Harris, but I have to think about Frankie He's

taking a huge risk and I have to prove to him and to me that he's doing the right thing. This is my life's dream. I don't think marriage is for me, at least, not right now."

"How much of this has to do with that other guy?"

"What other guy?"

"You know who I'm talking about. We've talked about this before. You can do both, put on your show and get married. Your show is Saturday. We don't have to get married until next summer."

"Harris, once Frankie allows me this, he'll do it again and then before you know it, I'll have my own studio or my own line out of his studio. This is just the beginning for me. You know that. Besides, Harris, I'm not the right girl for you."

"So when you say marriage is not for you now, you really mean we're not right for each other. Are you sure, Kat?"

"Yes. You know it, too." She took off the ring and handed it back. He wouldn't take it so she laid it on the dashboard. "I have to go." She opened the door and got out.

She felt Harris watching her as she left.

That didn't go as badly as she had thought it would. In fact, she thought he would have been more upset about things than he was. He knew that once she got this chance she wouldn't give it up. She's told him that often enough. She didn't want to talk about Scott. Harris didn't need to know about him.

Chapter 33
Scott

Scott sat at his computer, his fourth short story on the screen. He turned away from creating his character and plot and reasoned that he had seen the advertisements of Frankie's fashion show in the store and even seen them outside in the mall. His father did own the mall and the store in it and it was likely that he would see the flyers, he reasoned further. He knew the manager of the Hyatt and could get in without anyone seeing him. When he saw the advertisement, he was thrilled about Kathryn being in Frankie's fashion show. He recalled how excited she was about the fashion world and how desperately she wanted to have her own show. He knew this would be a start for her, and even after everything that had happened, he wanted to be there.

~~~~~~~~~~

The show, Frankie's spring line, and titled "Vivacity," was filled with big designers. Scott thought he recognized Oleg Cassini, Vera Wang, who Kathryn adored and Tommy

Hilfiger, but maybe he had hoped that they would have been present. His friend had helped him get in, like he had expected, and Scott sat along the side near the back, and unnoticed. A lavender curtain separated the models and the staging area from the audience and was decorated with what looked like baby blue, violet, yellow, and pale green streamers. Across the top of the curtain loomed "Designs by Sans".

When the show began, the lights dimmed so that only the runway was lit up with footlights. Scott saw how the audience "oohed" and "aahed" at Frankie's fashions, as the female models came out one by one, in twos and then groups and walked down the runway. When they reached the end, they held there in pose so the audience on all sides could get a complete view of each item. The clothes were feminine, but practical, even on the rail thin models. Scott looked down at what he was wearing and decided he would need a whole new wardrobe makeover and quick.

One model came out with a canary yellow sleeveless dress that seemed the epitome of spring. Scott could imagine a field of wild flowers as the model walked down the runway. When she turned around to walk back, Scott noticed a satin bow in the back. He thought how that dress would look on Kathryn. Another model came out with a sequined pale blue evening dress with an open back down to her waist. From where he sat, he could even see the sheerness and the delicacy of the dress. He sat watching until Frankie announced the designs by Agassi — Kathryn's mother's name, he remembered — entitled, "A Little Light."

Kathryn came out to the podium and stood beside Frankie to announce her creations. The pants suit, tailored seersucker with a lace design at the legs and sleeves, a below the waist jacket that flared out was first, and the crowd let out a series of "oohs" and "aahs" as the model strutted down the runway. When the model reached the end, the crowd clapped, before she walked back. Scott listened to the women around him and he heard things like "That's something I could wear" and "I would like to get that." When the last model came out wearing a lime green silk evening, dress, thin straps, tapered skirt the women went wild. As the model progressed down the runway the gold thread in the dress gave off tiny sparkles of light, and the women on the front row of each side, loudly chorused "ooohs," pointed, and whispered as the model walked by.

Scott looked around the room again and felt the desire from the women around him. He could see that every woman in that place wanted that dress and he knew just how the men in the room felt. They all wanted to buy that dress for the woman they loved, because he did. How could someone who designed something so breathtaking, so stunning, be anything but beautiful and loving herself?

Kathryn looked at Frankie and he gave her a hug. Scott remembered Kathryn telling him that Frankie had encouraged her to make and show that dress. He could see her now and could see that she was thrilled that Frankie had.

He saw Martin, eyes glued to his daughter, sitting in the front row, close to the podium clapping and yelling. He had looked toward Martin as the models had come out and saw Martin's face as his all-grown-up-little-girl described each article to the audience without a stumble. Kathryn had told Scott how much Martin had done for her over the years and how she wanted to make him proud. Everyone looking on had to know how proud he was of his daughter. Scott looked for Sylvia and Mary, but neither was there. Then he remembered Kathryn telling him about the problems the two of them had had and Scott guessed Sylvia didn't want to come, especially regarding the recent events of her daughter.

He continued looking around at the crowd and saw another face he recognized sitting in the back of the center section. He must have walked passed him when he slipped in. He was the man who had introduced himself as Harris Sweeney on the evening he went to Mrs. Fisher's house. He said he and Kathryn were getting married. He wasn't sitting with Martin; instead, he sat in the back. He turned to Kathryn to try to see if she was wearing an engagement ring, but even though he was on her left, he was not able to see a ring from his distance. Scott looked at Harris again and noticed he was not smiling or clapping or making awesome noises like everyone else around him. Scott guessed that their relationship was over, but he couldn't stay away. Scott understood how he felt. After all, he was there because he couldn't stay away from Kathryn, either.

As he sat there watching the crowd go wild over Kathryn, he knew just how she felt. He knew because since he'd been writing short stories, he had opened his heart and soul to the public and he wanted to see their appreciation just as Kathryn felt now as the people at this fashion show confirmed to her how much they loved her. He knew that the feeling extended beyond comprehension. That was the feeling he wanted to have, the feeling he needed.

At the end of the show, the crowd gave them both a resounding round of applause. Scott saw the woman he thought was Vera Wang get up and follow Kathryn and

Frankie to the back. Then he saw the other two important looking guests do the same. He imagined they were congratulating both of them and he couldn't help feeling a little jealous. Kathryn had found her way. Even though he was a little sad about himself, he also felt good that someone took the opportunity to tell Kathryn how nice her designs were. He wanted at least one of them to offer her whatever it was she wanted from this show. Scott wanted to wait, wanted Kathryn to know he was there, but quickly changed his mind and left the same way he had come in, unnoticed.

On the drive back to the office, he thought again about that relationship seminar. If he wanted a relationship with Kathryn, he would need to change. He would need to see her, the beauty of her. He would need to remember she had nothing to do with his mother and even tried to help him find the woman who saw everything. He would also have to remember that she had a career and she was on her way to becoming a top designer. He would have to make a change if he wanted from her what he needed.

Chapter 34
Kathryn

Kathryn was in a state of pleasant shock. She couldn't believe that the audience loved her. She thought her designs were good but she had no idea they were as good as the audience indicated. She heard them clapping, and shouting, and when she looked up, she saw some of the audience standing. She wanted to cry, she was so happy, but she held strong, smiling, and, bowing, while thanking them. When the clapping eased up, she thanked the audience one last time through the tears she was no longer able to hold back, and left.

When she got backstage, she hugged Frankie around the neck, jumped up and down several times, thanking him so many times that even he tried to get her to stop. Frankie saw Vera Wang enter back stage and he walked over to meet her and the other two designers.

"Hi Sweetheart," said Martin greeting his daughter with open arms.

"Daddy, did you like the show?"

"I loved it. Your clothes were breathtaking." They pulled back.

"Are you proud of me, now?"

"Sweetheart, I'm always proud of you." He leaned down and kissed her on the top of her head.

She looked over at Frankie and tried to hear what the three designers were saying to Frankie.

"Why don't you go and introduce yourself?" asked Martin, watching her and then the group of people.

"I don't want to be pushy or anything. You think I should?

"Why not?" asked Martin.

"Well, the fashion world is very strange. I'm hoping Frankie will call me over."

"And if he doesn't?"

"Then they don't want to talk to me. But, the fact that they came back stage is a good sign."

"You sure honey? Couldn't you just walk over and say hello, introduce yourself and say something about your work and be gone?"

"They would feel I wanted something."

"Well, you do, don't you?" asked Martin.

"Yes, Daddy, very much, but these people, they're rather peculiar. They don't want anyone to rush them or ask for anything. If they want you they will come to you."

"Okay, I understand. Whether they want you or not, your fashions are gorgeous, and all the women around me wanted to know where they could buy them. I almost took orders."

She laughed and gave her father another long hug. Kathryn and Martin watched as the three people nodded to Frankie, smiled, and laughed. She saw Frankie laugh as he said something and figured that he must have been nervous. She knew him well. After a few minutes, the two people took out their cards and each gave one to Frankie as they said something to him. Then they shook hands and left. Just before they walked out to the front, they turned around and waved to Kathryn. Martin elbowed her and she waved back. They stood and waited for Frankie to tell them what happened.

"Kat," began Frankie, "they just loved your designs." He held his knuckles to his mouth.

"See, I knew it," said Martin.

Kathryn couldn't say a word. She kept pointing to herself and nodding her head.

Frankie nodded back with a "yes, yes, yes," and then Martin joined in.

Frankie handed her Oleg Cassini's card. "He wants you to call him when you get your fall line together. He thinks he might be able to sponsor you."

Kathryn still was not able to speak. She opened her mouth to say something but could only get out the "O."

Martin put his arm around Kathryn. "I don't know why you're so shocked. Your designs were beautiful." Martin looked at Frankie. "She has a good teacher. Thank you, Frankie." Martin extended his hand and Frankie hugged him instead.

"Kat, can you say something?" asked Frankie.

"What about you Frankie? What did they say about you?" asked Kathryn.

Martin leaned over and kissed Kathryn in her hair.

"I got a card, too." He showed her the two cards that he held in his hand.

"Two cards, you got two cards," said Kathryn. She reached over and gave Frankie a hug.

"Frankie, no matter what happens —" began Kathryn.

"No, don't say it. Just don't say it," said Frankie. "All right everyone, why are you standing around like you're on a break or something. Let's get these clothes back on racks and ourselves out of here." He walked over to the models and crew, some still dressing and some standing around talking.

The crew slowly began picking up the clothes and putting them back on hangers and into plastic bags.

Kathryn and Martin went to help hang up the clothes. Martin watched Kathryn out of the side of his eye. Kathryn noticed, not sure how to broach the next subject. "The room was pretty full, Sweetheart. I hardly saw any empty seats," said Martin trying his best to keep a sleeveless blouse on the satin hanger.

"I was so nervous and worried that I'd forget what I had to say that I hardly took my eyes off my script," said Kathryn.

"You didn't seem nervous at all. In fact, when you talked about your things you seemed to know what you were talking about. You certainly seemed confident to me." He put the blouse on a rack and picked up another garment.

Kathryn hung up her lime green imported silk dress and picked up a pair of pants. She eyed her father. She was so familiar with his way and knew he wanted to talk about something, but she thought she'd draw it out, tease him a little.

"What did you think of the models?" asked Kathryn. "Did I get the best ones to represent my clothes?'

"Uh, the models? I guess so." He stopped trying to force the dress on the hanger and thought for a moment. "Yes, yes you did. I would say that every item that we saw stood out beyond the model. Isn't that what you want? The model is only the person wearing the item and the item is supposed to stand out?"

"Yes. That's right." Kathryn said it as if she was amazed at her father.

"I'm sure everyone watching saw that," continued Martin.

Kathryn realized what Martin wanted to say to her. "Okay, Daddy. Harris was there wasn't he?" asked Kathryn.

"Yes, he was. I saw him sitting in the audience. He did seem a little sad, I must say."

"Well, —"

"I take it he won't be coming to your after party either."

"No, maybe not, but, maybe he'll want a more amicable good-bye." Kathryn put the last item on the rack.

"Honey, there was someone else there, too. I think you should know about him."

"Who?"

"Scott. I saw Scott enter a little after the show started. He was alone."

"Scott? He was at my show?" Kathryn seemed lost in thought for a minute.

"Are we ready?" asked Frankie crossing the room and walking toward the two of them.

"Yes, we're ready," said Kathryn.

"Sweetheart, I've got to go back to work. Have fun at your party." He stood facing Kathryn as she seemed to want to say something.

Martin hugged his daughter and whispered in her hair, "Call him, go talk to him. Do something." Martin took a step back, gave Kathryn a smile, and turned to leave.

~~~~~~~~~~

Kathryn used to think that the studio where they worked

was small. When she and Frankie arrived back, someone had pushed back all the clutter and made room for the "party goers." A portable bar was set up on one end of the room and a table with finger foods was set up on the other end. She got a big glass of wine and took it to the window seat where she sat looking out on the employee parking lot.

"Hi," said Harris Sweeney, a wide smile on his face. "Mind if I sit down?"

"Harris? I didn't think . . . Were you at the show?" She didn't want to give away the fact that she already knew.

"Yes. You're on your way Kathryn. I understand now. I don't like it, but I understand. I just came to congratulate you."

"Thanks, Harris. That's really nice of you." She took a sip of her wine.

"So, what happens after this?' asked Harris.

"I don't know. I move to the big time, go to New York, maybe even Hollywood, star in a movie," she laughed.

Harris smiled, too. "After today, I think you'll get there."

"What about you, Harris? What are you doing?"

"My boss wants to move his operation to Paris. So, either I move or find another job somewhere. I'm thinking I'll get out of the fashion business and go into something else."

"I wouldn't worry about you. You always seem to come out on top," said Kathryn.

Harris turned his face away from her, looked down.

Kathryn didn't quite know what to say after she had just put her foot in her mouth.

"Come on you two. Let's make a toast," said Frankie.

Kathryn gave him a big "thank you" smile. She and Frankie each knew when the other was in trouble and he had come to save her from Harris.

"To Kat, a fully fledged designer. She has arrived folks. Kat is here."

They raised their glasses. Some tapped.

Harris tapped Kathryn's glass, "I'll drink to that." After he took a sip, he stood. "Take care of yourself, Kat. If you ever need anything, anytime, just call." Harris sat his glass down, waved good-bye to Frankie and left.

Kathryn felt a tinge of sadness as she watched him go.

"No, don't do that," said Frankie.

"Do what?" asked Kathryn.

"Get all sad. You have someone else you have to go talk to before you start your depressing stuff."

Kathryn laughed. She stood to move around the room, but gave Frankie a kiss on the cheek first. Then she took a big swill of her wine and went to the first group to mingle.

Chapter 35
Scott

Scott and Cameron had gotten word that after their first meeting with the board, three of the members had changed their minds about the project, due to Brian Hodge, and now they wanted to hold up the progress. He and Scott were on their way to meet with them to try to change their mind. Scott looked over at his father as he sped through the streets on their way to Rockville Pike. He could see that his father was angry and probably afraid that he wouldn't be able to make this happen for Laurie. He knew this school was something his father had to do for her. He wished there was some way to calm him before the meeting.

"Who is responsible for this, Dad?"

"Brian Hodge feels that the program will take the focus off the academics and college education and put it on vocations, or blue collar careers."

"Shouldn't a good school system have a variety?"

"You would think so, wouldn't you? I'm not worried, I have all of her plans, proposals, diagrams, correspondence; everything that she started."

"Sometimes I feel like these board members play the same games that our congress people play, taking everything personally," said Scott.

"That's the first thing that you must understand and you have to learn to play that game."

"How can anyone get anything done like that? The school board members are no longer high school students, and for the most part, have made successes out of their lives. Why is it so difficult for them to see that these students are not like them, that some kids, come from different circumstances, and these kids may need a different curriculum? What's so hard about understanding that?" asked Scott.

"You're right; they just want to do what they think is best, but they don't understand the needs. When they finally figure things out, it's too late, not to mention the competiveness that they have with one another and surrounding school systems. They are the better school system if they have more students graduating and going to a college or university."

"I don't think they like people telling them what to do either," said Scott.

Cameron laughed. "You seem to understand that school board all right."

"I don't understand how they think they can create a policy and have no idea what the kids are like. What is this country coming to?" said Scott.

"Sounds like you'll make a great politician."

Cameron pulled into the parking lot and drove up and down the lanes looking for a parking space. "Scott, I never thought that I would hear you talk like this."

"Me either." Scott laughed. "What's happening to me?"

They arrived just as the meeting began. The chair, Mr. Paul Delaney, introduced Cameron and Scott to the board members and reminded the members that they presented at the last board meeting. The superintendent introduced himself first, and then each board member. The board attempted to follow their agenda, but Cameron didn't wait for that. After the introductions, he got up from his seat at the long table that sat in front of the board members and a few feet away, stood at the mike in front of the table to speak.

"Excuse me."

All the board members looked toward the mike.

"I'm here to talk about the Laurie Home for Teens Project."

Scott got up and stood beside his father as he tried to figure out whom his father knew on the board. Generally, that was how things were passed, at least in congress that's what happened, Scott believed.

The Chair, Mr. Paul Delaney, smiled as he tried to interrupt Cameron to give a long discourse on board policy and the process through which the board accepts suggestions. At the end of his comments, he encouraged the board to go ahead with the planned agenda.

Cameron interrupted again after the policy harangue, but he didn't apologize for approaching the board out of turn. "At the last board meeting, I asked for a meeting to discuss my plans for the teen home. So you see, I submitted my request as Mr. Delaney has just suggested, but received no response. So, I decided to appear before you here today to restate my case."

The board members remained quiet, and a few looked at Mr. Delaney.

"I'm sorry if anyone was absent during the last meeting and missed hearing about the Laurie Home for Teens Project and because of that, I'm happy to discuss it again with you while the entire board is present, which, as I just said, is why my son and I are here today. I want to begin by saying that I have given this project a name, The Laurie Home for Teens Project." He paused, cleared his throat. He tried to begin again, "The Laurie Home for Teens Project . . ."

Scott saw how hard his father was trying to hold back his tears, but was unable to. Scott put his arm around his father's shoulders and led him to one of the chairs at the table.

"Son, just give me a moment. I'll be okay."

"No, Dad. I'll do it. Give me your notes. I'll do it."

"I just need a minute. I'll be okay. In fact, I'm okay, now."

"No, Dad, you're not."

"Is everything all right?" asked the superintendent.

"Yes, I just need a moment," responded Cameron. Then to Scott, "This is important and maybe our only chance to talk to the board." He took a deep breath, slowly let it out. "I'm okay, now."

"Dad, I need to help you. I'll do it."

"Are you sure, Scott?"

"Yes, I'm sure.

Scott took his father's notes and diagrams, plans and everything he had and stood at the dais. He cleared his throat, organized the notes, cleared his throat again, and looked at the table full of board members staring back at him. Beads of perspiration popped out on his forehead. He wiped them away as casually as he could. When he began to speak, he stuttered out his words and had to start again. He took a second to control his breathing. "You can see how much this means to my father and me."

He looked on the faces of the board members and saw that they had to know that what his mother began and father was trying to complete for these kids was the right thing and that the school board needed to make itself a part of the process. As he progressed more into the presentation a feeling of control, confidence seized him, and he presented one fact after the next with dropout rates of students who found it difficult for one reason or another to stay in school and they ran away from home.

He told them of his experiences when he went with his mother to volunteer at the center. "I saw young girls, teens so abused by their family members that they couldn't stand to be touched by anyone. I actually saw and talked to the girls. They're real people just like you and me. Can you imagine not being able to hug your son or daughter? I watched both boys and girls so strung out on drugs they didn't know where they were or what day it was. I want you to know that I had to watch because I couldn't do anything about it. Can you imagine how horrible that was? I saw girls who were pregnant. These girls were much too young to have children. I met teens who were HIV positive from prostituting themselves so they could eat. I was frightened out of my wits when one teen showed me a gun he'd found and told me that he had to carry it protect himself."

He showed figures of students dropping out of school every year for these things and told the board members how teens living this way turned his stomach. He found himself thanking God and his parents for his home and the love his parents showed him. He passed out charts Laurie had started. He challenged each board member to walk along the streets in areas that are depressed and see the number of students living in these conditions. He stated that those who are doing well are morally responsible for those who need help and he was here asking the school board to do a better job of serving their community by including these children.

He concluded by saying, "These children didn't ask to be borne under these conditions. I'm sure that if they were asked to select their parents and their living conditions, none of them would have said they wanted an abusive mother or father, or a father who would molest them, or a family who existed in poverty, or an uneducated mother and father who are always out of work. Each one of them would have picked better circumstances for themselves. Since they can't help who or what they are, we can. Help me help them. That's all I'm asking, that you help me help them. I'll pass out this detailed program description that my father, mother and I have written and we welcome any changes or comments that you have to make about it. Please remember that we're not asking the board for very much, but we do want you to support this effort. Thank you very much."

After which, he took a long sip of water.

The board members turned to each other, huddled in a group around the table, whispered, and nodded to each other.

Scott turned to his father, but Cameron didn't take his eyes off the members as they whispered to each other. Scott turned to watch the board members.

When they had finished whispering and nodding, Mr. Delaney said, "The board members are impressed that you two have done your homework and we can see the need. We will need to study this proposal and we will convene in two days. We realize your need and the fact that your hotel would be ready to open soon, and we agree to accommodate that need and meet out of our regular scheduling."

"Thank you, each one of you," said Scott.

When they settled in the car, Scott reached over to high five his father who high fived back.

"Scott, you did such a good job. You saved us in there. You delivered your speech with such passion, such confidence, such love that I know they'll approve it," said Cameron. He didn't seem surprised at how Scott handled himself.

The teen home was no longer just Laurie's project, something they were just doing for her. It had become their project. Scott was now wholly invested.

"Your mother would have been so proud of you. I'm very proud of you," said Cameron, a wide smile on his face. He reached out to hug his son.

"I want to make you proud," Scott whispered to his father.

Scott was surprised to hear his father say he was proud of him. He had waited his entire life to hear his father say that. He had to admit that he was even proud of himself.

~~~~~~~~~~~

Cameron pulled up in front of the hotel and the two got out. As soon as they entered, the electrician approached. He handed Cameron the inspection rejection. Just a few minutes ago, they were walking on air, high fiving each other for the sensational job that Scott did at the school board meeting, now in just a matter of minutes, they were brought back down to earth, and greeted with disappointment.

"What happened?" asked Cameron.

"Come take a look," said the electrician.

Max, the contractor, his electrician, Cameron and Scott all walked down to the basement where the main electrical box hung across the wall.

"Look, at this," said the electrician as he opened the large black box of wires extending and ending. "Since we did this you have asked for several more things. The box is not large enough to support everything you have asked for. We need to run new lines, separate some of these wires, and create several boxes. When we did the plans you didn't have that large kitchen area in there and those extra washing machines and dryers."

"Get your crew back here," said Cameron. "Fix the problem."

"We're all right here. Just waitin' on word from you," said the electrician with a wide smile.

Everyone but the electrician turned to leave.

"Mr. Kersey,"

Cameron turned around.

"I would expect that the same thing is happening with the plumbing," said the electrician.

Scott let out a light chuckle when he saw the plumber, wearing black rubber boots, headed their way. "Here comes the inspection rejection, now," said Scott.

The plumber heard the comment and he handed the inspection rejection to Cameron.

"We don't have enough —"

"Don't tell me," interrupted Cameron. "Just fix the problem. Do whatever you need to do to bring this teen home up to code." He turned from the electrician, to the plumber and to Max. "Look, I don't want any problems. I want us up to code and I want what we need for these teens so we can open this home. As far as I know, there will be no more changes to the plans."

The three men nodded their heads in understanding.

On the way back to the main lobby, Cameron told Max, that the school board would convene in two days. When they give their approval, he would want the home finished immediately after.

"We'll do the best we can to have things ready by then. I'll have every man working night and day. These are not normal circumstances," said Max.

"You're right," said Scott. "These are not normal circumstances."

"Why don't you two come see what we've done so far," said Max.

Scott and Cameron followed Max as he led them through the hair salon, kitchen, and all the places where the teens would work and earn credit. He left Scott and Cameron in the laundry room. Scott tried to imagine the big machines in use, bustling with bubbles and the back and forth rhythm of the washers and dryers.

"Let's take a look at the rooms," said Cameron. And the two of them began with the first floor.

When they opened the door to the first room, Scott, for a moment, forgot the hotel was a home for teens and thought it was really a hotel. The rooms were just as nice as any upscale hotel, each with its own bathroom, spaciousness — large enough for furniture including a desk and double bed. He could see pictures of football stars across one wall, rock stars on another wall. He could see books stacked on the desk and an open notebook with notes and diagrams scrawled all across a page. He could hear rock music coming from the clock radio on the nightstand. He could easily see a teen making this room their own. Scott went to the large window that almost stretched across one wall and saw that the sliding glass doors and balconies were removed, instead, turned into windows that didn't open all the way. Scott was surprised at this when he tried to open a window.

"Suicide prevention," his father whispered.

He looked over at his father, just as Cameron turned to walk out.

Scott realized that even though they were doing this for his mother, he couldn't get out of his mind that his father thought that he and Laurie would be doing this together. At first, this thought saddened him, but now, he saw that because of the tragedy his father immersed himself so deeply in the home, that ultimately, he will provide a much better home.

Chapter 36
Scott

The almost noiseless courtroom was beginning to fill up with people. As Scott sat next to his father watching the people enter, he wondered whom they were, where they came from. He didn't know any of them. The only sound was the thud of shoes against hard wood floors and sometimes a dull flop when someone heavy or tall sat down. Scott saw Martin and Sylvia as they entered and took seats up front across from him. After they sat down, Scott looked at them. Martin looked like he was disgusted and didn't want to be there, head down, hands clasped inside his legs. Sylvia had a curious look about her, almost as if she thought she was there through error and everyone would find it out just as soon as the judge arrived and cleared up everything. Scott turned his head slightly and looked around the entire courtroom. Kathryn was not there.

Lyle Green, Betty's attorney, entered in a rush, as if he'd just been told he had to take the case, and raced down to the table where he made loud noises opening his brief case and talking in a half-whisper to those around him. Duane Fandrey, the state's attorney, entered cautiously looking around the room as he walked down to the table on the right. He quietly shook hands with both Cameron and Scott, sat down for a minute. He opened his briefcase as he looked around the courtroom as if he had some secret papers that he didn't want anyone to see. Cameron looked over at Scott wrinkled his brow. Scott smiled at his father.

Scott didn't really know how he should have felt in that courtroom. He believed Betty when she said that it was an accident. He knew that she didn't want to bring his mother any harm. She didn't seem to be the type. He remembered a quote his father used to tell him when he was younger that "One of the tragedies of life is that once a deed is done, the consequences are beyond one's control." In this instance, the consequences were not out of their control. He and Cameron could control some of what would happen to Betty.

Scott turned around again and saw Kathryn sitting in the last row in the back. He looked at where Martin and Sylvia sat, and saw that there was room for Kathryn, but she evidently chose to sit in the back. He thought about the success of Kathryn's recent fashion show; she was on the rise. Betty could keep Kathryn from the success she deserved. Kathryn had worked hard trying to establish herself and this shouldn't happen to her. It shouldn't, but it could. Even though Kathryn changed her name, people will find out. People always find out everything.

Scott leaned over to whisper to Cameron, and Cameron didn't respond. Instead, he held his gaze on the judge's bench almost as if he was bracing himself for the wildest roller coaster ride and he hadn't buckled in yet. Cameron slowly turned his head toward Scott and Scott saw perspiration forming on his father's forehead. He heard his father breathing heavily, in and out rapidly. Cameron tried to stand. He grabbed the edge of the table, anchored himself, and tried to pull himself up, but he fell over into Scott's lap.

"Call 911. Someone, please. Call 911!" yelled out Scott. He got his father back on his chair and held him there. The two lawyers and the guard from the rear rushed to help. The guard radioed something to someone.

"Dad, dad. What happened?" Scott continued to ask.

Cameron tried to talk as others came to help. "What happened?" asked someone.

"Does he need a doctor?" asked someone else.

"Call an ambulance," said Scott, again.

"No, no. No ambulance," said Cameron, regaining his composure.

Scott looked up and saw the bailiff coming out of a door off to the side. He saw Cameron in the chair and people crowding around, he went back through the door. Judge Sickle came running out and saw Cameron seated at the table sipping water, Scott standing over him.

"Mr. Kersey, I have to call an ambulance for you."

"No, please. I just want to get this over with. I'm okay."

"A doctor. Is there a doctor present?" asked the judge.

No one responded.

"Sir, I'm fine. I don't need anything. I just, I just . . . I'm okay. Really, I am."

The judge looked at him as if he understood how hard it was for Cameron, how hard it was for him to go on without his wife.

"Okay, but if this happens again, I'll call an ambulance immediately. Understand?"

"I understand."

"Okay, then."

The judge went back through the door from which he came and Cameron took a few minutes. After a while, Scott leaned past Cameron to Duane Fandrey and whispered to him.

Just as Duane opened his mouth to respond to Scott, the bailiff entered again through the door in the front of the room. He looked around the courtroom, turned around and went back. A few minutes later, he reappeared and stood in front of the judge's bench.

"All rise," he began. "This is the courtroom of Judge John V. Sickle in the hearing of Betty Gilbert vs. The State."

Judge John V. Sickle came out through a door and sat down.

"Please be seated, everyone," said the Bailiff.

Judge Sickle began, "Good morning. This is the hearing —"

"Judge, could we approach the bench, please?" asked Fandrey.

Judge Sickle waited a minute then nodded his head. Both attorneys walked to the judge. Duane talked and then turned to Lyle. Judge Sickle spoke and then looked at Lyle, who nodded his head. The two attorneys walked back to their tables and whispered to their clients.

Scott and Cameron and Martin, Sylvia and Betty followed their attorneys out of the courtroom to the next room down, a conference room.

With a wave of his hand, Lyle offered everyone a chair.

Duane began, "Mr. Greene, Mr. and Mrs. Milner, Mr. and Mr. Kersey would like to offer what we call a plea before the hearing begins. If you accept the plea, we will just go back in and let the judge know and that will be that. You have to know that this is out of the ordinary, but your case is a case of vehicular manslaughter and it may behoove you to hear what they have to say." He looked at Lyle Green, still standing, who nodded back.

"I'm not privy to this information and you don't have to listen if you don't want to," said Lyle. "But, on the other hand, it might not hurt to listen."

"What is it?" asked Martin.

"Could I speak? Tell them what we want?" asked Scott. He pushed his chair back.

"Sure, but I'll have to stop you if you say anything that may hurt your position in this case," said Duane Fandrey. He pulled out a chair and sat down.

Betty looked as if she still didn't understand what was happening.

Scott looked at Cameron, thin lips in a slight smile. "My father and I would like to make you an offer. We don't think Betty meant to hurt my mother —"

"Stop right there," interrupted Duane Fandrey. "That could be damaging to your case."

"I need to finish," continued Scott. "Anyway, we would, that is my father and I would like to offer one year probation, one year loss of your driver's license and we would like to impose a fine. We would like you to work at the home for runaway teens, my mother's idea, for a period of two years."

"That's it?" asked Duane. "We can ask for five years jail time —"

"You heard my son. This is what we want," said Cameron. "This is the only and final offer."

Lyle Green leaned over to talk to Betty.

"We'll take it," said Martin without conferring with Betty or the attorney.

"Betty? What do you think?" asked Lyle.

"It doesn't matter," continued Martin looking directly into Cameron's eyes. "We'll take it."

"But, what about Betty? She needs to agree," said Lyle.

"I do. I do agree," said Betty finally.

"Tell the judge that this is what we want," said Martin.

Duane, Lyle, and Betty left the room to go speak to the judge.

Cameron and Scott stood up.

Martin stood and extended his hand to both men. "Thank you so much. I know Betty will appreciate what you two have done when she figures it all out."

He tugged at Sylvia and she stood to shake hands.

Scott noticed that she, the one who had so much to say on the day he went to look at their car, had nothing to say during the conference.

Duane Fandrey returned with a message that the judge wanted to see them all in his chambers.

"I understand that you want to plea bargain. Mr. Kersey, Mr. Kersey." He nodded to them. "You two have offered the following to Betty Gilbert on the charge of vehicular manslaughter. She shall be on probation for a period of one year, she shall give up her driving privileges for a period of one year, and she shall work without pay at your home for runaway teens for a period of two years. Is this correct?"

"Yes it is." "Yes." Scott and Cameron responded at the same time.

The judge turned toward Betty. "Do you understand what this means? You will not be able to drive for a year. You will have to report to your probation officer once a week which means you can't leave the area. And, you will have to work in the home for runaway teens for two years. I take it that this is full-time?" He turned to Scott.

"Yes, full-time," said Scott.

"And you will have to do that for two years. This also means that you will have to take public transportation or someone will have to drive you to this place." He watched Betty for a sign that she agreed.

"I understand all that." Betty looked down at the floor.

"Then, you accept this offer. Is that right?"

"Yes. Yes, I do," said Betty in a voice barely above a whisper. She continued to watch the floor.

"Well, then, if everyone is in agreement, so ordered. I'll have this written up. Thank you, gentlemen."

Scott could see that this whole process was tearing his father apart. Betty's punishment of being put away in a jail for only five years for taking his mother's life was not enough retribution and thinking about the injustice of this would only bring them both more grief. Making Betty work to support his mother's dream would do much more good and would take the worry off them. He knew this was the right thing to do. He knew that it was what his mother would have wanted.

Chapter 37
Scott

Sitting in his office, Scott couldn't get the school board meeting out of his mind. What did they mean when Hodge said they would discuss it? Why is he the one making all the decisions? Scott didn't think that the teens should have to wait until Hodge decided they could have an education. They needed this program now. He walked to his father's office. When he saw his father was alone, he gave a slight knock on the open door and entered.

"Dad, I think I know how we can get approval from the school board," said Scott, taking a seat in front of his father's desk.

"How's that?" asked Cameron, closing a folder he was evidently looking through.

"We need to have an "Open House" or more like an "Open Hotel.""

"We do, don't we?"

"Yes, we will invite them to look at the facility. Let them see the hotel and explain the programs that would benefit the students. We can have the students take them on a tour. They can ask the students questions and the students can ask the board members questions.

"I love it." Cameron pressed a button on his phone. "June, call the superintendent of schools and arrange a date for him and the members of the school board to meet us at the teen home, within the next two days."

"Yes sir." June's voice came back.

"We'll just have to wait to see what they do next," said Scott.

~~~~~~~~~~

Two days later, the superintendent of schools and all the school board members met at the home for runaway teens. One of the board members mentioned how everyone showed up for this trip, which was something because they had never had everyone present at sessions outside the school board meetings.

They were welcomed by the teens from Laurie's teen home, the mothers who worked in that teen home with Laurie and people from the community who came to finish painting or working to help get the hotel ready. Before the board members began the tour, Scott and Cameron once again, told them how the program would work. Cameron admitted that the vision could be a little idealistic since no one from the school system had called to work with them, so he really didn't know how far from workable, or practical the plans were. As far as he knew now, the logistics of the plans were workable and until he heard otherwise, he would continue to promote his plans as they were.

As they went from the kitchen to the dining room, to the

salon and laundry room, Scott spoke about the curriculum and the need for an alternative program of study for some students. He went on to say that, "The school system directed everyone to college, but everyone is not interested in pursuing a college education. Many people are needed to hold down jobs that are not college-type jobs." He continued by saying that, "when teens have problems at home and at school, they are not eager to stay in that environment and as soon as they drop out, they are automatically limiting their futures. Teenagers have two places to go – home and school. When they don't feel successful in either of those places then, they leave and go elsewhere. Except that the 'elsewhere' is not a good place for them either. They are not prepared in a world of prostitution and drugs, but their families and the schools have forced them into that world. We are just asking you to help us with a few of those students. Help us offer them a better life by supporting our school. All of these teenagers here today will help you with the tour and answer any questions that you may have as well as ask you questions."

One female teen walked with one of the school board members in the direction of the hair salon and asked him why no one had called Cameron back. When Scott heard her ask this, he knew right then that this day they would have some answers. He thought that the teens needed this and having them take part was a good idea. Maybe if these people could see in these kids the hope, love and future that his mother saw, they would be eager to help.

When the other people in the neighborhood thought that the school board members were taking a tour of the home for runaway teens, many of them showed up to see this huge place that would house teenagers. Scott tried to tell the crowd as much as possible, that there was no actual tour, but he soon saw that the crowd just wanted to look, so he gave up and went with a group to tour himself. He found his father with several school board members and when Scott saw his father smiling, he knew his father was feeling okay and everything was going satisfactorily.

About mid-afternoon, people began to leave and Scott caught up with his father again in the lobby. They thanked the neighborhood people for coming, and for their support, even though they weren't really invited. Many of the neighborhood people commented on the beauty of the hotel. Some of the teens stood around the entrance and Scott saw that Betty was there also with two teens and the assistant superintendent. He realized that she was beginning her two-year stint earlier than expected. The judge hadn't sent out the order yet. In the crowd of people, he saw Lisa just beyond Betty. She looked up and when she saw him, waved to him. Scott was nervous when he saw her, but waved back. He didn't go over to say hello to her and knew that was what she expected. The superintendent and two school board members came from the banquet room to Cameron and Scott who were now closer to the front door.

"Thank you for coming to take a look at things. I hope you now have a better idea of what we are proposing," said Cameron.

"We do. We do, indeed," said the superintendent shaking hands with Cameron.

The superintendent continued pumping Cameron's hands. "Thank you," he said and left.

Scott and Cameron watched the superintendent and board members walk down the driveway and to their cars waiting at the other end of the circle.

Just as he was about to return to the tour, Scott saw Kathryn, Frankie, and Martin get out of Martin's car. As they walked up the driveway toward the entrance, Scott's stomach fluttered. When they reached the door, Martin reached out his hand to Scott. "Are we too late for the tour?"

"How are people hearing about that?" asked Scott.

Betty, who had come to the front door, stepped forward. "I can take them if you'd like."

Cameron walked a visitor to the front door, they shook hands, and the visitor left. Cameron turned toward Scott. "I'll join you."

"In that case, Betty," said Martin.

Betty smiled and gave a "let's go" wave as she led the way.

Kathryn looked at Scott and said, "She feels good helping. This is the first time anyone has made her feel special. I want to thank you and your father for that."

Lisa came to the front door and stood watching as Kathryn thanked Scott. Scott wanted to go and say something to Lisa, thank her for coming, but he didn't move. He had been wanting her to support him for an entire year and she never had. She always thought about herself. Now, when he was no longer interested, here she was, giving her support. Maybe she finally figured out what change really meant. She looked down at the floor before she turned around to leave. When Scott looked for her again, she was gone. He let out a sigh of relief.

"It was what we had to do," said Scott.

A couple from the neighborhood interrupted them and Scott turned to them. Kathryn walked away.

At the end of the tour, Cameron walked Martin and Frankie back to the entrance. Just before he reached the front door, Martin turned around. "Before I forget, I have the people in my office and my clients supporting this project. We're all ready to go to the next school board meeting."

"Thanks, Mr. Milner," said Cameron

"What you and your son did. Well, I just don't know how to thank you and going to the school board, that's nothing."

"It'll mean more than you think."

~~~~~~~~~~

Martin kept his word. The next school board meeting was so packed that even Scott and Cameron couldn't find a seat. Martin placed an ad in his newspaper, asking people to pack the boardroom and support Cameron and circulated them all over the community. Scott saw it and showed it to Cameron. Cameron had his employees present, the teens and parents who helped give the tour and the people from the neighborhood, but Martin's friends and readership outnumbered Cameron's by a large margin. Martin had even gotten Sylvia to attend.

Sonya, a teen from years before had asked to speak. She read her personal essay paper, the one that Scott had helped her write There was a hush over the audience as she read about her harsh life.

"Thank you for allowing me to speak to you." She cleared her throat, took a sip of water, and straightened the skirt of her navy blue two-piece suit. "Sorry, I'm just a little nervous. But I am well prepared." She paused and looked directly at the board members. "When I was young my father encouraged his friends to have sex with me in my home. One day he slapped me and punched me several times, when one of his clients complained that my father charged too much money for what he got." The audience made an "oooohhh" sound, but she didn't turn around. "My mother was present during those times, but she was sick all the time. One day my mother just died. The doctor said from an overdose, but all I knew was that she was gone. I tried to take care of my mother when she was sick, even though she was part of my father's plan. But, when my mother died, there was nothing there at that house for me so I left. I ran away from home and ended up three states away." She cleared her throat again, and wiped at her face. "The best day of my life was the day Laurie Kersey found me wondering around the streets. She took me to their home where I stayed until I graduated from high school." The audience gave her a long applause. She turned around, wiped at her face again, and smiled.

"Today, I work full-time as a stylist with Tresses and Tresses where I have owned my own chair for the past three years. I love my job and get so many compliments from my clients. I can't take off because I'll hear about it from them. As you can see, I'm an example of what this program can do. Tomorrow, I'll travel to New York with my boss. There she is," she turned to point to her boss. "to one of the biggest hair shows in this country. My boss has chosen me to go with her. I hope you choose this program in the name of Laurie Kersey. Thank you."

The school board members clapped, nodded at Sonya. Some stood up when the audience did. The president told the audience that the school board had agreed to accept the plans. He also stated that curriculum specialists would provide the curriculum and would meet with Scott and Cameron to finalize the plans. They wanted to have everything ready by the opening of school in the fall. They had the spring and summer to get everything ready. Cameron stated that meanwhile he would have the teens and mothers from the old home move in immediately. All the teens stood up, high fived each other and cheered. The noise in the meeting room sounded like the cheering at a football game when the home team barely won. Scott saw his sister, Becky, and brother, Jack, as they started out of the meeting. Later, Becky introduced James to her family.

Cameron hugged Scott, "You did it, son. You made this happen. You did it," he whispered.

"Thanks, Dad, but we did it together. We make a great team."

"I love you, Scott, Don't ever doubt that."

"I love you, Dad. I love you."

Chapter 38
Kathryn

"Here, honey. You are just driving me crazy with that sad, depressed look and that little puppy sighing. I just can't stand it anymore," said Frankie handing Kathryn the phone that sat on her desk.

"Frankie, I can't just call. Are you crazy? I can't just do that," said Kathryn. She took the phone and put it back in its cradle. She walked over to the window where she had left her sketchbook and picked it up, took it back to her desk.

"You have to do something. You can't just sit around here moaning and groaning all afternoon." Frankie picked up several items of clothing and walked over to the door.

"Seriously Frankie? I know you're telling me to do something you wouldn't do," said Kathryn. She picked up the other clothes she saw lying on the table and walked over to the set of glass doors, pushed them out opening them for Frankie.

"In all seriousness, if I felt for someone the way you feel about Scott, I would. Anyway, I think he would want to hear from you." She followed him on the elevator and they got off at the next floor down.

"He would? Do you really think that?" asked Kathryn.

"Yes. It's your turn. You owe him an explanation about Harris, and an apology about Betty. Don't you think?" Frankie handed the clothes to Kathryn. He took out his key and opened the large window. He stepped inside and began undressing the mannequin.

"Apology about Betty? Do I owe him that?"

"Not really, but it's a good opener, don't you think?"

"Frankie, I thought you said seriously. I do want to call him and talk to him about Harris and if I need to apologize about Betty, I can do that too. I really need to thank him about Betty, again."

"That's for sure. He's a good man, Kat. How many other people would have done what he and his father did for Betty? I can't name any." He took an item of clothing off the mannequin and handed it to Kathryn. She laid that across the arm of another mannequin as she handed him a shirt to put on the mannequin.

"You're right Frankie. Remind me to kiss you sometime. Here I don't need these." She placed the other items that she had in her arms across the shoulder of the mannequin and went back up stairs.

She sat down at her desk and twirled the phone cord several times before she finally got up the nerve to dial his work number.

"This is Scott Kersey."

"Hello Scott. This is Kat."

The pause was unbearably long and Kathryn thought for a moment that he had hung up on her or she was somehow disconnected.

"Hi," he finally said.

Kathryn breathed a loud sigh of relief, one that she knew he would hear.

"Scott, I need to talk to you. Could we meet?"

Another long pause. Finally.

"Where?"

"At that little park behind your office."

~~~~~~~~~~

Kathryn and Scott met on the windiest and coldest day in March, when winter should have been winding down. When she arranged the meeting place, she must have forgotten to look at the weather report. She arrived at the park first and sat with her coat pulled around her trying to keep her hair out of her face. She watched Scott walk to the bench, the wind so hard that he seemed to be going backward, his coat pressed hard against him, his hair tossed around, head down.

When he got to the bench, he said not one word. He grabbed her hand, pulled her up and they walked to a little café hidden on a side street. There were few people in the café.

"You looked cold. I had to get you out of the wind," Scott said as they walked to a table in the back, a half smile on his face. Scott motioned to the person behind the counter that he needed two coffees. He pulled the chair out for Kathryn, unbuttoned his coat, and sat down.

She cupped the coffee cup and the waiter poured coffee in it. She looked across at Scott, his understanding eyes and couldn't remember how to start. She watched him pour crème in his coffee and take a sip.

"Coffee okay?' Scott asked.

Kathryn took a sip of her black coffee. "Yes. It's fine." When she saw him look down, she thought that she had her chance.

"Scott, I have so much to tell you, but I wish you'd let me finish telling you everything before you talk. Is that okay?"

"Sure." He took another sip.

Kathryn told him everything beginning with how she got to France and how badly she wanted to contact him to how she ran into Harris in Paris and about Betty and that, she didn't know what Betty had done. She apologized to Scott because she knew she had hurt him and she was so sorry.

"Even if we never see each other again, I have to know that you know all this."

Kathryn knew he was uncomfortable when he motioned to the waiter to bring them coffee refills. When the waiter came over, he asked the waiter to bring two crab cake sandwiches. She wanted him to look at her, but he kept looking away from her.

"I don't know what to say." He sat back in his chair, arms at his sides. "I never understood what happened. I thought maybe I'd done something, said something but . . ." He looked directly into her eyes. "I just wanted to know what happened."

"You didn't upset me. You did absolutely nothing wrong." Kathryn leaned across the table. "Don't believe that, you —"

"Look, I know we weren't seeing each other long but I thought at that time we might have enjoyed going out. We didn't know each other long enough for anything . . . ." said Scott.

He stopped talking, let out a sigh of relief when the waiter brought the crab cake sandwiches with fries and refilled their coffee. She could see that he was uncomfortable and felt the armor come down over him, shielding him from her. She could see what she had done to him.

"This little café is off the beaten path, but they have the best crab cake sandwiches I've ever tasted." He took an oversize bite and pointed to her sandwich.

Kathryn thought that the waiter came just in time. She hadn't wanted to make Scott uncomfortable, but she had. When she saw him motion to her, she took a bite of her sandwich even though she wasn't hungry in the least. She had to trudge on. She had asked to see him, so she had to tell him everything no matter how hard it was. "Scott, Harris and I are no longer seeing each other." She hesitated a moment, but she knew she had to continue. She looked at him, his kind, sweet face, the love that she saw written all over his face, like the depth of knowledge of a resource book.

"I miss you, Scott."

"Why aren't you seeing him?" asked Scott, his tone a little bitter.

"I never heard from you, either."

Scott looked up, laid his sandwich down, picked up the napkin, and wiped his face. "You were engaged."

"That was a mistake." She stopped herself from saying it, but inside she urged herself on. Say it. Tell him. It doesn't matter what happens. Just say it. "I want to be with you," she whispered. She put her sandwich down on her plate and watched him.

Scott stared at her for a moment. She could see from his half-smile and dancing eyes that he liked the fact that she wanted to be with him. She hoped he would answer, but if he didn't that was okay. She could see it in his eyes. If she could make a wish right now, she would wish he would jump over the table, and take her in his arms, tell her that she had always been his and that in his heart she never stopped. She knew it would take time before he would tell her anything like that.

"Kathryn, this is hard for me. I need you to understand that. It may be best for us to just let it alone for now. Thanks for the lunch." He stood, paid for the lunch and left.

On the way back, Kathryn decided that she would not allow herself to be hurt when Scott didn't respond to her comment. He didn't have to respond after all, it was not a question. She would have to give him more time, but at least she got things started. He came to meet her, a huge step for him, she recognized. She knew he still cared. She knew that he was just as in love with her as she was with him and she decided that she would not stop until she had won him over. If he wanted her to pursue him to show her love, she had to do it.

Three Weeks Later
Scott

He was waiting for her one afternoon on the bench in front of her store. Frankie told him that she was on her way back. When she saw him, she let out a wide smile and quickened her step.

He took her hand and they walked to the empty bench that overlooked the floor below. He sat on her left, half facing her, legs crossed. She sat turned to him, the smile still on her face. He took his finger and moved a strand of hair away from her eye.

"It's too soon," he said.

"I know."

He looked away, at the shoppers in the mall.

"You can't blame me for wanting to try. I'll keep trying," she said.

"I don't know when I'll be ready," Scott said.

"I know. When you are, I'll be here. I'll wait for as long as you need."

"You will?"

"Yes."

"Are you sure?" Scott asked.

"Yes. About everything," Kathryn said.

He looked at her again. He just wanted to take her in his arms hold her, kiss her and keep her with him forever. He didn't. Instead, he leaned over and kissed her on her head, got up and walked away. He didn't turn around to get another look at her. He knew that if he wanted to help himself, move forward, unstuck himself, he would have to come back to her and he had planned to do just that.

~~~~~~~~~~

"Hello Scott."

"Hello Kathryn," said Scott. He tried not to let on that he was happy that she called.

"I would like you to have dinner with me tonight."

Scott hesitated. He wanted to hear from her, but needed more time. She was taking him too fast. "Kathryn, I don't know."

"I understand. I really do. Why can't we just have dinner as two friends?"

"Do you think we can do that?" asked Scott.

"It would be hard for me, but I would like to try."

"I don't think so, okay?" He hung up.

~~~~~~~~~~

Two days later Kathryn called again. She wanted Scott to run with her that next morning. He met her at the park and they took off down the trail. They ran for six miles and she saw the ease with which he now ran.

"Wow, you've gotten much better. I could hardly keep up

with you," said Kathryn when they got back to the parking lot.

"I've been practicing."

"Do you like it better now?" asked Kathryn.

"You were right. I have learned to like running."

"Have dinner with me this evening."

"Why don't I take you home?"

"Scott, could we at least try?"

"I can't. I have something I have to do."

"Oh, I see," said Kathryn. "I hope she's worth it."

"She is. Very worth it."

"Oh, I see. Maybe you'd better take me home."

In front of her house and just before she opened the door, Scott reached over and took her hand. "It's a commitment that I made with my father. It's about my mother." He got out and opened the door for Kathryn to get out of the car.

When she got out and stood beside him. "I'm sorry, Scott, I really am."

"It's okay."

"I'll call you again, okay?"

"See ya," he said and walked around to get in the car.

~~~~~~~~~~

The next afternoon Kathryn called Scott again.

"Will you please have dinner with me this evening?"

"Who is this?"

"Scott, stop it. You know who this is. Will you? Please?"

He let out a sigh. "Okay," he finally said. "Where do you want to go?"

"What about the first place we had dinner?"

Scott hesitated again. He remembered the last time he was

there and how he sat, and waited, and waited for her and she didn't show up. He really didn't want to go back there again and have the waiter look at him as if he felt sorry for him. He wanted to suggest another place, but his heart wanted him to give her a chance to make it right. His father always said that you couldn't be responsible for what other people do.

"We had some happy times there, Scott. I could never forget our first date."

"Date? That was not a date. I just needed to see you to talk to you."

"To me that was our first date."

"Okay."

"Is that an okay for dinner tonight or an okay that that was our first date?" asked Kathryn.

"Okay to both."

"Scott you won't be sorry, I promise. Could I ask you to wear that suit you wore when you took me to that play?"

"Kathryn."

"Can you just do it? You won't be sorry, I promise."

"Okay. Okay to everything. I'll wear the suit and be there tonight. Okay?"

Scott was hesitant for a moment. Just as he told her he would be there, she began to give him the time again and then tell him what to wear again. After she repeated the instructions, he promised to follow them exactly as she asked.

~~~~~~~~~~

At the restaurant when Scott entered, the maitre d must have recognized his suit and asked him if he was Scott Kersey. He followed the maitre d' to the table, and when he saw that she was there he relaxed. As he approached the table, he saw how beautiful she looked in her low cut black satin dress and how nervous she appeared. He smiled to himself and knowing that she was nervous relaxed him even more. As he got closer, she gave him the most welcoming smile that melted him right away. This woman had some kind of spell on him, some kind of hold that wouldn't let go.

When the maitre d' pulled back his chair, Scott sat down. "Good evening Kathryn."

"Good evening, Scott. I know you like to do this, but this evening I have prepared everything. You can just sit back and enjoy it."

"Okay, I can do that."

"Are you ready mad'am?" asked the waiter.

"Indeed we are," responded Kathryn.

"No menus?" asked Scott.

"Now, I thought I just said that I have prepared everything."

"Yes, you did. Habit, I guess." He looked down at the white linen tablecloth and moved his fork around on the table. He had to look down because all he wanted to do was pull her toward him and kiss her. She was so beautiful with her hair parted to one side, her dark eyes telling him how happy she was to see him and her bottom lip with the tiny scar in the corner where she fell when she was seven. He realized that he, too, had a scar on his lip almost exactly where her scar was. He looked up and saw her place her hands on the table. He noticed that she had taken off her ring. Being with her felt good to him just like old times, as if nothing happened, as if nothing had come between them. She made him feel exhilarated.

One waiter poured California Cabernet Sauvignon in his glass, then her glass. Another waiter brought them an appetizer of mushrooms stuffed with crabmeat.

They ate, and talked, and drank, and smiled, and laughed. She touched his hand, and he let his guard down and let her touch it. Her touch sent a wave of electricity through his body. She told him more about her fashion show, and the things that went on behind the scenes, those things that the public never sees. He told her about things that happened at work, but careful not to tell her anything about his experiences looking for the car. He told her again, how he ran more and how he had built up speed and that he actually enjoyed running. She told him that she saw how much he'd improved and that she needed to run more often. He told her that he had almost completed four short stories and sent out three to magazines. He was waiting to hear back. But he didn't tell her that she influenced him. Eventually, they had finished all they were going to eat and the evening, unfortunately, came to an end.

"Why are you looking at your watch?" asked Kathryn.

"At the time."

She smiled. "Are you saying that you don't want time to move and our time in the restaurant to end?"

He stared at her, couldn't answer her at this moment. His body ached for her and he wondered if she felt the same way.

"I know. I don't want this evening to end either, but I know you have work in the morning." She summoned the waiter and asked for the check.

"Are you sure you don't want me to help."

"No, I'm not. But for this I am."

"That's right. You got that big check for the fashion show."

"Don't I wish."

The waiter came back with her tab and her credit card. She signed it and turned to Scott.

"I need a ride."

Her comment surprised him when he remembered that she arrived before he did. He didn't ask any questions.

"Okay."

When they got in his car, she had him drive to the Fairview Hotel a few blocks away. They got out and went in where she seemed to have things ready there as well. Scott didn't know what kind of surprise she had planned, but he went along with it, putting all his trust in her at this point. They were led up to the fifth floor and escorted into a beautiful suite. Scott almost expected people to jump out yelling happy birthday only it wasn't his birthday. He stood in the middle of the room and turned in all directions. He heard Kathryn close the door and he turned toward her. He looked at her and realized that the two of them were alone in a hotel room and what he had wanted to do all evening, he was about to do. He reached out and pulled her to him. Then he kissed her. He kissed her long and hard like a kiss that said you've kept me waiting much too long and now I can't let go.

He felt her body light and in harmony with his when he kissed her. He could feel her warmth and love, and he knew he needed her more than ever now.

"You know now, that there's no going back, don't you?" she mumbled out, not wanting to stop the kiss.

"I know." He mumbled back.

"I just wanna be yours forever."

He tightened his arms around her as if he never wanted her to leave him again and together they inched toward the bed.

The Meaning of Success

By Ralph Waldo Emerson

To earn the respect of intelligent people
and to win the affection of children;
To appreciate the beauty in nature
and all that surrounds us;
To seek out and nurture the best in others;
To give the gift of yourself to others
without the slightest thought of return,
for it is in giving that we receive;
To have accomplished a task,
whether it be saving a lost soul, healing a sick child,
writing a book,
or risking your life for a friend;
To have celebrated and laughed with great joy and enthusiasm
and sung with exaltation;
To have hope even in times of despair,
for as long as you have hope, you have life;
To love and be loved;
To be understood and to understand;
To know that even one life has breathed easier
because you have lived;
This is the meaning of success.

Made in the USA
Lexington, KY
19 January 2014